She lifted her face and Falke sucked hard for air.

Her almond-shaped eyes displayed her emotions like an expensive glass mirror. Every torment clearly distinct and apparent for all to see, yet imprisoned inside.

Kneeling to be eye level, Falke whispered, "Go ahead and cry."

Instead of relief, fear blended with Gwendolyn's despondency. "Nay, I'll not cry."

Falke pulled her into the nest of his arms. "'Twill make the grief easier if you don't hold it in so."

He could feel the erratic flutter of her heart next to his chest. "Pray, let me go." A half sob caught in her voice.

"Cry," Falke ordered. She would become sick if she kept all this sorrow inside.

"Nay, I cannot." She bit her lower lip. Her chin wobbled slightly, her voice filled with wistful remorse. "I've forgotten how."

Forgotten! Falke's mind flared at the notion. A woman who didn't cry…!

Dear Reader,

This month our exciting medieval series KNIGHTS OF THE BLACK ROSE continues with *The Rogue* by Ana Seymour, a secret baby story in which rogue knight Nicholas Hendry finds his one true love. Judith Stacy returns with *Written in the Heart,* the delightful tale of an uptight California businessman who hires a marriage-shy female handwriting analyst to solve some of his company's capers. In *Angel of the Knight,* a medieval novel by Diana Hall, a carefree warrior falls deeply in love with his betrothed, and does all he can to free her from a family curse. Talented newcomer Mary Burton brings us *A Bride for McCain,* about a mining millionaire who enters a marriage of convenience with the town's schoolteacher.

For the next three months, we are going to be asking readers to let us know what you are looking for from Harlequin Historicals. We hope you'll participate by sending your ideas to us at:

Harlequin Historicals
300 E. 42nd St.
New York, NY 10017

Q. What are your favorite historical settings?

_____

_____

Q. Which Harlequin Historicals authors do you read?

_____

_____

Whatever your taste in reading, you'll be sure to find a romantic journey back to the past between the covers of a Harlequin Historicals novel. We hope you'll join us next month, too!

Sincerely,

Tracy Farrell,
Senior Editor

Angel of the
Knight

Diana Hall

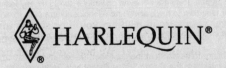

HARLEQUIN®

TORONTO • NEW YORK • LONDON
AMSTERDAM • PARIS • SYDNEY • HAMBURG
STOCKHOLM • ATHENS • TOKYO • MILAN • MADRID
PRAGUE • WARSAW • BUDAPEST • AUCKLAND

ISBN 0-373-29101-9

ANGEL OF THE KNIGHT

Visit us at www.romance.net

Printed in U.S.A.

Please address questions and book requests to:
Harlequin Reader Service
U.S.: 3010 Walden Ave., P.O. Box 1325, Buffalo, NY 14269
Canadian: P.O. Box 609, Fort Erie, Ont. L2A 5X3

To all my angels who helped me during Ricky's cancer:
Mom and Dad: I couldn't have made it through this time
without both of you. I can't thank you enough.

Tami, John and Mitch: Thanks for all the hugs, smiles
and hours of talking.

Savanna: I'm proud of you. Thanks for all your
help and strength.

Chuck and Maggie, David and Audrey—great friends
and wonderful listeners.

Tracy and Patience: Thanks for giving me the time
I needed.

All my writing friends at VFRWA and PLRWA,
especially Casey, Debbie, Joan, Kate, Orysia, Nancy and
Michelle: You keep me looking toward the future instead
of back to the past.

Prologue

England, 1144

Isolde clutched her protruding abdomen and prayed death would be merciful. Talons of pain raked her womb. Her scream bounced off the cold stone walls and reverberated in her ears.

"My poor lady. Curse that man and his evil." Ever faithful Darianne tipped a gourd of water to Isolde's chapped and bleeding lips.

Isolde savored each drip of lukewarm water, then asked, "Gwendolyn?"

"Outside the door."

Isolde braced herself as another contraction began. Her lady-in-waiting shoved a cloth-wrapped piece of wood between Isolde's teeth. She clamped down. Agony hypnotized her into a trance of torture and despair.

"Mother?" Her daughter slipped through the door of the cell. With iron determination, so like her mother's, the girl wrapped herself around a bed leg, clinging to the rickety frame. Long strands of snow-white hair hung in wild disarray around her face. Sapphire-blue eyes glistened with tears.

"Leave your mother be, Gwendolyn." Darianne gently tried to pry the child away. "Husband, you were to keep her from this sight."

A gnarled knight, just past his prime, entered. Battle scars marred his face, while tears stained his clean but frayed tunic. "You know how nimble she is."

"Let…her…be." Isolde's own hair was plastered against her skull with sweat and grime. She fingered her daughter's silvery tendrils and gazed into the startling blue eyes. Gwendolyn resembled her too closely. She'd bear Titus's barbs and beatings now.

Another contraction seized Isolde. The stab of pain tore deep. Despite the pain, she listened—stiffened when she heard the rough clunk of boots on the bare stone floor. She turned her head, warily eyeing the door.

Titus entered and swaggered over. "Has my bastard killed her yet?"

Loud booming laughter shook his muscle-bound body, but Isolde could see the effects of his extravagances. A belt of sagging flesh girthed his waist and jowls widened his coarse face.

"She needs a physician." Darianne hovered nearby, but out of Titus's reach. "The babe's turned and we may lose the both of them. I've done all I can with my herbs."

Titus sneered as he confronted Isolde. "No aid, no

relief until you sign all rights to these lands to me. Sign the contract or die in childbirth, unclean and unholy.''

''She's been in labor for two days. 'Tis more than she can stand,'' Cyrus begged.

The sneer hardened on Titus's face. ''Sign, woman, or die.''

The pain threatened to overtake her, yet Isolde fought on, not for herself, but for her daughter. Her response came out a scream. ''Nay, I'll not sign away my daughter's birthright.'' Her body ached to rest from the onslaught of labor. The brief reprieve between contractions was not enough. A cloud of white swept past her. ''Gwendolyn!''

Her daughter tackled Titus and sank her teeth deep into the flesh of his leg. The burly man yelped, then picked up his attacker by the scruff of her wool shift. With a careless toss, he heaved her from him. The petite form hit the wall. Gwendolyn's head cracked against the hard stone. Her body lay slumped in the corner like a discarded rag. A low moan escaped her lips. The knight and his lady gasped but did not move.

''That was foolish.'' Isolde fought to make her mind clear. Her fate was sealed, but Gwendolyn still had a chance, a hope of surviving. ''You may forge my signature and have no repercussions from King Stephen, but what of Henry?''

The cold sneer melted from Titus's features. Isolde had only moments before a contraction pushed reason from her mind. In a deceptively calm voice, she argued for her daughter's life. "Henry will drive you from Cravenmoor, wrest from you your ill-gotten gains should he be crowned. Gwendolyn, as legitimate heir, is your only protection from Henry's ire."

Titus gripped Isolde's hand, his fingers digging into her wrist. "You should have wed me when I offered."

"And burn in hell for marrying my husband's murderer?" She waited for the slap that would follow her retort. 'Twas not a long delay. Her cheek stung from the blow.

"My brother died from a hunting accident. I would think you would learn by now not to cross me." He rubbed his knuckles against the red mark he'd produced.

Isolde wished she could spit in his face, but she didn't have the strength. In a quiet voice, she requested, "Leave me to die."

Titus's face grew mottled with anger. "Then you die for nothing."

"Nay, Titus, do not think so." This time, Isolde used the pain, used the months of torment to summon a will beyond her own. "For with my death, Gwendolyn's survival is assured. Kill her, and your wealth is lost. And know this—my death brings me strength. I will not lay in consecrated ground and thus will not rest. Draw my child's blood, and I will seek you out, though I must travel from the bowels of hell to do so. Neither heaven nor hell will keep me from you."

Titus stumbled away from her, his eyes wide, his jaw slack. She had penetrated his thick skin, for a man as evil as her brother-in-law must believe in an evil more dark than himself. Believe in that power and fear it.

Recovering, he jerked his head in Gwendolyn's direction. "I may not be able to own the lands, but I'll be the whelp's guardian. I'll grow rich off her." He rose and moved to the unconscious form. He nudged the child with his toe and gave Isolde a lecherous stare. "She reminds me of you—same hair and eyes. She'll provide me with entertainment longer than you did." His laughter lingered in the room as he left.

Darianne and Cyrus rushed to the child. Gwendolyn wrapped her arms around the woman's neck.

Isolde sucked in her breath and cursed Titus's evil. Her limbs grew strangely numb, the life seeping from her. Only moments remained, but what of her child?

Cyrus knelt at her bedside. "Gwendolyn's battered, but she'll mend." He rested his palm on the dagger in his belt. "Release me from my vow, Lady Isolde, and I'll kill the hell-spawned devil."

"Nay, Sir Cyrus." Isolde had to speak before the pain made thought impossible. "Titus has too many men to be taken unaware. If you should die, who would look after my Gwendolyn?"

Darianne cradled the child as she knelt near her husband. Isolde reached out and caressed Gwendolyn's black-and-blue cheek. Eight short years her daughter had lived, and few of them joyful. Would she remember the happier times, before Titus's lust and greed had driven him to arrange William's murder?

Time grew short and precious. "Darianne and Cyrus," Isolde murmured, "I give you my child to protect as your own." She fingered the soft straight hair and mumbled on. "Heaven has cursed her with my beauty. Spare her the ravishment my looks brought upon me. Do not let Titus destroy her."

The couple intertwined their hands. "With our last breaths, we will protect her," they vowed together. Tears streamed down Cyrus's weathered face. Darianne kissed Gwendolyn's temple.

A knife of pain sliced thorough Isolde. Her eyes opened wide in shock at the intense agony. Then she felt a disattachment from her body. A brilliant white light blinded her, and within it stood a tall, familiar figure, beckoning. William!

Light and young again, she rushed to her husband's arms, but stopped just before being engulfed in their welcome embrace.

"William, what of our child?" How could she leave her daughter alone in the world?

"Come, my love, your time of suffering is over. Darianne and Cyrus will look after her." William's rich voice soothed her fears. "And we shall watch over her from above."

Isolde closed the distance and embraced her husband.

Darianne gently closed her lady's eyes and drew the moth-eaten blanket over her face. In death, the serene beauty of Isolde's face reappeared from the ravages of pain.

Cyrus wiped his tears on the back of his sleeve. "I should kill that bastard now and be done with it."

Darianne batted him with her arm and motioned for him to help her rise. Still holding Gwendolyn, she tottered to her feet. "Nay, his death is not so important as this child's life. The next years will be hard. We must have our wits about us or we'll all end up supping at death's table."

Cyrus looked at the sleeping child's face. Marred with dark bruises, it still foretold a beauty to come that might even surpass her mother's. "Our lady spoke true. Titus will want Gwendolyn as he desired Isolde. He'll not care that the child is his niece. What can we do?"

Darianne clutched the girl closer to her bosom. What could she and her husband do against Titus's evil? They were both past their prime, with only their wits as weapons. Titus kept her alive only because of her knowledge of healing herbs. Herbs! Aye, there was a chance, though a small one, that they could save the child from Titus's evil touch.

She gave Gwendolyn to Cyrus and began to gather up some small twigs and leaves into bags. "Take the child to our rooms and then inform a servant to bring a pot of boiling water."

"What are you about, woman?" Cyrus readjusted the child's limp form in his arms.

"I mean to erase the gifts heaven sent this child." Darianne pushed her husband out the door. Before she left, she turned back to the body of her lady, wrapped in a makeshift death shroud. "From this day on, Gwendolyn will cease to resemble you, my lady. I pray you will forgive me for what I'm about to do to your child." She closed the door and whispered a prayer for the dead woman, the child, and for herself. The last few years had been torture; the years ahead would be worse.

Chapter One

England, 1154

"Hurry up, lass. He's sure to wake soon." Cyrus cast a baleful gaze toward the snoring drunk sprawled across the straw pallet on the floor. "Besotted before the midday meal." He shook his head in despair. "'Twould not be so in your father's time."

"Almost done." Gwendolyn dipped her quill into the inkwell and scrutinized the list in front of her. "I can change this one to a four. This three to an eight." Tallying up the numbers in her head, she smiled. "The total's the same. I've just rearranged the assets."

The man on the floor muttered in his sleep and scratched his groin. He chomped his teeth and yawned. The smell of sour wine drifted toward her.

"Let us be gone from here." Cyrus tugged at her sleeve. "'Twould not go well should the steward find us."

"He's not found us these many years, and at the rate he drinks, 'tis not likely he ever will." Disgust and resignation echoed in her voice. The conditions at Cravenmoor never changed, never would until she could find a way to remove her uncle as lord.

She hopped down from the tall stool and wiped the ink from the tip of her quill. "I gave Sir Demark enough potion to ensure sleep long into the night. None will know of our involvement."

Opening the door just enough to poke her head through, she scanned the corridor. No sign of guard or servant. Not that she expected one. Cravenmoor had settled into disrepair and ruin since her uncle had taken control. 'Twas all she could do not to fall into the same state. She had to hold on to a shred of hope, if not for herself, then for her people.

As much as she suffered from her uncle's hand, they fared even worse. Worked from dawn to dusk, and barely allowed enough food to fill their children's stomachs, her villeins lived a dismal existence. With Cyrus's help, she managed to sneak food from Titus's storehouse to feed the village, but credit for the gifts were given to Isolde's ghost. Gwendolyn did not mind. To starving people, loyalty was a luxury. One word to her uncle about her pilfering, and a serf would have a full belly and she a far more brutal life than she now endured.

"'Tis clear." She motioned for Cyrus to follow her. Merging with the gloom of the castle's dark areas, Gwendolyn slipped out the door and raced to the stairs. The elderly knight joined her, the creak of his knees cutting the quiet of the upper tower.

"I'll boil you some lineament for your legs," she whispered. A small reward for Cyrus's years of devotion and love. Gwendolyn prayed she could someday repay the knight and his wife for their selfless loyalty to her and her secret.

The old man shrugged his shoulders and nodded. "'Tis too old I am for this duplicity."

"Nonsense, you get around well for a man of more than half a century," she chided, but a meddlesome doubt tickled her conscience. Ten years was a long time to keep up a charade. The mental anxiety wore her thin at times; Darianne and Cyrus must be exhausted. She and her adopted family walked a tightrope. One false step, and all three would be brought down.

Noise from the noon meal drifted from the great hall to the landing. Everyone should be downstairs by now. The busy servants would present the joints of meat and fowl, while the nobility of Cravenmoor consumed the food in front of the near-starving staff.

With light steps, Gwendolyn scampered down the stairs and jumped the last three steps to the gallery. The rotting wood complained. Again she waited and listened. The curses and unsavory jests from the tables below became clearer. Her uncle's jeering laughter made the hair along her neck tingle.

Cyrus reached her side, his breath coming in loud puffs. "Sooner or later, Titus is bound to discover you've been altering the books. And when he does…'' His aged palms came together as in prayer.

Gwendolyn knew her plight, but was at a loss to end it. She sought the one sight in Cravenmoor that gave her solace: the effigy of her mother.

Wormholes ate at the mahogany banister. A bench, broken in a drunken brawl, littered the gallery hall. The floor rushes reeked of animal and human excrement. Intricate wall designs had decorated the great hall years ago, but now were faint tracings. Only one item remained of Cravenmoor's splendor, and Gwendolyn crossed to it.

A life-size effigy of her mother stood sentry on the gallery, gazing down at the great hall and all the assembled men and women. Gwendolyn did not know whether Titus feared or revered the image, but he insisted the effigy be flawless. Regularly, a new wash of platinum paint highlighted the hair, and artists renewed the sapphire shade on the eyes.

Carved for her father, the statue flaunted tradition by showing a true likeness of Isolde. No wimple framed her mother's face; instead her long hair tumbled to her waist. A sapphire kirtle with knotted sleeves draped the image, displaying the curve of her breasts, the narrow width of her waist and the gentle swell of her hips. The hardwood statue enabled Gwendolyn to remember her mother's beauty, and offered an opportunity to spy on her uncle's entourage. Hiding behind the base, she listened to the mayhem below.

Peering down, she spotted Titus at the high dais.

He stuffed his mouth with roasted meat with one hand, while slipping the other down the blouse of the serving wench. The young girl trembled as she tried to refill an empty goblet. Drops of dark wine spilled across the stained linen tablecloth and spattered her uncle's tunic.

"Idiot." He released the wench and batted her away like a bothersome insect.

Gwendolyn leaned against the smooth wooden effigy, drawing courage from her mother's image. As she closed her eyes, she felt her aged protector's strong hand on her shoulder. "Dear Cyrus," she murmured, releasing a long slow sigh. "If not for you and Darianne, that would have been my fate long ago. Titus keeps me alive now as an amusement and because of my mother's death vow. Greed is Titus's king and treachery his most beloved mistress. Should he discover the true profit my lands bring, I would have no hope of ever escaping. He would keep me prisoner till my death."

"Aye, the man's got no soul. And thus he fears your mother's death vow."

"But those words will not protect me forever."

"Nay, but there have been many sightings of Isolde's ghost." Cyrus gave her a wink. "Trust that when King Henry hears of your plight, all will be put to rights."

"King Henry?" She snorted. "He's still trying to restore order in the civilized parts of England. 'Twill be some time before his judges and his influence reach us here in Cravenmoor." The stairs creaked, and Gwendolyn hushed. She peeked from behind her sanctuary.

Ferris, the worst of her uncle's bastard sons, stood at the far end of the galley. His dark eyes searched the hall below, then settled on her. The handsome lines of his face twisted into a familiar sneer.

Gwendolyn let the tangled mass of her dark hair cover most of her face. The hatred, the fear, the disgust churned away inside her soul, but she kept a vacant stare in her eyes as she lolled her head to the side.

Ferris approached and tapped her with the point of his sword. "What do you spy on, fat cow?" He stared down his long thin nose at Cyrus. "Why is she not waiting on her betters?"

"'Twas another fit, milord. I brought her upstairs so she'd not disturb your meal." Cyrus pulled on her arm and led her from the hiding place. Gwendolyn kept her eyes downcast and her hands pushed deep in the folds of her gown. The coarse material snagged on her hangnails.

"Get the sow downstairs. Titus wants her." Ferris slapped her leg with the flat side of his sword and waited, his black eyes exploring her face for a reaction.

The sting from the sword burned. A show of pain would only lead to more slaps and taunts. She buried her cry by squeezing her hands into tight fists. Cyrus patted her upper arm and guided her toward the stairs.

"Phew! Don't you ever wash her?" Ferris sniffed

the air with disgust. "Even if she is as fat as a sow, she needn't smell like one." He pushed them aside and headed down the steps.

Gwendolyn peered from between the strands of knotted hair. "What can Titus wish with me?"

Cyrus shook his head and scratched his beard. "Probably just planning sport at your expense. Mind, do as I've taught you. Keep your head down. 'Tis hard to mask the spark of life in those brilliant eyes. Keep your tongue quiet and carry yourself as Darianne instructed. Have faith, my child."

"Aye, a bit of playacting and faith 'tis all that stands betwixt Titus and I." She slumped her shoulders and hunched her back. To cover her eyes, she combed more hair over her face with her fingers. The transformation complete, she motioned for her knight to usher her downstairs. As she walked, one foot dragged over the rough planks of the floor. Occasionally, her foot snagged on the rushes and she had to lean on Cyrus for support.

Breathing hard, Gwendolyn made her way to stand in front of Titus in the great hall. Her uncle continued to gulp his ale. Drink dribbled down his greased beard. He wiped his chin with his hand and then flung the moisture away. Drops splattered her face. She shoved her hands deep into the slits of her kirtle and swallowed all her emotions.

Titus patted his stomach and belched loudly. "God in heaven, Ferris, it took you long enough to find her."

His son remained quiet, but the tight line of his jaw showed his anger.

"Mayhap he was out searching for his angel again," a nearby knight called as he drained his wine goblet.

The room grew silent. At a lift of Titus's finger, Ferris's blade rested at the blundering knight's throat. Pressing the knife as well as his point, Ferris growled, "I think you talk too much, Hercule. Isolde lays moldering in her grave, not walking the lands of Cravenmoor."

"Aye, Ferris. I talk too much," the knight agreed with an eager but stilted nod. Ferris removed his blade; the knight rubbed his neck and swallowed several times as if to verify that his throat still worked.

Titus's gaze flickered upward to where the sunlight haloed Isolde's effigy. A tick attacked his left eye and a flicker of fear crossed over his face. The one chink in Titus's evil came from Isolde's threat. Gwendolyn whispered a prayer of gratitude for her mother's gift.

The village talk of a wandering night angel, a silvery figure that appeared by night, ofttimes had instilled in Titus the only terror Gwendolyn had ever really seen in the man. Titus might not fear retribution in this world, but retribution from the hereafter scared him to the marrow of his bones.

"Why search for angels when we have such a lovely one here?" Titus's gaze lowered, centering on Gwendolyn. A chill racked the wicked man's body, as if an icicle ran through his soul.

The room took a collective breath. The knights and their women gave her rancorous looks and jeering smiles. Like Romans at the lion dens, they waited to see the cruel sport made of her.

Her uncle tossed a ham bone at her feet. From under the trestle tables, hunting hounds jumped at the morsel. Snarls and snapping teeth lashed out as the animals vied for the bone. Standing taller that she, the wolfhounds buffeted her from side to side. Their square-jawed heads collided with her knee. Daggerlike teeth sank into her calf.

Laughter and taunts clanged in Gwendolyn's ears. Cyrus kicked at the pack, putting himself between her and the fighting beasts. The leader gripped the bone in his long yellow teeth, then slunk off, followed by his pack. Gwendolyn lifted her hem and gave thanks that the wounds did not run deep.

"God, but she's stupid," a woman declared, then drained her cup of wine.

"Aye, and ugly enough to make a cow look beautiful." A knight nuzzled the woman's ear. "Hair as soft as nettles. A shape to mirror a pregnant sow. 'Tis no wonder the girl's the only virgin left in Cravenmoor. None of us are that desperate to bed a wench."

"But all of that is soon to change, my dear niece." Titus rounded the table and towered over her. Evil glittered in his eyes and warned Gwendolyn that misfortune would soon befall her.

"My friends, let us raise our goblets to the fair Gwendolyn on her coming marriage." His hand whipped out and grabbed her by the hair. With a sharp tug, he forced her face upward. Another tug, and her lips parted from the pain.

"Drink, fair maiden." He swept a cup from the table and poured the strong wine into her mouth. Hot fire swept down her throat as she tried to both swallow and spit out the brew. She started to choke from the forced drink and her uncle's words.

Marriage! Was deliverance soon at hand, or an even crueler master? A crystal of pure hope burned in her soul and she suffered the abuse by focusing on that light.

"To Gwendolyn." The nobles lifted their goblets high in the air and toasted her in mock salute.

Laughter at her expense echoed off the dreary stone walls. Titus released her, pushing her head toward the flea-infested rushes.

Gwendolyn scooted across the floor. Outrage and anger boiled in her heart and threatened to erupt, but her foster parents' schooling helped her hide the turmoil. *Keep all within. Do not show the pain.* To distract herself, she stared at the rip in the seam of her shoe. Her fingernails dug into the palms of her hands. She could not afford to let Titus know of the person that existed beneath the dull outer shell she presented.

Her uncle, weak from laughter, waved his hand impatiently for another tankard of ale. A bone-thin page ran to fulfill the command.

"So, Niece, how do you feel to know of your coming nuptials to Lord Merin's heir?'' Titus chuckled under his breath.

''Milord?'' Cyrus approached with hesitant steps. ''Lord Merin's son died some years ago.''

''Aye, and 'tis his good fortune he did, or else he'd suffer the fate of marriage to the cow.'' Titus grabbed the fresh tankard and downed a hefty swallow. ''Lord Merin has adopted a new heir and decided to bind the man to the agreement made between himself and his lifelong friend, Sir William. For the new heir to inherit, he must marry my lovely niece.''

A groan sounded in the hall. Gwendolyn heard the condolences to her unknown betrothed. ''The poor man. What bad luck.''

Titus withdrew a wrinkled parchment from the bag on his belt. ''Lord Merin demands I deliver the lady Gwendolyn to his northern keep of Mistedge before Easter or his troops will come to take her by force.''

''He threatens war for her!'' Ferris pointed his reedy finger at her. Surprise animated his face, erasing the usual sneer.

''The man hasn't set sight on her since she was two. Lord Merin'll turn her away at the door.''

''Then why not let him come to us?'' Ferris suggested.

''Because if I carry out Lord Merin's request in good faith, only to be refuted, I'd have to be compensated for my travel. Then again, the contract has been signed and delivered to the king. Lord Merin would have to compensate my poor niece for her broken heart and embarrassment at being so publicly humiliated.''

Her uncle's laughter tore at the last threads of self-control Gwendolyn possessed. Her desire for revenge caused her muscles to ache for action. Her fingers curled, begging for the chance to scratch out Titus's eyes. Hidden beneath her kirtle, a dagger tempted her to finally end the years of torment, and impulse caused her to slide her hand toward it.

Cyrus saw her movement. His gray-white brows crinkled as he shook his head to warn her off. She returned her hand to her pocket.

Ferris gave his father a thin smile. ''Pray, who is the unfortunate man destined for Gwendolyn's hand?''

Titus slapped his thigh. ''I know you'll find much pleasure in the knowledge that my niece's betrothed is Falke de Chretian.''

Ferris's smile tightened to a snarl and his voice dripped with hatred. ''So the rogue's luck has finally run out.'' He shoved aside his gaudily dressed mistress and marched to Gwendolyn's side. His eyes scrutinized her. ''Still, Chretian is known for his uncanny luck.''

''Not this time, which is why this tastes so sweet. Chretian will pay well not to wed Gwendolyn.'' Titus's gaze again lifted to the image of Isolde. A brilliant shaft of light shone on the white-blond hair, and the statue's eyes seem to sparkle with life.

Titus's voice lowered and Gwendolyn strained to hear him. ''She has no power beyond Cravenmoor

land.'' A cloud passed, casting a shadow over the
statue. The spell broken, Titus waved to Cyrus.
''Take her away and pack up what belongings she
has. We leave tomorrow.''

The old knight bowed low, so only Gwendolyn
saw the white line of anger across his lips. ''Aye,
milord. I'll prepare her stallion tonight and—''

''She's not riding that stallion. He stays here.''
The glimmer of another torture glinted in Titus's
green eyes.

The steady thump of Gwendolyn's heart stopped.
Not take Greatheart? Without her to care for her father's charger, he'd die of neglect. Somehow she had
to convince Titus to allow her to take him. *Show no
concern,* her inner voice cautioned. *Titus is only trying to torment you more. Think! Outsmart him!*

''I...ride...white...mule, like real lady?'' She labored over each word and spoke in a childlike voice.
Through the strands of hair, Gwendolyn watched her
uncle's reaction.

''By Hades, I wouldn't waste a horse on the likes
of you,'' Titus shouted back.

''But she's got to have an animal, milord. The trip
would take too long if she's to walk the whole way.
And 'tis a long and taxing journey—hard on man
and beast.'' Cyrus gave her a quick wink. He had
caught the direction of her plan and fallen in step.

''Aye, that it is.'' Titus yawned, the drink and
heavy meal beginning to slow him down. ''Take the
old stallion. No one but she can ride him anyway. If
the animal dies en route, 'twill be no loss to me.''

Gwendolyn's heart resumed a steady beat. She wanted to rejoice, hug Cyrus and rush out to Greatheart.

"Now get her the hell out of here. I'm tired." Titus dismissed them and grabbed the wrist of the woman nearest to him. Her eyes glazed with drink, she followed him up the stairs to the main bedchamber.

"Let's go," Cyrus whispered in Gwendolyn's ear.

Ideas and speculation raced in her head as she followed Cyrus down the stairs to the first-floor pantry. How was Falke de Chretian connected with Titus and Ferris?

"Gwendolyn?" Darianne hobbled from the tiny cell she called her chamber.

"Here." Gwendolyn hurried to assist the elderly woman to a stool. "Are your joints aching again today? Did you drink the tea I made for you?"

"Hush, child. Someone may hear you," Darianne cautioned, looking about the room.

"Do not worry. The serfs are off sleeping or drinking. Why work when the filth is tolerated? Why serve palatable meals when the food is strewn across the floor? We'll be alone until 'tis time to break our evening fast on the scraps from my uncle's table."

Cyrus brought over a cup of hot water and Gwendolyn dug about in her pockets until she found the right leaves. She steeped several dark, aromatic stems in the cup and pressed it to the pained woman's lips.

"It seems I'm to be married," Gwendolyn stated in a dry voice. "Lord Merin has a new heir and wishes to honor the contract he made with my father.'' Again a surge of hope washed over her. For so long, not even a beam of light had made its way into the darkness of her life at Cravenmoor. Disappointment threatened to snap the thin shaft of longing in her heart. She was afraid to believe, afraid to dream.

"Thanks be to God." Darianne took a long sip of the hot liquid and rocked back and forth. "At last you're to be saved."

"Titus is sure the man will pay handsomely to be released from the contract. 'Tis the only reason he's letting me go."

"But if we tell this knight the truth…" Darianne's gnarled and twisted fingers brushed the tangled curtain of hair from Gwendolyn's face. "If we show the man the truth, he'd not refuse a union."

"And what if he's akin to Titus? If I tell this man that I do have my wits about me, that my dowry is rich, that I am not what I seem—and he tells my uncle—I am doomed."

"She's got a point, Wife." Cyrus rested on a keg of ale. The strong yeast smell permeated the wood and the pantry area. "We must gauge what kind of man Chretian is. 'Tis plain Ferris and Titus have dealt with him before, and by their reaction, I would reckon the outcome was not in their favor. No offense, Gwen, but the thought that Chretian had to marry you brought them pleasure."

"Aye. But what does that tells us? Any man who would deal with my uncle cannot be reputable."

"But any man that bests them can't be all bad." Cyrus crossed his arms and asked, "So what's it to be?"

"We go. We listen." Gwendolyn pulled a handful of dried marigold flowers from a pocket to prepare a decoction for Cyrus's joints. Placing the withered petals into a pot of boiling water, Gwendolyn formulated a plan as she worked.

"If Falke de Chretian is honorable, I'll tell him everything. If not, I'll keep up the disguise and wait for another chance." She tried to keep the fear from her voice. How many more chances would there be? This was the first real opportunity she'd had in ten years to escape the horrors Titus heaped on her.

"What of Titus's steward?" Darianne asked. "How long can you be away before our other little game is found out?"

"Come harvest I must be home to fix the numbers, or I must wed. That gives me nigh on seven months. I foresee no problem, for either Lord Merin's heir will send me straight home or he'll honor the contract. I should be safe either way."

"I pray you're right, child." Darianne's voice wavered with emotion.

Gwendolyn prayed also, under her breath. She looked around the dank, unkempt kitchen, and faint memories haunted her. Long ago this room had held happy, busy servants, the walls had sparkled with cleanliness. Her mother had… The rest eluded her. Each time Gwendolyn tried to picture her life before Titus, the image blurred more and more. Was she forgetting, or was desperation clouding even the pictures in her mind?

"Our luck is changing, love," Darianne sang as she began to gather their meager belongings.

"But for the worse or the better?" Gwendolyn couldn't help asking under her breath. Would her betrothal be her salvation or destruction?

Chapter Two

"I tell you he murdered him." Outrage rang in the knight's voice as he crashed his fist onto the trestle table.

Falke watched the reaction of each of the seated lords. Suspicion darkened their eyes. These men were to be his vassals, but now sat in judgment of him. Falke directed his comments to the panel. "I have witnesses, Laron. Uncle Merin's horse stumbled on the path. He hit his head on a rock."

Laron spat on the floor. "Witnesses! Two of your own men." Facing the assembled noblemen, he summed up his case. "All of you heard their argument. Just before the hunt, Lord Merin threatened to disinherit Chretian unless he wed the daughter of William Duberque."

"'Twas not an argument, Brother, just a conversation." Tall and willowy, Lady Ivette rose from her stool. Her fine linen kirtle hugged her hips, and as she walked toward Falke, the tiny links of her girdle tinkled like bells. She touched his arm with her fingers and turned her dark eyes back to her sibling. "The accident occurred as Sir Falke stated. I was there and saw it all."

As she turned to the tribunal, her voice wavered. "'Tis a crime the manner in which my brother throws accusations at Sir Falke. I know Laron believed our uncle would name him as heir. But King Henry approved of Sir Falke."

"Only because Falke was lucky enough to take a blow meant for Henry and thereby gain the royal favor," Laron sneered.

"Aye," Falke agreed, "luck placed me on the battlefield with our king. Pray, what kept you safe within the walls of Mistedge while men died to protect their king?"

"You accuse me of cowardice?" Laron's hand rested on the pommel of his sword.

Falke snickered at the knight's implied threat. Standing, he crossed his arms and raised an eyebrow, daring Laron to attack.

"Fellow knights." A scarred warrior stood and glared at Laron and Falke. "We are here to solve the death of our lord, not cause yet more."

Laron chewed the side of his mouth and sat down, pouting.

The older knight then addressed the panel. "Lord Merin's widow insists Chretian is innocent, and Lady Ivette supports the alibi. We've naught more to do but bury our lord and see that his last wishes are carried out."

Disgruntled ayes closed the proceedings, but Falke could feel the nobles' animosity. He brushed an imaginary speck from his amber velvet tunic and returned to his seat. Winking at his second-in-command, positioned next to him, Falke gave a cheery smile. "I told you, Ozbern, there was naught to worry over. Justice prevails."

"You and your eternal luck. Just how eager do you think Lady Ivette would have been to support your story if she didn't have hopes of being the new lady of Mistedge?"

"Which is why I cultivated her friendship when first I arrived. She bats an eye and the most seasoned warrior melts at her beauty." Falke tilted his head in the direction of the lady in question.

"But you're in an awkward position." His friend raised his dark brows. "How do you appease your uncle's vassals and keep Lady Ivette dangling? The lords insist you fulfill Merin's contract of marriage."

Falke chuckled. "In due time. At present, I must properly thank my staunch supporter." He rose to his feet in one fluid motion. Looking down on most of the men in the room, he gave a regal nod to those that most opposed him. He sauntered across the room to where Lady Ivette waited with her maid. Her delicate face, framed by a cream-colored wimple, bore not a pox scar or irregularity. If Helen of Troy launched a thousand ships, a thousand more would set sail for Ivette.

"I wish to thank you for your words." Falke gave her a gallant bow and his most charming smile.

Welcome flashed in her blue-black eyes. "Nay, do not thank me. 'Twas only the truth." Ivette waved away her maid. "I hope you do not hold my brother's behavior against me."

"I am thankful you do not share Laron's opinion of me."

She smiled and slowly ran her tongue along her teeth to her lip. "There are many things I would share with you."

He slanted one brow. "Really? Pray, can you elaborate? I would be most interested."

A titter of laughter answered his question. "Aye, I would show you...someday. For now, let us walk in the garden and leave the staring eyes of these men."

"Gladly." Falke took her arm, then led her past the glaring eyes of his vassals. The heat of their anger beat against his back as he walked out into the fresh air.

Leaving the winter scents of old rushes and smoke-lit rooms, Falke inhaled the perfume of the newly arrived spring. New shoots eagerly reached for the morning sunshine. Stark trees and shrubs showed an array of tiny leaves. A lone bird chirped from the whitewashed trellis, its song a hymn to the season.

"What an ugly little bird," Ivette clucked. "All brown and drab. What a dreary existence it must have."

"'Tis a wren. A delightful song, is it not?" The bird's melancholy notes caused his heart to flutter. His second sense, which some called luck, clicked inside his head. The little bird cocked its head and stared at Falke intently, then began its song over again.

"Delightful? Nay, 'tis a rather sorrowful melody. Mayhaps it knows its lack of beauty and laments its fate." Ivette snapped shut her fan and laughed.

Her voice halted the bird's serenade and it retreated to a maple tree. The song did not resume, but Falke's instincts remained charged with energy.

He watched the bird hop along a branch and perch its bit of weight on a thin twig. "Its lack of splendor is only more apparent because of the beauty before me."

The flattery melted Ivette's pout. She gazed at him through the dark fringe of her eyelashes. "Sir Falke, you are too kind."

"Kindness has nothing to do with my words. 'Tis not gratitude I seek, lady." He cradled her cheek in his hand.

"Then perhaps you should be more aggressive in your search, Lord Falke." She emphasized his title and thereby his rights as her liege.

All gentleness left his caress and he pulled her to him. Eagerly, she sought his lips and molded her body to his. The nubs of her breasts rubbed against his chest, inflaming his lust. He held a practiced seductress in his arms. With full knowledge of her intentions, he cupped one full globe, his finger massaging the hard tip.

"Sir Falke." A breathless page ran down the cobblestone path. "They're here."

Releasing Ivette, Falke vented his frustration at the lad. "God's blood, make sense of yourself. Who is here?"

Red faced, the page stumbled to a stop and gulped deep breaths into his wiry rib cage. "Cravenmoor. Sir Falke, your bride has arrived."

Ivette sucked in her breath and a quiet pall settled on the garden. Cravenmoor here already? Crafty old Merin must have sent for the girl as soon as Falke accepted his offer of inheritance.

"Milord, they're entering the castle gate now." The lad shifted from one foot to the other, obviously impatient to see the queue of guests.

"I suppose I should be there to greet them." The page raced off before Falke could even finish. Taking Ivette's hand, he strolled toward the castle, his mind churning with ideas on how to handle the Cravenmoor dilemma.

For some reason the melody of the little bird wouldn't dislodge from his mind. A speck of a shadow flew off into the sparse green of the woods beyond the garden just as Falke climbed the forebuilding stairs.

The men and women of Mistedge already huddled in tight groups, awaiting the arrivals. Ozbern came to Falke's side, shrugged his shoulders and nodded toward the mayhem entering the inner bailey.

The procession dragged through the barbican gate in a cloud of noise and dust. Sir Titus, seated on a hide-scarred palfrey, shouted curses at the servants.

His crop slashed across the back of a bearer. "Drop that trunk and I'll open your back with fifty lashes."

Falke watched the display of cruelty and noted to his friend, "Titus hasn't mellowed with age."

Ozbern nodded and wagged his finger toward where Ivette stood with a cluster of ladies. She ripped the lace from her handkerchief as the women gossiped. Tiny shreds of thread floated to the ground like snowflakes. "'Tis plain Ivette is worried. Am I correct in assuming you knew not of this arrival?" Ozbern queried.

"Aye, Merin must have been certain I'd agree to the arrangement." Falke scratched his chin. "Or he thought 'twould be harder for me to deny the girl if she stood before me."

"Perhaps this girl will not be as sordid as her guardian."

"Growing up in a household ruled by Titus?" Falke crossed his arms and widened his stance. Revulsion tensed his muscles. "That man is the vilest human being I know. My aunt is certain he arranged his brother's death and the widow's. Just the fact that his niece is still alive tells me something."

"Titus is known as a lecher. Any man would be a fool to leave his daughter alone with him." Grimness settled in lines around Ozbern's mouth. "'Tis said Isolde, her mother, was the fairest woman of the realm."

"If Isolde's daughter has any looks about her, you can be sure Titus has already tasted her wares. She's probably as twisted as he is. Mark me, my friend,

I'll not wed away my freedom just to honor a dead uncle's wish. Mistedge is mine, marriage or no. Henry has decreed me heir.''

"Aye, so he has." Ozbern cocked his head toward the assembled lords. "But should these vassals plan rebellion, with King Henry busy setting London to rights, your throat could be cut and a new lord in place before Henry has time to act in your behalf. A sliced gullet or marriage?'' He rubbed his neck tentatively. "Of the two, I suggest the wedding. At least you would be able to enjoy a fine feast.''

"As always, my friend, you add a bit of sunshine to my dreary day." Falke slapped Ozbern on the back. As the party cleared the inner bailey gate, Falke sighed. 'Twas time to greet his guests.

Horses and servants huddled around Titus, hesitant to move before he gave the signal to dismount. When the dust settled, Falke addressed his guests. "Lord Titus, welcome to my home." He paused to allow the meaning of the words to sink in.

Titus's beady eyes searched the crowd for Lord Merin, then he smiled. The wide grin of chipped and crooked teeth reminded Falke of neglected tombstones. "So, Merin's dead already. Didn't waste much time, did you?''

"My uncle died from a hunting accident." Falke kept his eye on the cagey older man, but he searched the group for the girl. He saw no young maiden in the assembly, only a few knights and camp followers with the servants.

"Hunting accident? I know a bit about those myself.'' Titus gave a hearty laugh. "'Twas the same that happened to my poor brother. Now I'm lord of Cravenmoor because of it. 'Tis strange how fate unwinds…ain't it?''

"Lord Titus, we are all in mourning for my husband.'' Falke's aunt spoke with displeasure as she joined him. "Now, where is Isolde's daughter, Lady Gwendolyn?''

Titus's mouth curled into a sneer. "So, Lady Celestine, I didn't think you dirtied yourself with the likes of me.''

"That will be enough, Titus.'' Falke stepped in front of his aunt, protecting her from the foul man. Ozbern rested his hand on his sword hilt, his thumb massaging the emerald in the pommel. Tension rippled through the inner bailey. The men of Mistedge stood ready to defend their lady's honor.

A dark-haired Cravenmoor knight sidled up to Titus. "Shut up, you old fool, before you get us all killed. We're outnumbered ten to one. You'll get your say.''

"Wise advice, Ferris.'' Falke looked back at the older man. "I suggest you take your son's words to heart.''

The snarl on Titus's lips changed to a secretive smile. "My apologies.'' His crop flew out and sliced across Ferris's cheek. A thin line of blood seeped from the high cheekbone. "And you would do well to know your place, bastard.''

Ferris's face turned white with rage, making the

wound even more pronounced. His jaw clenched and a blue-white vein pounded in his neck.

Titus motioned a ragged boy forward. He carried a mahogany stool with an embroidered top. The boy positioned the ottoman on the ground, then guided the grossly overweight knight's foot to the pad.

Curiosity drove Falke closer. His aunt and the crowd of noblemen followed him. Titus swaggered forward, a gleam of pleasure in his small, swinelike eyes. The hair on the back of Falke's neck prickled. The old codger had nothing but ill wishes for Mistedge, and anything that brought happiness to him could not be good for the keep or Falke.

"I can see you're eager to meet your bride." Titus waved his hand impatiently. "Cyrus, fetch her."

A gray-haired man approached. Although past his prime and dressed in cast-off clothes, he walked with dignity and strength. Behind him, a charger followed. Aged with gray, the warhorse moved with the same regal assurance as the elderly servant. A small form perched on the back of the beast. Lady Celstine gasped and covered her mouth with her hand. A fist of shock slammed into Falke's gut.

Titus kept his gaze on Falke and ordered, "Come, Niece. Climb down and let your betrothed get a good look."

The girl wrapped her arms around the horse's throat, leaned forward and slid to the ground. She kept one hand on the horse and with the other leaned on Cyrus's arm. It took her several minutes to balance on her own feet.

Falke had never seen anything so pathetic. Matted with tangles and knots, her mud-brown hair bushed out wildly and covered her face. An earth-colored kirtle, patched with bits of rags, strained to cover the girl's ample girth. A dirty toe stuck out from a hole in her leather slipper.

Titus's chilling cackle brought Falke back to reality. His aunt's fingernails sank into his arm and he felt her tremble. In a hoarse whisper, Lady Celestine said, "By the saints, she wasn't like this as a child." Then loudly, she demanded, "What did you do to her?"

"Me?" Titus raised his eyebrows in surprise. "I did nothing. Many a towheaded child's hair has darkened with the years. And sadly, after her mother's death, in the throes of bereavement the child threw herself against a stone wall. Now she's an imbecile, an idiot. Suffers fits and such. There's a body, but no soul." Every word was uttered with undisguised relish and stabbed at his aunt's strained resolve.

"Enough, Titus." Falke refused to allow the base knight to hurt his aunt further. He motioned an attending lady forward. "Take Lady Celestine to her chamber."

"Falke, believe me, she was a beautiful child." His aunt's voice faltered, and tears came freely. "So like Isolde." Her attendant led her away and into the protection of the castle.

Titus clicked his tongue as he gave his niece a fatherly gaze. "Such a dreadful accident."

"Like her father's death?" Falke let the tone of his voice resound with recrimination.

"Like your uncle's death?" Titus threw back the innuendo. The silence the statement drew from the crowd made him crow louder. He grabbed hold of his niece's shoulder and pulled her forward. "Come, Gwendolyn, let the crowd see your pretty face."

The girl dug in her heels and fought Titus's touch. The stallion stretched his bony head forward, bared yellow-stained teeth and clamped down on Titus's hand.

"Damn you, demon of hell." Titus's roar of curses and pain caused the ladies present to blush. Cravenmoor knights and villeins clustered around in a vain attempt to free their lord. Using his other hand, Titus clobbered the animal's head. Still the horse held on. Not until the gray-haired servant gave a brisk command did the stallion free his prisoner.

The crowd parted suddenly with another of Titus's curses. "Let the devil take the animal. He'll not taste my blood again." Cradling his injured hand, Titus whipped a long thin dagger from the folds of his mantle. "'Twill give me pleasure to slit the devil's throat. Grab the reins so the beast can't move."

Ferris jerked the leather strips from Cyrus. The deadly sharp blade was raised high in the air. Falke raced forward, ready to protect any warrior, man or animal, that drew Titus's blood.

"Nay!" As the blade descended, the docile girl lunged at her uncle's arm, deflecting the blade. It swooshed harmlessly in the air.

Titus's ham-sized fist swung at her, but she had expected the blow and rolled away. Knights that should have served and protected her actually kicked at her as she scrambled beneath the feet of her charger. Falke noticed that none of the men dared to venture within striking distance of the stallion's war-trained hooves.

Titus bellowed, "You'll not escape this beating."

"Aye, she will." Falke positioned himself between the horse and the furious knight. Serving as a shield and protector, Falke ordered, "Ozbern, take our guests inside and have someone look at Lord Titus's injury."

"Get out the way, Chretian. That whelp is getting a whipping, then she'll watch me feed that horse of hers to the dogs." Titus wrapped a dirty cloth around his mangled hand and took one step toward Falke.

The sound of twenty blades leaving their scabbards stopped the old man's advance. Falke's trusted regiment of men widened their stance. A few knights and lords of Mistedge aligned themselves with Falke's men. The majority waited with Laron, offering no aid.

"Fine." Titus backed off. "Have your *show* of chivalry." He peered around Falke at the girl still under the stallion. "Don't think he'll protect you, girl, not when it counts. I'll have my day with you yet."

Ozbern gave a cavalier wave of his hand toward the castle door and did a fair imitation of Falke's sarcastic smile. Titus snorted, then marched toward the castle. His men followed, their gazes staying on the line of armed Mistedge soldiers.

"Milord." The elder man's voice from behind him startled Falke, his perfect French betraying his birth and nobility. "I and my lady thank you for your intervention on her behalf."

"No thanks are necessary. You are a knight?"

"Was." The aged man nodded to the girl, and she crawled from the protection of the horse's feet. "I served Lord William and Lady Isolde. Now I and my wife, Darianne, serve their child, Gwendolyn."

Falke started to address the girl but stammered to a stop midsentence. She stood staring at the back of her uncle. For the first time, Falke could see her face uncloaked by hair. And what he saw took his breath away. Her eyes, large and wide, shone with the fires of consuming hate. Titus was wrong about the girl— a soul did reside deep inside her. Only a soul could hate so completely.

"My wife is riding in the cart and will be along soon. Pray, Lord Falke, is there a place where we and the child could chamber? Somewhere out of the way, where no one will bother us?"

The knight's questions tugged Falke's attention from his bride. "She can sleep in the women's dormitory." His gaze flickered back toward the girl, but she had once again hidden her face behind the wild tangle of hair.

"We do better on our own. A high tower room or a cell in the pantry."

"Those are for servants, not noblemen."

"'Tis what we're used to. The more out of the way the better. Away from staring eyes and hurtful phrases."

"A high tower room then, Sir..." Falke waited, unsure how to address the knight turned maidservant.

"Just Cyrus, Lord Falke. I and the girl will put the stallion in the barn and wait for my wife. If you'd be so good to have a boy show us our room, I'd be most grateful."

"As you will." Falke studied the two as they led the charger to the stable, then rejoined the Mistedge nobles, the back of his neck tingling with expectation. For what, he could not say.

"'Tis a perfect match." Laron clapped Falke on the back. "I assume you'll be having the ceremony immediately."

"Laron, stop your jesting." Ivette waved her shredded handkerchief under her turned-up nose. "The whole crowd from Cravenmoor smell like a sty. I can imagine what that creature must have smelled like." A sly smile came to Ivette's full mouth. "She reminds me of that little bird we saw in the garden. Ugly, fat and brown. What was it, Falke—a wren?" Then a soft laugh tumbled from Ivette's lips. "Why, 'tis not Lady Gwen, she's fat, little, drab Lady Wren."

Collective laughter floated over the group. Amused men and women congratulated Ivette on her witty remark. The haunting memory of the bird's song returned to Falke's mind.

A bird singing in the garden. But not just any

bird—a wren. A bird ofttimes associated with strange happenings. Did the visitation only signal the coming spring or more? Why were his instincts stinging like raw nerves?

He watched the last of the Cravenmoor procession enter the crenulated castle walls. A dust-covered woman separated herself from the line and joined Cyrus and Lady Gwendolyn at the door of stable. The three embraced, and Falke wondered again about the creature who was his intended. Lady Wren? The name did fit her—small, brown and unassuming. And sad. Along with the hate, her sapphire eyes had registered sorrow and longing.

"Falke, are you coming?" Ivette looked up at him with eyes that promised a warm bed filled with pleasure.

"Of course." Falke entered the castle, but his thoughts remained with the three near the stable. There was time enough to delve into the many questions he had. For now, flirting with Ivette would be a pleasant diversion.

Chapter Three

The servant boy paused outside the fourth-floor chamber and cast Gwendolyn a cautious glance. He whispered to Darianne, "She ain't dangerous or anything, is she?"

Gwendolyn quelled the urge to start a low wolf howl and really scare the rude child.

"Nay. As long as she's left alone," Darianne advised.

The lad pushed open the heavy oak-and-metal door as Darianne ushered Gwendolyn inside the chamber. Cyrus followed, carrying their meager belongings.

The freckle-faced boy handed Darianne an earthen jar. "The chambermaid said there be a lamp on yon wall. Here's oil for it."

"Thank you, lad." Cyrus spoke with regal reserve.

"There's not many 'twill be up these stairs," the boy advised gently in a thick English accent. "If'n ye be in need, me name is Lucas. I'm not worth

much, but I'll help ye if I ken. From the look of this
room, ye'll be needin' me.''

Through the high arched window, afternoon sunlight filtered in, creating a drowsy spring warmth.
Crates and trunks lay strewn about the tiny cell. Spi-
derwebs coated with dust laced boxes and the corners
of the room. The stone walls were blank of any
whitewash, murals or tapestries. A pile of musty
smelling straw lay on the floor as a pallet. Compared
to her room at Cravenmoor, these accommodations
were majestic to Gwendolyn.

''Tis fine.'' Darianne threw her tattered scarf and
mantle across a box and shoved at a trunk to clear
space. She motioned for Gwendolyn to sit on the
floor. Gwendolyn hesitated, not willing to let her
aged friends do all the work. Her foster mother
pointed to the boy and again signaled for her to sit.

Lucas cast a wary eye at Gwendolyn sitting cross-
legged on the floor. ''I'm thinkin' ye'll not get much
help from 'em. None are partial to climbin' those
stairs or to waitin' on the likes of her. And then
there's not many here who are jumpin' at the new
lord's command.''

''Why is that?'' Cyrus kept his voice casual, but
both he and Gwendolyn waited with impatience for
the boy to answer.

''Well, 'tis his manner.'' Lucas scratched his head
and shrugged his shoulder. ''Things just seems to fall
'is way. And then there's the business of the old
lord.''

''What happened to Lord Merin?'' Darianne fished

about in her bag while she asked the question. Gwendolyn prayed the boy wouldn't comprehend the inquisition they were putting him through.

"Yesterday, the two of 'em had a row about..." Lucas dropped his voice to a whisper "...marryin' her." His voice resumed a normal tone. "Lord Merin rode off at a gallop during the hunt. Weren't but a short time later, the new lord returns with Lord Merin's body strapped to the back of his horse and claims the old lord fell from 'e's palfrey. But for Lady Celestine and Lady Ivette's standin' up for 'im, Sir Laron would have had Lord Falke's head."

"And do you think 'twas only an accident?" Darianne wiped off a crate to serve as a table.

"I think..." the boy hunched his shoulders and looked down the hall to see that no one approached. "...Lord Falke is one lucky man. His friends are always sayin' that Sir Falke was kissed by an angel as a baby 'cause he was born on the seventh day of the seventh month and 'e's the seventh son born. And I think..." his voice grew quiet again and his head nodded like that of a wise old abbot "...that what's good luck for Lord Falke ain't always good luck fer everyone else."

Cyrus raised his white brows and lowered his voice. "I think now you should be on about your business."

"Aye, I'll get me ears boxed for sure if I tarry." A smile flashed across the boy's lips as he flew from the room. Darianne almost caught his foot in the door when she rushed to seal the chamber.

"Falke's as bad as Titus." Gwendolyn jumped up and forced her arthritic foster mother to take a seat. "He killed his uncle for the land. Falke de Chretian could be one of my uncle's bastards, they're so much alike."

"We don't know that for sure." Cyrus spread their blankets onto the straw pallet. "Remember, Falke stood up for you against Titus."

"Was that because of an inner goodness or a wish to show up my uncle?" Gwendolyn played devil's advocate. She could not forget the anger in Falke's gaze. His pale blue eyes, so like the clear spring sky, had turned brittle and hard. Full of menace and danger. Like the gleam of a sharp-edge sword. Was that ire directed at Titus because of his treatment of her or from some past confrontation with her uncle?

"We can't afford to make a mistake about my intended husband. Once he knows the truth, we're at his mercy." She pushed her hands deep into her pockets and paced the room.

"Then we wait. And pray." Darianne spoke the obvious.

Gwendolyn hopped up on a trunk and, on tiptoe, peered out the window. The sun burned through a cloud-filled sky and the tower's shadow stretched out long and thin on the ground. A group of knights passed below her and the sunlight highlighted the tall blond figure of Falke de Chretian. Wide shoulders moved with casual ease along the upper defense wall. A breeze danced through his long, unbound hair. The rich amber of his velvet tunic shone in the sunlight, and as he moved, the muscles in his arms and legs strained the material.

He walked past the infantrymen stationed on the wall. None of the men came to full attention. Falke passed without seeming to notice the insult given him.

So Lucas's opinions were shared by the fighting men as well as the serfs. The boy had mentioned that a knight had opposed Falke. Sir Laron. A decision might be taken out of her hands if he ousted Falke from Mistedge. Would he be a better choice to unveil the truth to?

"I need more information." Gwendolyn turned to her friends. "And I can't get it here."

"And how do you mean to get it?" Cyrus's voice told her he already knew her answer.

"The usual way. When the nobles are their most talkative…after they've drunk their fill of wine and ale."

"Nay, Gwendolyn, don't put yourself through that today. There will be time enough tomorrow, when you've rested."

"Time is exactly what we don't have, Cyrus." Gwendolyn turned and watched the guardsmen. Their animosity toward Falke blanketed the keep even more than the afternoon shadows. With a sigh, she muttered, "I'm afraid 'tis even shorter than we thought."

Falke strolled along the defense wall and chose to ignore the black looks the guardsmen threw his way.

Give them time and the gossip would die down.

Ozbern placed a restraining hand on Falke's elbow, then pointed over his shoulder at the soldiers. "They hate you. Your vassals don't trust you. Laron is no doubt plotting to depose you as lord, and you're stuck marrying an imbecile."

"Don't call her that," Falke barked, then softened his voice. "Whatever she is, I saw a spark of life in those eyes."

Ozbern shook his dark curly head. "Whatever she is, or isn't, do you intend to marry her?"

"God's blood man, nay. I'm not my father. No one will make my decisions for me."

The shorter knight let out a long, slow sigh. "Falke, whatever you do, will you think beyond yourself?"

Giving his friend a glib smile, Falke asked, "And what is more important than me?"

"Your uncle and aunt. Crispen's last wishes. The people of this keep." Ozbern gripped the stone wall and looked out over the meager peasant village huddled a few miles from the bailey walls. The pitiful huts wallowed in mud, along with the livestock in the small bare pasture. A stench even more imposing than that from the Cravenmoor nobility wafted in the air.

"'Tis not much, I grant you that, but don't throw away this opportunity in a vain attempt to prove you're not an honorable man."

"I'm not." Deep anger drove straight through

Falke's heart. He tensed his jaw and snarled. "My father taught me well that empty code of chivalry, what it was to be governed by what others think of you. For that hollow code he threw away the love of his life." Taking a cleansing breath, he looked over the castle wall at the squalid village. "Honor is nothing but a shackle around a man's soul. I rode to Crispen's side in battle because he was my friend and my heart told me to do so, not because of some false sense of duty. And despite my actions, Crispen died."

Disgust sharpened his tone and hardened his face. "And in a farce of nobility, along with King Henry's strong urgings, my uncle made me his son's replacement. Merin couldn't abide me. To him, I was nothing more than a ne'er-do-well who lives off his uncanny luck."

Ozbern shook his dark head. "'Twas no angel's kiss that made your sword arm strong, but hours of practice. Nor did any seraphim plot your battle strategy. Despite all your bravado to the opposite, Falke de Chretian, you're a good man. You deserve this keep. And by heavens, in spite of you, I intend to see you keep it."

Falke gave Ozbern a rueful smile. "I'm not sure whether to call you friend or foe."

"Friend. Believe me, only a friend would put up with your attitude." Ozbern shared a laugh with his leader. "Now, we need a strategy to expedite you from marriage to the lady Wren."

Falke rubbed his face with his hand and racked his

mind for a plan, any plan. Afternoon heat beat down on the wide expanse of his back and he felt like the weight of the huge celestial body rested on his shoulders. Aunt Celestine was adamant about him upholding the contract.

Six years as a mercenary for King Henry had left him and his men bone weary. Falke desperately wanted a place to call his own. But he wasn't ready to forfeit his freedom to gain his dream. Somehow he had to find an acceptable way to halt or at least postpone his wedding.

"Of course!" He slapped his friend on the back. "I can't believe how simple the solution is."

"What have you devised now, my crafty friend?" Ozbern nearly staggered from the blow.

Falke hummed under his breath. "I just need to approach my aunt in the proper contrite mood and I will buy myself at least a year."

"How?"

"I believe 'tis customary for a period of mourning to pass in honor of the death of a loved one. Also, after today's shocking revelations about my betrothed, I think 'twould be perfectly understandable for Aunt Celestine to retire to a nearby convent for her mourning. A place of quiet and serene surroundings where my poor aunt can collect her thoughts. And we could have no wedding without her."

A wry smile came to Ozbern lips. "And with your gift for glib talk, you're bound to pull it off. 'Twill buy you a year, but what of Laron? He'll have a year to forge a wedge between you and your vassals."

"And I'll have a year to gain their faith." Falke began to hum a lively peasant song under his breath.

"You're that confident your plan will work?"

"Don't they always?" With a jaunty skip, Falke resumed his stroll and hummed louder. He even gave each surly guardsman he passed a wide grin. This plan would work. His plans always worked.

The great hall echoed with the voices of knights and ladies ready to begin the evening meal. Falke scanned the room from his seat at the high table, beaming with self-pride. After hours of cajoling, sympathizing and nodding serenely, Falke had convinced his aunt that she had conceived the idea to enter the convent. Even now, a group of Falke's own men were escorting her to an abbey. All that remained was to inform the assembled nobles of the delay.

As if drawing up battle lines, the nobility had separated into two sides. Men and women of Mistedge crowded together on the tables to his right. On his left, with ample room to spare, sat the Cravenmoor contingent, minus his betrothed and her servants.

"My cup is empty," Titus bellowed. Jumping into action, a page rushed to pour scarlet wine into the knight's cup.

"Give me that." Titus yanked the jug from the boy's grip and gave the page a backhanded slap.

"That will be enough." Falke spoke in a low tone but made sure his voice carried the length of the

Cravenmoor table. "My people will not be manhandled."

The room's din quieted to a churchlike silence. Titus patted his bloated stomach and belched. "You ain't the real lord till you marry my niece."

"The man has a point. Just when will the ceremony take place?" Laron asked from his seat next to Ivette. His lips tilted in a smug smile, a caricature of Falke's own cavalier expression. "After the wedding, the vassals of Lord Merin will swear their allegiance to the new lord of Mistedge. And not a moment before."

Mistedge knights turned frosty glares to the high table. An angry mutter of agreement spread from man to man.

"And a wedding will take place." Falke spoke to stamp out the resentment Laron's comments had rekindled. "But, as you all saw today, my aunt is in need of rest. Today's incident has strained Lady Celestine. Therefore, she has decided to enter a convent for a year of mourning. At the end of that time, the contract between Mistedge and Cravenmoor will once again be evaluated."

"A year!" Laron jumped up from his place, an angry snarl on his face. "You're just juggling for time."

"I'm showing proper respect for my deceased uncle," Falke retorted.

"Laron," Ivette's scolding tone interrupted. "A year is the minimum time required to show our loss at the death of our lord and uncle." She flashed Falke a crafty smile. "In the meantime, Sir Falke will lead us wisely, I'm sure."

"Brat, get out here," Titus shouted.

From the shadows, the girl materialized. With her face hidden by her hair, she walked with slow, agonized steps toward her uncle, then stopped well out of arm's reach. How many slaps had it taken for her to gauge so effortlessly the length of her uncle's grasp?

The urge to slash the lecher's arms from his torso ripped into Falke. His hand clenched the dagger at his belt, turning his knuckles white with checked anger. No living thing deserved the abasement Titus shed on this poor lass.

Falke rose and motioned to the table where her knights sat. "Lady Gwendolyn, you must be hungry. Won't you be seated and partake of some nourishment?"

Mean-spirited laughter from Titus and his crew greeted Falke's remark. A flush-faced woman spoke, her gown displaying her soiled chemise beneath and dark love marks on her throat. "Now don't that sound so fine, Lady Gwendolyn?" Slapping her thigh, the woman threw a gnawed bone at the girl. "She eats with the dogs, like the rest of the animals."

From the Cravenmoor table, bones, pieces of bread and apple cores rained down on the hapless girl.

"Halt!" Falke's unbridled contempt and his half-drawn sword stopped the rain of trash. "God's wounds, Titus, how can you treat your own blood this way?''

"Don't be high and mighty with me." The lecherous old man leaned his elbows heavily on the table. "Your own serfs and nobles call her names. 'Tis Lady Wren they call her."

Falke's gaze sought out Lady Ivette's. The corners of her full lips tilted in a slight smile. Pride in her little rhyme rimmed her mouth.

He looked at the girl scrambling to pick up the leftovers. If she lived on scraps, how had she accumulated so much weight? He doubted he could span her waist with both arms. A streak of empathy coursed through him. Her life with Titus must be miserable.

"Lady Gwendolyn." Falke rose and knelt beside her. "Pray, come and share my trencher." He touched her shoulder to draw her attention away from the scraps among the rushes.

Like a frightened rabbit, she froze. Her hands stilled. For such a short woman, she possessed large hands. Long slender fingers ended in torn but clean nails. In fact, although the rest of her was filthy, her hands were scrubbed raw with cleanliness. The smell of strong lye soap overpowered the damp, woodsy odor of her hair.

"Milord, thank you for your kindness." Her elderly guardian rushed forward. "But 'twould be best if we leave now." Cyrus helped the girl to her feet. She leaned on his elbow, her left foot dragging as she walked.

"See to it you have hot food from the kitchen." Falke issued the order, but doubted the man would see the command carried out. The two looked like beaten dogs retreating from a fight.

"You'll not get away with this scheme." Laron's pale face was mottled with fury.

"Aye, that he won't," Titus agreed, and gave Falke an evil grin. "I've brought her here for a wedding and I'm not taking her back. At least not without compensation for a year's keep."

"Of course." Falke had been prepared for Titus's ultimatum. Untying the heavy leather pocket at his belt, he dropped the bag in front of Titus. With a greedy gleam in his eye, the old swine grabbed the gold, gauging the weight of it in the palm of his hand.

A sliver of conscience sliced through Falke. Could he really send the girl back with this depraved man? In his mind, the ominous voice of his father rebuked him for the dishonorable act. Falke forced himself to muffle the voice and harden his emotions.

"I appreciate doing business with you," Titus cackled. "Mayhap we can do a bit more business before I leave."

An underlying evil lay in his words and slithered along Falke's spine. Repulsed, he answered, "I think our business has concluded."

Titus rose and smirked. "'Twould be to your benefit to hear me out." He gave an evil laugh, then stalked from the room. The rest of the table dispersed quickly, except for Ferris. The willow-thin knight refilled his goblet with wine and cursed his father between sips.

"Robert," Falke called to one of his younger knights, seated at his right. "'Tis enough wine for tonight. What will Sir Laron think if my men make drunkards of themselves?"

"But, Falke," his man protested, "'tis only my third...nay, my fourth cup." He lifted his glass high in the air and spoke in a slurred voice. "Sir Laron...is a knight...who appreciates a good press." Robert, his fine auburn hair covering his bleary eyes, brought the cup to his lips, overestimated the distance and sloshed wine down the front of his gold tunic. A dark stain spread across the wool.

"I'd expect as much from one of your men." Laron sniffed with disdain.

Ozbern gave Falke a quizzical look. "He's too far into his cups to stop him now."

Falke laughed, then smiled at Robert, who staggered across the room, balancing two wine jugs and several cups. When the young knight reached a bench near the fireplace, he sat and poured another goblet of wine. Robert raised the cup, took one sip, then grew limp. The knight passed out, the crack of bone against wood making Falke flinch in empathic pain.

Robert rolled off the bench and landed facedown in the rushes. Falke rose, surveyed the passed-out figure and commented, "A night in the cold and a heavy head will teach him a lesson."

The comment dispersed the nobles into small gos-

siping cliques. Ozbern rose, cocked a brow toward
Laron, then sauntered off toward the gallery.

Tension gripped Falke's neck like a hawk's talons.
He wanted a breath of fresh air and a moment or two
of privacy. He strode through the hall to the courtyard.

The fragrance of new grass hung in the cool evening air. Mistedge blossomed with spring's promise
of new beginnings. And the keep offered Falke a
promise also, of remaking himself from a cavalier to
a lord. With time and patience, all the pieces would
fall into place. The vassals. The villeins. Lady Wren?
The girl would take much thought, but somehow he
would arrange to end the betrothal.

Worry nagged at the back of his mind. His feet
followed the garden path as it curved away from the
castle. A whiff of old urine and spoiled wine warned
him of who waited ahead.

Emerging from the pruned shrubs, Titus broke into
a ragged-toothed grin. "A year will come and go
afore you know it. What will you do when the time's
up?"

"As I said, I'll rethink the situation." Falke tried
to sidestep around the corpulent knight.

"'Tis a dangerous trip home." The malice in Titus's voice brought Falke to a quick stop. Titus
rubbed his beefy hands together. "For fifty gold
pieces and a deed to her lands, I'll see she finds the
sharp edge of a sword should we be attacked by,
say…bandits. None of those high-and-mighty lords
will be able to connect you with her death."

An unexplainable fear replaced the villainy in his stare. Falke detected a slight wavering in Titus's voice as he finished, "But the deed must not be done on Cravenmoor soil, nor can a Cravenmoor knight spill her blood."

Revulsion gagged Falke and he restrained the urge to beat the old man senseless. He could feel the steady throb of blood pounding in his head and heart. And questions. Why was Titus so adamant about the where and who? And why the fear?

"Do we have a deal?" Titus held out his hand as a gesture of goodwill.

Falke ignored the outstretched hand. "I'll think over your proposal."

The criminal huffed with indignation and hooked his thumbs on his leather belt. "You were quick to seek me out when foul work was needed before. When you needed information on Stephen's troops, you came knocking on my door."

"That was before I realized how you tortured those men for answers. Before I saw their broken bodies in your battle camp." The tentative grip on his ire slipped. Falke emitted a low growl under his breath.

Titus's face blanched. He scurried down the path toward the castle. Tension racked Falke's shoulders and he mentally forced his muscles to relax. God's blood! Titus had a soul blacker than the pits of hell. Falke would like to wipe the old robber baron's grin right off his face. More specifically, Falke would like to force every crooked tooth down the bounder's throat.

Desperate to work off his anger, Falke decided to leave the castle for a brisk run. The evening sun melted to a golden arc just above the horizon and the temperature dropped with springtime quickness. He ambled through the inner bailey gate and noted the marshal dozing at his post. Lack of a sure leader was fast turning the troops soft. If Falke didn't gain his vassals' allegiance soon, Mistedge would be ill prepared to ward off an attack.

As he entered the outer bailey, he noted the guards' chambers. Infantry troops bedded down in the chamber halls and supplies of weapons were housed in the lower levels. Bombastic laughter and ear-burning curses echoed from the row of windows. Several colorful phrases involved Falke and various types of torture devices. Reason wasted little time convincing Falke 'twould be best to steer clear of the soldiers for now.

Set off by itself, the stable offered respite from the chill and a place to collect his thoughts. Postponing the idea of leaving the castle, he slipped inside, and plopped down on a pile of sweet-smelling hay to watch the glorious sunset through the open doorway.

"Thank you." A husky voice floated to him from within the barn in accented English. "Tell me about horse." Falke scooted to the shadows to investigate. A shuffle came from the back of the stable, and he spotted a boy's brown cowlick bobbing inside a stall.

"I couldn't find Cyrus or Darianne to tell them

about the animal's legs. Ye could have knocked me
over with a quill when ye spoke to me. In me own
tongue, no less. There's nobles around here who
can't speak it as well as you. And to think ye be a
know'n the heal'n ways, too.''

"Don't speak much, Lucas." Only a head taller
than the child, Lady Gwendolyn moved from one
side of the stall and disappeared again behind the
wooden gate. "No tell anyone. My uncle. Go hard
on me."

The boy nodded his head with vigor. "I've heard
about 'em. I'm thinkin' 'e's like me da, Lady
Wren—" He stumbled on an apology. "I-I'm sorry,
Lady Gwendolyn. 'Tis just that everyone's been cal-
lin' ye that."

"'Tis no harm. Hold this bowl. I soak the rags."

The desire to peek over the gate and survey the
operations nagged at Falke. He ducked into the
empty stall next to the pair and sought a crack to spy
through. The girl's disclosure intrigued him. She
spoke English as well as French? Titus called her an
imbecile, but the boy was right—there were many
nobles who could not communicate with their serfs
as well as she.

She moved with ease around the tiny boxed pen.
He couldn't hear any dragging feet against the wood
floor. The limp was another facade. What else did
she hide from Titus? Falke remembered a young
girl's wooden doll he had seen in the Holy Lands.
In reality, it had been a series of dolls, each smaller
than the next, all nested together. How many inner

layers resided within the outer shell of Lady Gwendolyn?

"'Twas too long a journey for him." Genuine concern cracked the even timbre of her voice.

A finger-wide split between two boards offered Falke a view into the next stall. A short candle sputtered light onto Lady Gwendolyn's hands. Again Falke found himself mesmerized by that part of her body. The muscles in her fingers flexed and contracted while she massaged the inflamed tendons of her mount's legs. With skilled efficiency, she rubbed a sharp-smelling ointment deep into the horse's joints.

"Now I'll wrap them." She withdrew long strips of brown cloth from the bowl the boy held. The smell of juniper and camphor mixed with the aroma of the liniment. She swaddled each leg with even, parallel turns of the wraps, then wiped her hands on the front of her skirt.

"Will that fix 'em up?" The boy stayed close to Gwendolyn and away from the stallion's sharp teeth.

"Aye." She stood and shook the hay from her gown. The kirtle ended in a ragged rip across the front and exposed her ankles to the cool night air. A glance at the wrapping and the gown confirmed the origin of the strips of cloth. How many of the patches on her gown were due to wear and how many due to use as bandages?

"What should I do tomorrow? Remove them strips?" The boy offered his aid, but kept his gaze on the huge head of the animal.

"Nay. Greatheart…not like strangers. Save with me."

The boy flattened himself against the wall of the stall. Gwendolyn stretched out her hand and rested it on Lucas's head. She brushed back the curtain of hair from her face, and once again Falke found himself amazed at the color of her eyes—two jewels of brilliant sapphire light.

Her voice deepened and grew steady. "Cyrus or I will nurse him. And Lucas, if anyone asks, tell him Cyrus wrapped the legs. Can you do that?"

Her blue eyes suddenly grew worried. They no longer shone with youth. Instead, Falke saw them dim with ancient wariness. She bit her upper lip and cupped the boy's chin with her hand. "Lucas, 'tis very important."

Lucas nodded his head and gave her a big grin. "Lady Wren—I mean Gwendolyn—ye can trust me."

"Good." She tossed her head and the matted dark mane again covered most of her face. Her voice became hesitant again. "Check outside. No one can see." The boy ran out the gate. Falke duckwalked to a corner and waited for the two to leave.

"Goodnight, Greatheart. We lived another day." Sorrow and courage colored her statement reminding Falke of an old woman who has outlived all those she loved.

"Lady Wren, there's no one about." The boy gave her a quick wave from the stable door.

Light, sure steps danced across the floor, then the

only sounds were the even breaths of the livestock. Falke peered over the gate. The boy's and woman's forms flittered past the stable window and disappeared around the corner.

He braced his arm on the top board and jumped the stall gate. At the door, he searched the dusk for signs she had succeeded in reaching the castle unseen.

From the garden path, Ozbern emerged breathless and panting. "There you are. I've been looking for you."

"Why? Did you see anything?" Had Lady Gwendolyn been spotted?

"Nay, not see. But I heard from Robert." Ozbern's tone was rueful and admiring at the same time. "I don't know what possessed you to have him play the drunk for Laron, but it worked. After the rest of the knights withdrew, Ferris and Laron had quite a conversation. They let their tongues wag until they passed out drunk. Guess what plan they devised?" Ozbern quirked his mouth in an all-knowing grin.

"Ferris offered to kill Lady Wren—Lady Gwendolyn—and frame me for the woman's demise." Falke squelched the smug smile on his friend's face.

"Blast it, Falke, just once I'd like to supply a bit information that you don't already know." Ozbern shook his dark mane of hair in self-disgust.

"Titus offered me a similar deal. Though I think Ferris acts alone on this. Titus was adamant that no Cravenmoor people be involved. But father and son are much alike."

"What kind of people are we dealing with?" Distaste hardened Ozbern's tone.

Falke walked back to the castle with Ozbern matching his strides. 'Twas a good question his friend asked. A man who offered to kill his ward, a bastard who offered to kill his cousin, and a woman-child who played the buffoon but hid an ember of humanity... The image of her strong hands working with practiced ease created in Falke a desire to erase the sadness that dulled her azure eyes.

"We must keep her here." The tingling sensation that had nagged at him disappeared with his words.

"And guard her well. Her death would be all Laron needs to set the rest of Merin's vassals against you." Ozbern combed back his hair with his fingers.

"See that one of my men is with her at all times," Falke ordered in a harsh whisper as he pushed open the castle door and entered.

Red-hot embers in the fireplace pulsated with heat, driving away the chill of the outside air. Ivette embroidered near the wide hearth. Her gaze traveled up the stairs toward the solar and main bedchamber. Instead of returning her inquiring smile, Falke slumped into a chair near the fire. The sharp snap of a fan and the stiff crinkle of silk marked her displeasure at his refusal of her unspoken offer this night.

"Go to bed, Ozbern," he ordered as he stared into the coals. Alone with his thoughts, he stirred the ashes with an iron poker and watched the embers fly up the chimney, wishing his worries would disappear as easily.

His errant vassal and the men of Cravenmoor offered him no real danger. But the girl's danger materialized because of him. He couldn't allow her to
be hurt due to his plan. He crinkled his eyes in disgust. God's wounds, if he wasn't careful he'd start
to sound honorable. And that was something he
couldn't allow. Even for the sake of Lady Wren.

Chapter Four

Robert careened around the corner, swept the great hall with a glance, then bounded up the stairs three at a time. Falke watched the anxious young knight race across the upstairs gallery.

"Lost her again?" Ozbern positioned his rook to capture Falke's bishop.

"Aye, 'twould seem so." Falke saved his bishop, the move putting Ozbern's white rook in danger.

Falke's squire, Harris, stumbled into the great hall, then strolled casually across the floor. When he reached the stairs, he, too, raced up them. Lady Wren's two bodyguards exchanged shrugs on the balcony.

"Harris doesn't know where she is, either?" Ozbern moved a pawn to block his rook's capture.

"'Twould appear so." Falke stretched his long legs and propped his fingers together as he pretended to study the chessboard. Seated in a small alcove at the far end of the room, he had a location that enabled him to survey the hall's activities.

Servants bustled around the trestle tables, collecting the trenchers from the midday meal. Hounds milled through the floor rushes, eager to find scraps. Indulgent villeins threw bones and pieces of meat to the appreciative dogs. Though nearly waist high to the women clearing the table, the dogs remained docile, wagging their tails and licking the hands that fed them. Would that Falke's vassals were as easily subdued.

Upstairs near the solar, Ivette and the ladies of Mistedge had retreated to their sewing and embroidery. His dismissal nearly a fortnight ago had Ivette playing the wounded lover, though they had shared but a kiss.

Seated near the hearth, Laron and Ferris shared a bottle of Norman wine, speaking in low tones and occasionally throwing a speculative glance toward Falke. Titus snored heavily near the high dais, his overindulgence of rich food and strong wine sapping his alertness. 'Twas one enemy Falke need not worry himself with.

He nodded slightly toward the expansive room. "All those who could do the lady harm are accounted for." A wisp of a smile tugged at Falke's lips as he slanted a glance toward the shadowy alcove just to his left.

Ozbern leaned across the board and whispered, "'Tis good to see you enjoy this duty."

"'Tis naught but self-preservation," Falke insisted.

"But 'tis an honorable decision nonetheless." Ozbern smiled as he moved his queen.

"Do not read more than is there. I have no honor, wish no honor. I do and say as I please to get what I want." Falke swore as he spied a bit of skin. A big toe, in fact. Light wavered through the high window behind him and lit on the corner of the alcove, illuminating a worn leather slipper with a toe protruding from the tip. Lady Wren.

Wrapped in a mantle of charcoal gray, her bulk melted into the lengthening shadows. If Falke squinted and scrutinized the varying shades of gray and black, he could just make out her form standing motionless, eavesdropping on the conversations in the great hall.

She's good. Very, very good. The lady played the same game as Falke, but substituted herself as an imbecile for Falke's chosen drunk. Either way put tongues and men off guard. "Checkmate, Ozbern." He played his knight, cornering the white king between his bishop and rook.

"Again." Ozbern slumped back in his chair. "I suppose we should help Robert and Harris."

"Aye, I suppose we should." His voice just a trifle louder than necessary, Falke advised, "Send Robert upstairs to her chamber. Harris to the chapel. You take the halls." With his men so dispatched, Lady Wren would be able to make her daily pilgrimage to the stables without bumping into any of them.

"And you?"

Settling back and gaining an unobstructed view of

the alcove, Falke smiled. "I will savor my victory."
The shadows shifted. The toe vanished. Lady Wren
disappeared in the darkness.

Ozbern muttered complaints as he strode off to do
his leader's bidding. Falke waited a few minutes, just
long enough of a head start so the girl would not
know he followed her. She was too fleet of foot for
him to give her much of a head start. He strolled
toward the garderobe, then ducked down the adjacent
hall to shadow the girl.

He had wrestled with informing his men of her
lack of handicap, but had decided to keep mum. The
more people that knew of her secret, the more likely
'twould to be revealed. The girl needed as many
tricks as possible to elude Titus. Cyrus and his wife,
Darianne, had instructed her well. None save Falke
knew of her deception.

If not for the night in the stable, Falke would never
have guessed the girl possessed such stealth. Nor
would he have been watchful for her quiet moves.
For nearly a fortnight, he had been mindful of her
silent presence among the shadows. When the hall
rang with music, the nobles sipped fine wine and the
servants busied with finishing up the day's tasks,
Lady Wren cloaked herself in mourning colors and
spied.

As long as her would-be assassins remained in
Falke's sight, he allowed her to roam. He would give
her what freedom he could as long as she remained
at Mistedge. But with reason. He had followed or
beat her to the stables each day.

Dampness seeped through the walls of the curved passageway, chilling his skin. Fur-soft moss clung to the stone. Thankfully, the floor rushes were winter old and had long ago had the snap crushed from them. Soundlessly, he made his way through the hall and down a set of stairs to the first floor.

Clatter from the kitchen broke the silence. Falke stilled, then inched closer. The fire snapped and popped as grease and water spattered onto the embers. Servants laughed and spoke in harsh English accents as they consumed the last vestiges of the nobles' meal.

Poised at the kitchen door, Lady Wren waited, her entire body swathed in a dark mantle. With the kitchen crew engrossed in merriment, she scampered past and slipped out the door to the yard.

The butler rose from the table and approached the kitchen archway. He turned his neckless body toward the door, listening. Falke crouched against the wall, the cold stone pressing into his back. Releasing a sigh, the butler withdrew and returned to the ribaldry in the kitchen.

On tiptoe, Falke crossed the hall, paused to listen for any approaching steps, then carefully opened the door and followed Lady Wren.

A small, square shape shuffled along the inner bailey wall. Carefully, she made her way to the gate and the outer bailey. Above, the guards lounged, unaware of the figure's presence.

Lady Wren would make the stables without detection. Falke would give her time to inspect the steed's legs and apply the aromatic herbs, though the animal seemed to have recuperated. This morning, when he had ventured to check on the animal, the old war-horse had tried to kick his teeth in just for peering over the stall gate. A few days rest and the destrier would be well enough to travel, though a journey back to Cravenmoor might cause a recurrence.

More than a gentle nag of guilt pricked Falke's heart. He never tolerated abuse of an animal, and Lady Wren and her mount jousted with his deter-mined aloofness. How could he stay distant from the girl's plight? But he would. He'd not make the same mistake as his father, forfeiting all he truly desired because of honor.

Nay, he had seen his father wither into a bitter man. 'Twas said misery loved company, and Falke's father had strived to have his wife and sons join him in his disappointment with life. Especially Falke, who had ignored the dogma of honor and sought to savor all of life's pleasures.

The pungent scent of fresh hay and horses cleared Falke's thoughts of all except his quarry. Lady Wren. He listened outside the stable door, expecting to hear her soft husky tones calming her horse. Only the shuffling of hooves across sawdust and the quiet snores of horses broke the quiet. Slipping inside, he scanned the rows of stalls. Lady Wren's horse rested his head over the gate, his eyes closed.

God's wound's, where could she be? Discarding all discretion, Falke ran from stall to stall, searching for the plump shape. Dozing horses, a few mules and goats complained of his intrusion. He climbed the stairs to the loft and found two stable boys napping in the soft hay, but no Lady Wren.

Dashing out of the stables, he walked toward the fishpond, retracing his steps mentally from the castle, across the inner bailey, to the outer yard to the… Would she leave the castle proper? The tiny hairs along his neck tingled as he strode toward the outer wall.

"Falke." Ozbern trotted toward him. "Harris found her."

"What?" Falke shortened his stride, but continued toward the barbican. "Where?"

"In the chapel." Ozbern puffed his reply. "Lady Wren and the old knight were lighting prayer candles."

"But it cannot be." When Falke pulled up short, Ozbern nearly plowed into his back. "She came outside."

"I know not whom you saw, but Lady Wren is inside the keep. I saw her myself. No other would willingly don her rags and arthritic step."

Raking his fingers through his hair, Falke shook his head. "I could have sworn…"

"Falke, no one can be in two places at the same time." Ozbern waved his hand toward the gray stone castle. "Your betrothed is in her room, guarded once again by Harris and Robert. And by two other experienced men. Though why two healthy young men cannot keep up with one crippled imbecile, I know not."

"Ozbern." Falke kept his voice patient. "Do not call her cripple, and do not call her imbecile. Lady Wren is many things, but neither of those."

Lifting his brows, Ozbern dropped his chin, looking stunned. "And pray, has Falke de Chretian finally discovered honor to fight so for a lady?"

"Nay, you should know me better," Falke countered.

"Then why so fierce when I but speak the truth?"

"Because *I* speak the truth." Falke waited as his friend and second pondered the information. "The girl has no impediment to her legs. 'Tis but a ruse."

"And you just now tell me." Ozbern voice rose in pitch. He patted his palm over his heart.

"'Tis my thought she plays this game to put Titus off guard. I fear the more that know the more likely Titus will find her out."

Appeased, his second asked, "'Tis true, and Titus is not a man to forgive. But what of her wits? Is she as dull as she seems?"

"Nay. I have heard her speak, both French and English. But not well in either language. She is not as weak-minded as she appears, yet I know not how strong a mind she possesses."

"Why is it, my friend, that nothing associated with you is as it seems? Not even this poor woman?"

"That is why I keep your company, Ozbern." Falke slapped his friend on the bank. "You are ever constant."

"Are you saying I'm a boor?"

"Nay. Only...predictable. 'Tis why I always win at chess. You think overmuch."

"'Tis my lot, since you act first and think later. But that will change."

"How so?"

"Now you have something to lose." Ozbern gave Falke a paternal smile. "Come. After the evening meal the musicians will strike up their instruments, and a poet has stopped by to recite an epic. 'Twill be almost as much entertainment as watching Ivette pretend to hate you."

"Pretend?"

Ozbern chuckled. "No woman that harbors ill feeling toward a man would walk past him so oft and with that gait." He let his hips swing gently back and forth.

"She is a woman. She will use what she has to get her way." Tugging at his chin, Falke gave the barbican one last glance. If 'twas not the Lady Wren he had followed, who was it? 'Twould be several hours before they ate the light evening meal. "I would explore my demesne, Ozbern. Stay here, with an eye to Lady Wren. See that she is escorted wherever she may wander. I will return by nightfall."

"What is about?"

Years of friendship and countless battles had melded a bond between the two men. Falke could hide little from his second. 'Twas a feeling of both comfort and concern. What could he say to his friend? That the hair along his neck tingled? That he felt restless?

"Nothing, save a wish to stretch these long legs and free me from Ivette, Ferris, Laron and Titus."

"Very well, I will be on my guard. And mind you, you do the same. I've no wish at this late date to find myself without a liege and friend." Ozbern walked back toward the castle.

Falke strode toward the barbican, his strides lengthening with each step. After his conversation with Ozbern, he realized the mysterious woman could be anywhere. He scanned the landscape.

The one road to the drawbridge dipped into a shallow valley. Standing on the rise, he could see the hovels that made up the village. His uncle had wasted no income on his serfs, and as such, they had no loyalty to Falke.

The grassy fields surrounding the village claimed the hearts of his villeins and freemen. Fertile soil waited to be plowed, sowed and harvested, the bounty of which would feed his people over the long harsh winter. With Lord Merin's death and the arrival of the Cravenmoor nobles, the planting had been delayed but a few days. Tomorrow he would order the reeve to begin the plowing. For now, he planted his fists at his hips and scanned the grass for the woman he had been following.

There! Just at the forest's edge, a short form, dark and shapeless, slid into the woods. He marked the spot in his mind and loped across the fields toward it.

Cautiously, he made his way between the trunks of oak and maple trees. Insects hummed near his ear, and he batted away the flying pests. The ground sagged as he walked, the spring thaw soaking the accumulated dead leaves and soil.

Afternoon sun sneaked through the canopy above his head and spattered light like an artist flicking his brush. From somewhere deep in the shadows, a mournful bird called. A wren. Falke followed the sound, mindful of the tingling at the base of his neck and the racing of his heart.

Chapter Five

A warm breeze ruffled Falke's hair as he paused in his search. His uncle's woods—nay, his woods—bowed with stately greenery. With surprise, he noted the brushstrokes of turquoise and rose in the sky above. Hours had passed since he had first entered the forest and heard the wren.

He must have been wrong. 'Twas some villein or poacher he had spotted at the forest edge, not Lady Wren.

With the sun sinking, 'twould be best to make his way back to the castle. Looking about, he realized he had ventured far into the woods. Far enough that he was unsure of his landmarks. He headed off to the east, believing he would either run into fields or find the castle.

Speaking out loud to the muse of nature, Falke questioned the wind. "Where is my infamous luck now? How could this sixth sense of mine lead me so far astray?"

Luck served as his aegis, a way to hide his intelligence and prowess...and irritate his father. Bernard de Chretian hated the fact that his son accomplished military coups so easily and brushed them away as just a manifestation of good fortune. Falke always kept his planning hidden under the guise of carousing and wenching. Now, when he could really use some good fortune, not even a glimmer of hope burned.

Ozbern was right—Falke did not want to lose this keep. Mayhap, at last, he had a home. And luck aside, he was determined to secure Mistedge as his own. Despite Laron and the dismal village, Falke knew he could build Mistedge to a prosperous keep, if given the chance.

He let his feet pound against the leaf-littered forest floor. Down a steep vale, a jump across a narrow creek, then a scamper up the other side. He crested a ridge and scanned for some telltale mark that he was on the correct path.

Daylight battled with the coming night, but twilight would last only so long. Already he spotted the cold face of the full moon as the sun dipped below the treetops. Disheartened, he trudged on as the darkness deepened, until he heard again the wren's serene song, a splash, then a gasping chortle.

He pivoted, his instincts telling him the sound was feminine in origin. Aye, he could hear it plainly now, an odd, scratchy-throated laughter, but womanly. He followed the sound as he made his way through the forest.

Pushing aside berry brambles and wild rose

bushes, he entered a clearing. A small pond nestled in a gentle groove of land. Wildflowers, their colorful heads nodding like sleepy children, sprinkled the mossy green banks. Moonlight glided across the water, the silvery beams twinkling like underwater stars.

Kneeling on one knee, Falke cursed his foolishness. There was no woman here. Whomever he had spotted earlier must be long gone by now. In an attempt to relieve his frustration, he skipped a flat stone across the water.

He followed its path as a shadow against the moonlight, and then stumbled to his feet and gasped. Just where his stone disappeared into the depths of the dark water, the moonlight came to life.

Rays of silver-white light turned to strands of floating hair. From the blue-black depths, two arms surfaced. Then a chest, with full, uplifted breasts, followed by a narrow waist and slim hips.

His own chest constricted and his heart demanded he take a breath of air, yet Falke could not. The image before him made movement a forgotten act. At the far shore, the petite figure emerged from the pond. Artemis, goddess of the moon, stood on the bank opposite him, clad only in the glorious light of her hair. She disappeared behind a clump of vines and at last Falke found his breath.

A dream…a fit brought on by his troubled mind. Falke tried to rationalize away the mirage as he wove in and out of the shadows toward the mysterious woman. Like a thief, he stalked a hidden treasure, afraid it was all a dream. Afraid the vision might be real.

His answer came on the breeze. Gentle humming called to him as the Sirens called to Ulysses. As helpless as the Greek mariner, Falke could not help but seek out the songstress.

Seated on a pallet of lichens and moss, his goddess brushed the tangles from her moonbeam hair. She was dressed in a modest linen chemise, and his eyes lingered on the way it clung to her damp body. The material molded to her tiny waist and the full curve of her breasts. Alabaster skin peeked from the open throat. Dainty ankles invited his mind to explore the rest of the hidden contours. Her face, tilted up toward the sky, remained obscure.

He leaned forward, straining to see her features. A dry branch snapped, the sound deafening in his own ears. Falke watched with dismay and anticipation as she turned toward his hiding place. Beauty, so pure as to blind him, stared at him with eyes the color of a star-filled night.

She rose and sped off like a deer, silent and swift.

"Nay, do not go." Falke crashed through the undergrowth after her. "I'll not harm you."

She bolted, a flash of white streaking against the growing night. Falke rushed after her, loath to end the encounter. His legs stretched to shorten the distance between them.

Ahead, like an animal caught in a poacher's snare, his nymph tugged at the hem of her chemise trapped in some thorns.

Slowly, he approached. Her actions became more frantic. The thin chemise clung to her trim waist and the smooth curves of her backside. Falke felt the embers of lust ignite to the heat of passion. Never had a woman's features so moved him. Beautiful women had begged him to make love to them, but never, until this night, had he ever thought to beg a woman to lay with him. He wanted this woman, and he wanted her to desire him just as much.

"Rest easy. I'll not touch you." His words stuck in his throat.

Her beauty transcended any mortal vision. The high cheekbones and delicate chin reminded him of a marble sculpture. Each fine line drew attention to her magnificent eyes. Eyes now filled with terror. Tiny whimpers came from her graceful throat as she tried to rip her covering from the tangle of thorns.

Falke bit his lower lip and raised his hands to show he had no weapon. With care to keep his movements small and precise, he pulled free the threads of her chemise, then dropped his hold.

Immediately, she turned to flee.

"Nay. Stay." He wanted to run after her but fought the need. If he chased her in the fading light, she might stumble and hurt herself. Tamping down the fear that he might lose her, Falke remained near the brambles.

A few strides down the trail, close to the water, she stopped and turned. She combed back the wet hair from her face. The action tickled Falke's instincts. Somehow the movement seemed familiar. From a secure distance, she scrutinized him.

Pulses of excitement raced through his body. Falke schooled his features to show none of the rampant desire in his loins. "Are you real or a dream created in my fitful wandering?" In the depths of his soul, he believed she might evaporate into the fingers of mist rising from the water, but prayed she would answer. What would her voice be like? Music? Bells?

A voice of strength answered him—feminine, yet deep, with layers of wisdom and understanding. "I am no dream." She tilted her head and her eyes narrowed. "Do you oft walk alone, Sir Falke? I thought you kept your nights occupied with other pursuits."

A sardonic laugh rolled from his lips. "If only the gossip about me were true, I'd be a happy man."

"And you're not happy? Pray tell me what more you could desire. You have a fine home and riches enough to please any man." Her voice held a hint of reproof at his ingratitude.

"And responsibilities." Falke settled himself on a fallen tree and waved his hand to her. He patted the space next to him. "Pray, have a seat so that we may converse in comfort."

Her full lips puckered into a pout while she shook her head. "Nay, I think 'tis close enough."

Falke opened his eyes wide in mock indignation. "I give you my word I'll do nothing improper."

"Your word? Are you not the knight who proclaimed you have no honor and are not bound by such maudlin customs?"

"Who are you that you know me so well? I'd stake my life I've never seen you before. Have you been hiding in the village?" An eerie feeling of premonition slithered along his spine. Who was this woman?

"Nay, but do not let my absence stop you from visiting the village." Again her voice seemed to reproach him for some unknown crime.

Falke rested his elbow on his knee and cradled his chin in his hand. For some reason his usual charm and wit were failing to win the woman over. He gave her his seductive smile, the one that displayed both of his dimples. "And if I came, would you be there for me to find?"

"Nay, but you might find a way to help the people of Mistedge."

No effect? Falke shook his head. Something was terribly wrong. That smile never failed him.

"Lord Falke? Did you hear me? I understand the blacksmith is a terrible bully. He's drunk most of the time and beats his family—"

"How do you know all this? Who are you?" Falke shot off the log. How dare this woman lecture him? How was she privy to so much information about his keep? Perhaps Laron had sent her to spy on him.

"I keep my eyes and ears open." She backed away from him, her eyes wary and distrustful.

Falke pondered his next move. If Laron had set her up in this espionage, she would tell Falke nothing out of fear. Better to gain her trust. If so, she might slip and reveal her identity.

"As will I, now that I have something to search for." He gave her a wink and waited for her expected blush.

It did not come. Instead she straightened her back and tilted her head up in a vain attempt to look down her nose at him. "Will you take nothing seriously?" The sapphire blue of her eyes darkened to black. "One pretty face, and you forget the heartache of your serfs. These people till the soil and plant your fields. In return they expect your guidance, justice and protection."

Falke rubbed the spot between his brows. Never had a woman so disregarded him. If he wanted a lecture, all he need do was return home to his father, who was quite capable of making Falke feel like a failure.

"Woman, that is enough. What business is it of mine if a man beats his wife?"

An outraged snort was her only reply. This conversation was not going as planned. He should be plying her with sweet words and tender names. Names! He had yet to know hers.

"Who are you that you know so much about me?"

She dropped her gaze to the ground. Her naked toe scraped the soft dirt back and forth. Again Falke felt a glimmer of recognition in the act, as though he should know this woman.

"I do not think my name important." Her voice rose, as did her gaze. Falke expected to see condemnation; instead hope filled her eyes. "Will you do something about the blacksmith?"

Disapproval he could have swept away without a thought. He could not ignore her heart-touching favor. ''Aye, little angel, I'll see to the blacksmith. Does that ease your worry?''

''I'm sure you'll sleep better this night for your decision.'' A riot of platinum curls cascaded across her slender shoulders. Falke had to stop himself from reaching for the riches before him. There'd be no peaceful slumber for him this night. Dreams of the woman before him would keep him awake for many evenings to come.

''Come, angel, do not fear me. Tell me your name.''

Why was she so hesitant to tell him who she was? Every nerve in his body jumped when she took a few hesitant steps toward him.

''I'm not afraid. After all, 'tis I to whom you owe your lot.''

In the depths of her eyes, Falke saw a quickening of spirit and the heavy footprint of grief. She looked at him with eyes that had seen too much pain, experienced life's hardships and survived. The mixture made her more alluring, less a child-woman, more woman-child.

''I'm afraid I don't understand.''

''You call me angel. Was it not a kiss by an angel that granted you exceptional luck?'' When she moved closer, he could smell the scent of lavender soap from her skin and hair.

'''Tis nothing but an old wives' tale. Village gossip.''

With each word, her stance grew less rigid, more relaxed. Falke shrugged his shoulders, nonchalantly kicked a stone off the trail and scuffed his boots in the dirt. His shuffling steps brought him to within arm's reach of his prize.

"But I would gladly turn the myth to reality." He winked at her and pulled a persuasive smile from his arsenal of charm.

"Nay, one kiss from an angel brought you good fortune. If you should have another, 'twould turn the favored luck to bad." She swung away from him, her dainty foot raised to escape down the path.

"A risk I'm willing to take." He captured her wrist in his hand. A quick tug and he pulled her to his chest. He buried his lips into the wealth of hair and inhaled her scent. She twisted in his arms, arching her body, seeking to be free. The brush of her breasts against his chest thickened his longing.

With practiced seduction, he trailed kisses down the delicate line of her jaw, then captured the moistness of her lips. Deep carnal hunger ached to be fed on the sweetness of her mouth. The kiss took on a life of its own, feeding from his passion and her awakening desire.

Confident of his victory, Falke relaxed his hold and lifted his mouth from hers. Her upturned face mesmerized him. Lips swollen from his kiss parted, offering more delights. Quick breaths made her chest rise and fall, rubbing her stiff peaks against his chest. She slipped her arm from his grasp and rested both hands lightly on his chest, feeling the nap of his velvet tunic.

"I thought I could make you see reason." Falke winked at his now pliant hostage.

"Aye, that you have, Lord Falke." Her breath danced across the hollow of his neck, warming his skin. "You've made me see how blind you really are." With a mighty shove, his dainty angel hurled him backward into the pond. Dark cold water swallowed him. He sputtered to the surface in time to see a flash of white disappear over the ridge and melt into the forest.

Staggering to his feet, Falke trudged to the shore and twisted the corner of his tunic to wring out the water. Each squish of his wet boots as he walked up the rise reminded him of the beauty and his desire. He'd have that woman, and he would torture her with passion, until she cried for him to bring her relief. Standing atop the high point, he saw the flickering lights of the castle.

A few miles and he would be home. He walked on, his thoughts occupying the time. He had Laron plotting against him, Ivette ready to scratch his eyes out and a plain, daft woman as his betrothed. Not to mention a mysterious woman bathing in his pond.

Half an hour later, Falke entered the castle and shuffled over to the nearest fireplace. Ozbern rounded the corner. "Where in blazes have you been?" Noticing the damp clothes, he added, "And what have you been doing?"

"Aye, Lord Falke." Ivette entered in turn, with an

entourage of knights and ladies. Titus, Laron and Ferris pushed their way to the front.

"I've had an encounter with an angel."

"What?" Ozbern wrinkled his brow. "Have you gone daft?"

"Nay." Falke took a seat on the hearth and pulled off his boots. Water sizzled on the hot stones. His clothes hung like weights on his shoulders. "I have seen a face Helen of Troy would grow jealous of. Eyes like twin jewels, blue with fire in their depths. Hair made of moonbeams. The exact same shade as—"

"Strands of silver. Small like a young girl, yet a body that tells all she is a woman." Titus drew away as he spoke, his eyes wide, his voice shaking. "She knows! She knows and follows me here! Ferris, gather our men! We leave this place come the morrow." The errant knight raced away, leaving behind a perplexed crowd.

Ferris crossed his arms over his narrow chest. His small dark gaze studied Falke with unhidden intensity. "This woman—you spoke with her?"

"Spoke. Touched. Kissed." Falke smiled at the memory.

"Falke!" Ivette screeched. "You shame yourself as you shame me." She turned and waited for the ladies to follow. Falke could see their desire to hear his story and their fear of Ivette's wrath. A snap of a fan, and the ladies meekly fell into step behind Ivette.

"So you are certain this woman was real? No

specter? No ghost?'' Ferris continued to interrogate Falke.

''Aye. Those lips were warm and inviting.''

''And where is my cousin?'' A gleam came to Ferris's eye, one Falke found strangely unnerving. Titus was evil, but Ferris added cunning and youth to the mixture. By far, Falke found him the most dangerous.

''In her chamber,'' Ozbern answered. ''You'll find four men posted outside her door.'' The information served as a warning. ''While Lady Wren—Gwendolyn—resides at Mistedge, she'll come to no harm.''

''I would think nothing else.'' Ferris's thin lips drew into a sly smile. Letting his voice rise so that the nobles could hear, he added, ''For the only way Falke can escape his commitment to her would be should she die. A man not held by honor might resort to murder to free himself. Or luck.'' Placing the ember of suspicion in the minds of the assembled knights, Ferris sauntered away. Laron threw Falke a smug smile, then followed his newfound friend. The remaining knights departed, but with whispers and mumbling.

''An angel, Falke?'' Ozbern murmured. ''Do you seek to turn these men against you? And what of Titus? I thought the old man feared nothing except the devil himself. What has this strange woman to do with him?''

''I know not.'' Falke warmed his hands at the fire.

"But one thing is certain—I will find her again. And she will not escape me."

"This woman can wait. But Titus cannot. Lady Wren cannot leave come the morrow."

A deep growl rumbled in Falke's chest. Ferris and Laron must have sealed a deal. If Gwendolyn died suspiciously, Laron would have a good chance of stirring the vassals to mutiny. Falke had counted on Titus's greed to keep him at Mistedge longer, giving him time to arrange a convent stay for his betrothed.

"Give the Cravenmore men ample drink. 'Twill be hard to move so many with heavy heads. We may delay their leaving for a day."

"And then?"

"I will think of something."

"'Twould seem our luck has gone from good to bad." Ozbern stirred the fire with a long iron poker.

Falke brought his head up and stared at his friend. The warning of the woman in the woods reverberated in his mind. Who was she? How came she to know him so well? Once again he wondered if she might be in league with his enemies. Hadn't the mention of her sent Titus scurrying for his home?

Falke had been kissed by angel twice now in his life. Was he twice blessed? Or twice cursed?

Chapter Six

Gwendolyn peered out the window of her room, watching the serfs in the inner yard just beginning their daily chores. The knotted strands of hair over her eyes seemed like prison bars, trapping her soul within. Why couldn't she be outside, laughing and singing in the sunlight? Why couldn't she dress in soft gowns and flirt with young knights?

Defiance exploded her well-built armor of caution and she combed back her hair, exposing her face. The filtered light from the room's only window bathed her cheeks with warmth. She closed her eyelids and let the sunshine cause speckles of light to dance on the insides of her eyelids. The soft warmth made her remember Falke, the way his hand had felt on hers, and the heat of his lips when he had kissed her last night.

Nay! Falke had not kissed *her,* Lady Wren, the plain, squat woman who was his betrothed. The knight had tried to seduce a beautiful woman. A stranger to him.

Jealousy raked a stinging wound in Gwendolyn's heart. Falke had no idea that his angel near the pond had been, in truth, drab Lady Wren. To him, she was a dullard, a jest of nature. Gwendolyn snorted at the absurdity of her emotions, how could she be jealous of herself?

Temptation teased her better judgment. Just a bit of hair dye, swaddling around her waist and play-acting built her disguise. Falke would welcome a union with his night angel, but Gwendolyn dared not tell the truth, not yet. She still had doubts about the knight's integrity.

"My child?" The door creaked open as Darianne entered, followed by Cyrus.

With reluctance, Gwendolyn opened her eyes and gave her foster mother a quiet smile. "Titus should be ready to leave soon. I've just a few more things to collect." She bit back her disappointment and returned to packing her few possessions in a vain attempt to drive away the heartache.

Word of the "angel" in the woods had swept through the castle. Her carelessness had levied a heavy toll. Titus had ordered all of the Cravenmore entourage to depart. As dawn brightened the sky, her optimism dimmed. Looking around the tiny cell, clean and tidy now from their work, she sighed, "I don't know if I can stand going back."

"Only for a year," Cyrus said, trying to reassure her. He gave his wife a helpless glance. "'Tis just this talk of ghosts and such that has Titus running scared. We'll be back for another chance."

"Gwendolyn…" Darianne folded her fingers together and studied her foster daughter. "The talk is Lord Falke spoke with…kissed…this woman, this angel."

Heat blossomed across Gwendolyn's cheeks as warmth swirled in the pit of her stomach. "He saw me before I had time to reapply the dye to my hair. Falke has no inkling 'twas me he tried to seduce."

"And did he, child?" Darianne tilted Gwendolyn's chin up and studied her. "No man would wait a year to claim you."

Gwendolyn shook her head. "He took but a kiss, but I've lived under Titus's roof long enough to know he wanted much more. Would he have taken more and showed the true mettle of his worth? I know not, for I escaped before he had the chance. Now 'twill be another year before I can find answers."

Another year with Titus. Another year of groveling at his feet and pretending not to understand the cruel jokes and blows. Despair washed over her like a summer flood. The wavering flame of hope washed away in the tide. Why couldn't Falke de Chretian be a man she could trust and believe in?

Her arm still tingled when she remembered the warmth of his fingers. Goose bumps ran down her neck as she recalled the soft whisper of his words against her ear. Flutters of excitement buffeted her stomach. A gentle touch and kind words, the first she'd ever experienced from a man other than Cyrus… Then to have it all collapse with that ominous announcement of their departure. Another year!

"Have you discovered anything of Lord Falke's character, other than he is enraptured by this angel?" Darianne asked with a smile.

Volumes, Gwendolyn thought. Though nothing that helped their cause. Falke de Chretian disavowed any trace of honor. Grimaced at the code of chivalry. Thought a witty smile would buy him anything or anyone he chose. Ignored his villeins and disregarded the soldiers' disrespect.

But one trait remained dear to her heart—the camaraderie he shared with the knight Ozbern was forged in true friendship.

Two men, so vastly different. Falke, tall with broad shoulders and the gait of man at ease in battle. Hair the color of sunshine, a smug grin on his full, sensual lips. Ozbern, shorter than many knights, yet taller than most when it came to conscience and morals. His dark curly head was ofttimes shaking in censure over some sharp retort of Falke's. They would share a laugh, a toast, a bawdy remark, and then Gwendolyn would experience the pangs of loneliness.

No one knew that in the shadows of the castle, occasionally right at their heels, she listened attentively. But always alone. Never included. Seeing the ladies dressed in fine wools and silks made Gwendolyn long for the trappings of feminine youth. What she would give for an opportunity to dance in the hall, to share laughter with a friend, to share life with a man who loved her as she was!

'Twas useless to wish. Her dreams would not come true. As she plopped down on a trunk, Gwendolyn answered, "Though tongues wag about me, thinking I cannot understand, I have learned little. Chretian's men brag of his fighting ability and quick wits. His enemies condemn him for his brashness and uncanny luck."

"Someone's coming. 'Tis probably the guard." Darianne spread her skirt to hide Gwendolyn from view. "Hurry, cover your face."

The racing footsteps echoed off the stone walls, heading toward their tiny room. "'Tis me." Lucas's pale face peered around the door. His sandy topknot waved like a flag of friendship. "I come to say ye need not hurry."

The sound of her foster parents' collective sigh resounded in the room. Cyrus asked, "And why is that?"

"The ale and wine flowed freely among Cravenmoor last night. Lord Falke entertained the whole crew, with orders that as this was to be their last night, their cups should never be empty. There's not a man among them that can seat a horse. Titus is nursing a heavy head and a churning gut. The only one with clear senses is the dark one."

"Ferris?" Gwendolyn asked.

"Aye," Lucas agreed. "He's out swearin' in the stables. 'Twill be noon before most Cravenmoor knights rise, and then they'll be sufferin' the drops and thick heads."

Gwendolyn shot her foster parents a worried frown. Overindulgent hospitality did not seem a likely reason for Falke's sudden generosity. Why didn't he want Titus to leave the castle? How long did he intend to detain them?

Lucas sidled over to Gwendolyn and looked at her with wide brown eyes. "The salve ye gave me for me back eased the pain from them bruises."

"I'm glad my medicine—" Gwendolyn clamped her lips tightly together. She had almost forgotten to stammer. "—help." Darianne shot her a chastising stare.

Lucas's smile faded. "Milady, it's been three days that me mum's been feelin' poorly. Da says she's just lazy, but 'tis not like her. I wish ye could see her and help her."

Gwendolyn's heart melted, for she knew well the fear the boy experienced. But wandering the castle unnoticed was difficult enough. To enter the village and administer there undetected would be nearly impossible. Tending the ill required that she ask questions. Insightful questions that would strip her of her masquerade.

She took a scarf from her bag and reached into her pockets. "Mayhap an infusion of chamomile and yarrow will comfort her." Her arms went around his thin body and she hugged him to her waist.

"Mum needs help. Me da's naught but a drunk. Beats me and Mum and the little 'uns. The whole village looks down on us because of 'im.'' Great tears rolled down his cheeks. He looked at Gwendolyn for guidance. She could only hold the child close.

"Don't let them see how their words hurt you." All pretense of her dull wit disappeared as she tried to comfort him. "You need to be strong for your mother's sake." She sank down to be at eye level with him. Between loud sniffs, he nodded and wiped his face with the sleeve of his oversize shirt.

"You let that boy see too much," Cyrus said critically.

"He's a good boy," Gwendolyn murmured. Lucas's tears soaked through her thin overtunic and straight to her heart. The lad was a good child. He had kept quiet about Greatheart and had even aided her in nursing the animal. And it tore at Gwendolyn's very fiber not to share her herbal knowledge. A quick trip shouldn't be too hard to cover up, with all of Cravenmoor sleeping off a drunk. Especially if Darianne and Cyrus helped. But getting to the village... She would need Greatheart for that.

"Lucas, come here." Cyrus pulled the boy away from his charge. "Lady Gwendolyn still must be very careful. If anyone were to find out that she is not what she seems, it could go hard on her."

"I understand." The hope in the boy's eyes diminished, replaced with sorrow.

"I'll see her." Gwendolyn pretended not to notice her foster parents' looks of disapproval. "If my uncle's men are still in a stupor, we will go. But we must be quick.''

Gratitude lifted the despair from the boy's shoulders. ''Thank ye, Lady Wren. I just know Mum is sick and ye will be able to help her, just like that horse.'' He rushed forward and hugged Gwendolyn tightly around the waist once more. His pale face blushed with color, then he rushed from the room. The clatter of his steps faded with his retreat.

''You can't see that woman.'' Cyrus rose and pointed his finger at Gwendolyn.

''She's sick. If I can help her, I will.'' Gwendolyn straightened her back.

''You can't afford to expose yourself that much,'' Darianne argued.

Tears started to form in Gwendolyn's eyes. Anguish flooded her heart and threatened to rip it apart. ''I'm sorry, but I can't not help her. I can't keep from Lucas's mother the medicine that might heal her. That would make me as guilty as Titus.''

The older woman's gnarled hand stroked through the tangles of Gwendolyn's hair. ''Ah, child. I pray each night for the Lord to take the nightmare away from you.''

''Nay, Darianne.'' Gwendolyn rose and wiped the tears from her eyes. '''Tis that memory that fuels my hatred for Titus and gives me the will to survive his tortures.''

She rummaged in their bags. ''I will need Cyrus to attend me in the village. Tell Ferris you must walk Greatheart to see if his legs are sound. I will meet you outside the wall. Darianne, should I need more herbs, I will send Lucas to you.''

"But what of your guards?" Cyrus raised both hands high in disgust. "Lord Falke is having you watched. I've yet to determine if it's for your safety, or…" He let the rest of his statement hang in the air. 'Twas plain Gwendolyn was in peril, but from Falke or some other?

"If Darianne assists me, none will know I've left.''

The older woman shook her finger at Gwendolyn. "'Tis too dangerous.''

Unmindful of her foster parents' warning, Gwendolyn pulled Darianne's faded crimson mantle from a parcel. She stuffed her extra gown into the front of her chemise, forming a loose-hanging bosom. From her medicine bag, she grabbed a handful of fine white powder and sprinkled her hair and face. Turning in a circle, she rounded her shoulders and clutched her hands in an arthritic curl. Like magic, the young girl transformed herself into an old woman.

"This is not Cravenmoor, with knights and serfs besotted with ale,'' Cyrus argued in a low hiss.

"They've been fooled before. We go unnoticed. None wish to take a close look at me.''

Bringing the younger woman's hands to her lips, Darianne kissed each. "Go, but be on your guard.'' Her voice sounded tired and old, but resigned to the decision. She wrapped herself in Gwendolyn's gray mantle, covering her face and assuming a hunched and crippled walk. "I have lit enough candles in that chapel to light all of London."

"And pray God heeds your messages, or no amount of subterfuge will save us."

"Christ's blood, I should put an end to this madness." Cyrus looked into his foster daughter's eyes and sighed. "But I know you'll not rest until you've seen the woman."

Lucas barreled into the room, delight plain on his young face. "They's all asleep, Lady Wren. Are ye coming?"

"Aye." Gwendolyn slipped from the room, followed by Cyrus and Lucas.

Outside her room, Cyrus chatted with the guard. "I must see to the stallion, and my wife needs to gather herbs for Lady Gwendolyn's medication. The girl is still inside." He pointed to Darianne, who, posing as her foster daughter, was seated on a trunk. "She may wander to the chapel later. Stay with her. She tends to be careless with a flame."

The handsome, auburn-haired knight eyed the mantle-wrapped figure rocking slowly on the trunk. "I will see to her."

"Come, Wife, we shall not be long." Cyrus stressed each word as a warning to his adopted child.

With Lucas ahead, scouting for observers, Gwendolyn made her way down the steps to the great hall. There Cyrus left her, heading directly for the stable.

Keeping near the wall, Gwendolyn avoided the ladies gossiping near the hearth as they sewed new gowns. Ferris sat at a trestle table, deep in conversation with the thick-necked knight, Sir Laron. Although her back was to the knights, Lady Ivette nodded her head occasionally, as though agreeing with them. Gwendolyn pulled the scarf over her face and scurried out the door.

Down the central steps and across the inner bailey, she retained the slow steps of an old woman. Lucas pulled on her hand, his eagerness to help his mother jeopardizing Gwendolyn's disguise. Even with her head down, she sensed something amiss.

People were working, but halfhearted. Instead of a sentry at the outer bailey door, only a lance rested where a soldier should be standing at attention. A glance to her left showed the infantryman on his knees gambling with another soldier.

Wet laundry remained in a basket near the wall, mildewing in the shade. Women gossiped near the well, neglecting their duties. Sir Falke needed to take control of his holdings and quickly, before there was nothing left to take.

The marshal in the tower barely noticed as she and the boy left the barbican. Presently, Cyrus appeared, leading Greatheart. The old stallion sniffed her shoulder, then curled back his limber lips, smiling a horsey grin.

Cyrus gave her a leg up. Thankfully, the wall guards took little interest. She doubted her ride into the village would be reported. Reaching down, she lifted Lucas up behind her, then Cyrus climbed on. The weight of three would slow the stallion, but as a destrier he was accustomed to carrying the weight of a grown man in full armor.

She would be to the village and back before any were the wiser.

"What possessed you to keep that dingy animal here?" Ivette cornered Falke in the great hall. Her fingers latched onto his arm in a possessive lock.

"To what are you referring?" He opened his eyes wide and acted obtuse. His plan had worked better than he hoped. Not a single Cravenmoor knight, aside from Ferris, could sit upright, much less seat a horse. Wasting his fine wine on the doltish Cravenmoor nobles had been a painful loss, but had achieved the desired results. Nothing made a man sicker than too much of the fermented grapes from Champagne.

Ivette clutched his arm. All trace of demureness vanished. Her blue-black eyes glinted with irritation. "Do you intend to marry her?"

Falke freed himself from her grasp. Now the lady showed a glimpse of her true self. No sweet words or gentle carriage here. "Lady Gwendolyn stays because it suits me. That is all you need know."

Her demeanor softening, she trailed her fingers up his arm and brushed his ear as she licked her lips. "Falke, I beg pardon if I sounded harsh. 'Tis only that I don't want you to make a mistake you'll come to regret." Ivette waited to see if her change in tactics proved more successful.

"I appreciate your concern for me, but 'tis for naught. I can take care of myself."

Her chest rose and fell, her full lips creased in an inviting smile. "'Tis just that I'm afraid you might feel honor bound to do something about that creature."

"Honor bound?" He spread his arms wide and stepped back. "Dear lady, I thought you knew me better than that. If 'tis honor you wish to discuss, then you'd best seek out my sire, Bernard de Chretian. If you do not know his reputation, I assure you, he will be more than glad to inform you of it."

Today Ivette's beauty suffocated Falke. Her perfume stuck to his skin.

"Come, let us not quibble over so insignificant a thing," Ivette crooned. "The girl is nothing, and even if you do have to marry her, we can still be together. You can send her off to a convent and I can remain as your chatelaine. 'Tis obvious that girl cannot run a keep."

A crooked smile formed on his lips. "Really?" Falke didn't like the way Ivette planned his future for him. 'Twould do her good to be put in her place. "I think with a good washing she might be presentable. I mean, I only have to bed her often enough to get a child on her once or twice. The room would be dark."

Ivette's lips formed a perfect oval. Her face flushed with ire. "You're impossible. First I must contend with your halfwit bride, then your escapade last night with another woman. Do not think you can treat me this way!'' She flounced off.

"Well, now you've done it.'' Ozbern lazed against the stone archway. "Now there's none at Mistedge on your side.''

Falke shrugged one shoulder and strolled over to his friend. "'Tis easier that way—I know whom not to trust.''

"Aye, everyone.'' Ozbern chuckled. "What about the girl?''

"In her room. Neither she nor her servants know of the danger. Keep the guard. I want proof of Laron and Ferris's deviltry. When Laron is discredited, the mutiny against me will falter.''

"I put Landrick on the day watch and Alric at night. I've said nothing to them of her not having a twisted leg.''

Falke caught a glint of amusement in his friend's gaze. "A lonely night vigil will be just what the amorous Alric will want. Have you two been dicing again?''

"Alric won, but I win this game.''

"Ozbern, I do believe I'm getting to be a bad influence on you. When we first met, you'd never have thought to use your position for such petty revenge.''

"When we first met, I didn't have a position,'' Ozbern reminded his commander.

Falke glanced down at the one man he could really call friend. Ozbern's shiny armor of respectability was tarnished by their friendship, yet he never mentioned it. Falke's second served as a very vocal conscience, while Falke in turn provided the too-serious knight an outlet for fun and humor. They were a good match for command. A good enough match to find a way out of the predicament Falke found himself in.

"What of this woman you say you met in the woods?" Looking dour, Ozbern broached the tender subject.

"Did meet," Falke corrected. "The wine loosened many tongues last night in the Cravenmoor rooms, but all became silent when I spoke of the woman. She is real. And just the mention of her puts the fear of God into them all. Not an easy task."

"The archangel Gabriel with his fiery sword would find Titus a challenge." Ozbern's frown tipped to a knowing smile. "What power does this beautiful woman hold over Cravenmoor?"

"I know not. But I will find out." Falke scratched his chin. "For now, we must find a way to keep Titus here another day. Post the gossip that the woman I met was a girl whose parents live in the woods for fear her beauty would be too much of a temptation. That may lessen Titus's fears and, along with his greed, make him stay a few nights longer."

"As you will. But we cannot postpone his departure forever."

"Harris has ridden to a nearby abbey. I would have Lady Wren enter those walls, where she would be safe until I can deal with Titus and Laron. We need but stall him until my squire returns."

"Robert is the gossiper, and already has eyes on

a kitchen wench. He will drop the information as he whispers sweet words in her ear. Before the midday meal, all will know your angel is flesh and blood.'' His second gave him a jaunty salute and headed for the soldiers' dormitory to find Robert.

Falke strolled into the garden, welcoming the warmth of the sun and the absence of Ivette. Flirtation and seduction had withered to nagging and impatience. As far as Ivette was concerned, in Aunt Celestine's absence she was the lady of Mistedge manor. Falke could no more see sharing a life with her than with Lady Wren. So far, the quiet, plump girl had intrigued him more in just a few days than Ivette had since he'd met her.

A loneliness settled around his heart—loneliness for a mate, someone to share long stories with, to laugh at a silly tale or help lighten a sorrow. His cousin had found such a woman, one that matched him in temper and love. Roen's wife could not be classified as a beauty. She stood toe-to-toe with her husband, having her say, never backing down, though Roen stood a head taller and bore the physique of a warrior. And at such moments, Falke would swear Lenora's fiery mane of hair sparked, as did her whole person. Aye, when Lenora had her passions inflamed, she glowed with a beauty all could see.

What would it be like to have such a woman? A woman whose passions came from a natural state and not from a seductress's instruction? Falke pushed away the irritating questions. Women such as that didn't seek out men like himself. Oh, he was good enough for a short tumble when their husbands were away, but not the sort they married. Nay, a man like Ozbern, steadfast and loyal, was what a woman—a true lady—sought. And Falke was none of those things, nor would he ever be.

Chapter Seven

The black fields lay fallow as Gwendolyn and her friends rode past. Oxen that should be tied to the yoke grazed idly in the pasture. Spring sowing was already dangerously late. Seeds of barley, oats, peas and beans should already be lying in carefully plowed rows. If work continued at this pace, the winter would be hard indeed.

Time-worn paths from the huts to the various fields formed a mosaic of avenues. Gwendolyn reined Greatheart toward the center of the village. Chickens squawked as the warhorse disturbed their search for insects along the muddy lane. Near the well, which usually bustled with activity, only a few women gossiped, while their children played in the dirt.

A woman grabbed her toddler when Gwendolyn smiled at him. "She's got the evil eye," the mother warned her child.

"Devil's spawn is what I heard," another woman added.

The hateful whispers hung in the air and Gwendolyn felt their sting, though by now she should be impervious to insults. But Falke's kiss had opened a fissure in her heart. Daring to dream of a life with him also made her painfully aware of how others saw her, how Falke no doubt saw her. Ugly, dull and a cripple.

"There's our place, milady."

Lucas's excited shout tugged Gwendolyn back from her melancholy. The boy pointed to a broken-down hut with a partially caved-in roof. The whole structure leaned dangerously to one side. Gwendolyn reined Greatheart to a stop and Cyrus dismounted, then gave Lucas a hand down.

Thick mud oozed into Gwendolyn's worn leather slippers when her feet hit the ground. Leaving Cyrus to tether the warhorse, she grabbed her bag of herbs and followed the boy into the hut.

The smell of old rushes and animal feces stung her nose when she passed the hut's arched doorway. Food scraps and empty gourds littered the earthen floor. A rotting trestle table filled the center of the single room. A skinny hen snagged spiders from beneath it. To the left, a lean-to separated a scrawny cow from the living area.

A feeble voice called, "Who's here?"

"'Tis her, Mum. Lady Wren's come to tend ye." Lucas ran to the back and knelt next to a thin straw pallet. Covered with a ragged blanket, a frail woman tried to lift her head and peer past her son. Sweat darkened her red hair. A flush covered her wan face.

Gwendolyn approached the ill woman. "I can help." Pulling her extra gown from her tunic, she plumped it up and gently put it under the woman's head. She noticed the shallow rise and fall of Lucas's mother's chest and the rasping sound of her breath.

The woman's eyes grew wide and she waved Gwendolyn away while trying to pull her son closer. "Leave me and my son be. Don't lay your evil eye upon us." A spasm of dry coughs shook her weakened frame.

"Mum, Lady Wren is a good woman." Lucas gave Gwendolyn a beseeching gaze. "'Tis just the fever that's got her talking so."

Like a salve, the boy's faith eased the bite of the mother's words. Gwendolyn ruffled his hair until the cowlick stood at attention. "Do not worry, Lucas, I understand."

From behind her, she heard Cyrus clear his throat, a reminder that she must not forget to play the dullard. She laid her palm against the woman's forehead. Heat burned her hand.

"Lucas, need clean water." Gwendolyn worried her lower lip as the boy rushed from the room. The fever was much too high, and the labored breathing did not bode well. This was no simple illness, to be cured with an infusion or tea. Gwendolyn could afford no pretense. "Pray tell me, how long have you had the fever?"

"Gwendolyn, be careful!" Cyrus cautioned.

The woman on the pallet fluttered her eyelids and fought to form words with her cracked lips. "Two days a headache. Fever came today." Teary eyes studied Gwendolyn with despair. "Ken ye help me, like the boy says?"

"I can try." Gwendolyn ignored her foster father's dark looks.

The sick woman swallowed and rested her hands on her chest. "Take care of me boy when I go. Nesta, she's me oldest, ken take care of herself after I die."

"You're not a dy'n, Mum." Lucas stood in the middle of the room with a leaky bucket of water. A muddy puddle formed and increased the odor of staleness. He dropped the bucket and ran to his mother's side. "Lady Wren ken fix ye up, just like she did me back and her horse. Ye'll see."

"I need you to be strong so that I can help your mother." Gwendolyn pulled the lad aside. "There are ways to pull down the fever and clear her lungs, but 'tis hard work."

Waving at the debris around her, she ordered, "First, all of the old rushes must be taken out and burned. Burned, mind you, not just thrown in the refuse. These blankets must be washed in hot water."

"I ken do it, Lady Wren." The boy jumped up and scooped a handful of rushes from the floor. As he headed out the door, his thin legs pumped with new vigor and determination.

"A cough and the fever." Cyrus emptied the water bucket into a cook pot and placed it on the hearth embers. "And her breathing?"

"'Tis slow. I can hear the fluid in her lungs."

Rubbing her temples, Gwendolyn added, "'Twill be difficult to tend her with all this filth—"

Cyrus threw his arms into the air. "Tend? You can't do it." He lowered his voice. "Already you have shown that boy and woman too much. If you stay, all will know you have your wits about you. At Cravenmoor, Darianne and I could cover for you. The serfs believed Isolde's ghost left the medicines. But here—"

"Is a woman in need," Gwendolyn answered. "'Tis but one woman. She will keep my secret."

A dark shadow blotted out the meager light from the doorway. Gwendolyn turned and gasped. A mountain of a man stood in the doorway. In one hand he held a hammer like a weapon, in the other a chipped crockery jug. From the overpowering smell, she knew both the jug and man were filled with strong ale.

"Wife, get your arse up and fetch me some food." Grabbing the table corner to stabilize himself, he pulled himself to a seat and rested his head upon the rotting table.

Lucas skipped into the room and skidded to a stop. One look at the drunken man and the newfound hope in his young eyes drained away. His knees quivered and his upper lip twitched. Keeping his eyes on the large man, the boy made a wide berth around the table.

"Boy!" The man roared to life and dug his thick fingers into Lucas's thin shoulders. "Get me some drink."

"Aye, Da." Lucas's voice shook with fear and pain. "I'll get ye a new jug."

Appeased, he released Lucas. The drunk struggled to focus his bleary eyes on Gwendolyn and Cyrus. "Get outta here afore I throw ye out." He took in his wife's form on the floor. "I said for ye to get up and get me some food."

"Your wife is ill." Gwendolyn motioned for Lucas to join her.

"She's lazy," the drunk roared back.

"She's sick," Gwendolyn shouted, and then stiffened. Ten years of living with Titus had taught her one thing—there was no reasoning with a drunk. "I'll get you something to eat."

"See to it fast, wench. And bring me my jug."

"Oh, I'll see to it," Gwendolyn muttered. She grabbed the fresh jug of ale from Lucas's hand and pointed to her bag of herbs. Cyrus brought her the satchel and watched silently as she stuffed a handful of dry, dark leaves into the jug.

"What are you up to?" Cyrus asked.

"Bringing him his jug, and I hope he chokes on it." Gwendolyn slammed the container down on the table and watched with a satisfied grin as the smithy took a long swig.

"Food!" Lucas's father ordered.

"'Tis coming." Gwendolyn returned to the hearth. Whispering, she advised, "Go sit with your mother, Lucas."

"But, Lady Wren, me da's a mean one when he's drunk."

"He won't be drunk or mean for long." Gwendolyn gave the boy a cryptic smile and a wink. Glancing over to where Lucas's father gulped ale, she slowly began to count. By the time she reached five, the potion began to take effect.

"Saint preserve me. What did ye do to me, ye old crone?" Doubling over, the blacksmith clutched his gut and staggered outside. The instant he cleared the door and took a deep breath of fresh air, he spewed out the contents of his stomach. Between crying bouts and the dry heaves, he croaked, "Help me, someone. The witch from the castle's poisoned me."

Spectators assembled around Gwendolyn, Cyrus, Lucas and the sputtering, cursing, still-vomiting smithy.

"About time someone did something about that drunk blacksmith," one woman sniffed.

"Aye, that Arry and his family are a disgrace. Drunk more'n half the time." A man passed judgment with a sanctimonious air. None of the villeins made a motion to assist the smithy.

Weak and still suffering from the stomach cramps brought on by Gwendolyn's herbs, Arry begged for mercy.

"So, you've only let one boy, his mother and now this drunk know you've got your wits about you," Cyrus commented dryly. "Are you planning on telling anyone else?"

"Just a few," Gwendolyn admitted. Turning to the assembled men and women, she informed them of the situation. "Arry's wife is ill. I need help in tend-

ing her.'' Her announcement brought a marked un-
easiness to the crowd.

The villagers took a collective breath and made
the sign of the cross as they realized Gwendolyn
spoke clearly and intelligently.

''Arry's done me no good deed.'' A woman
brushed her sun-spotted hands back and forth as
though brushing away crumbs. ''I owe him nothing.
Nor ye.''

''But I can't stay here. I can show you how to
tend her. What herbs to give.'' Gwendolyn searched
the tiny group for one caring soul. She found none.

''What ails Cadel?'' From the back of the crowd,
a bulky woman pushed forward.

'''Tis headaches, followed by fever. I've seen it
before.''

''Is it…deadly?'' the woman asked as she placed
a hand over her heart. Fear stiffened the lines on her
square face.

''Aye,'' Gwendolyn answered. ''Especially to the
old and the very young.'' The terror that appeared in
the serf woman's eyes made Gwendolyn ask, ''Do
you know of someone else who is ill?''

''Nay!'' The woman fingered the collar of her tunic and glanced about at her neighbors. Her voice
softer and near to breaking, she asked, ''Can you
heal Cadel and any others?''

''With help, I may, though I can promise nothing.'' Gwendolyn could see panic in the woman's
eyes. Looking over the group of villeins, she noted
the same expression mirrored in the eyes of several

men and women. "If any of you feel ill, or have sick families, bring them to the smithy's hut. We must work together if we are to save any."

In an unnatural quiet, the villeins dispersed. They exchanged anxious glances as they ducked into their huts or wandered to the fields.

"One boy, one woman, one drunk and now a whole village. What am I to do with you?" Cyrus shook his head in dispair. "And what are we to do with him?" The knight pointed to Arry, who had managed to crawl to his hands and knees.

Gwendolyn stood over the prone man and kicked his shoulder with the tip of her leather slipper. It hurt her protruding toe, but she got the blacksmith's attention. "Arry the blacksmith, do you hear me?"

A groan came as a reply. She decided to interpret it as an agreement. "I did not poison you, only purged your body of the ale you consumed. For the moment, you are sober, and for that you can thank me. But to remain sober—that rests on your head. Your wife is in sore need of a husband, your son in need of father."

Arry squinted open one dark brown eye. "Cadel is really sick, isn't she?"

"Aye, that she is." Thankfully, a glimmer of caring showed in the giant's eye. That faint light encouraged Gwendolyn to go on. "She'll die unless my orders are followed exactly."

Shuddering, Arry staggered to his feet. He wiped his face with the back of his sleeve. "I'm not much of a man—the drink swallowed up what there was.

But Cadel has always stood by me, so I'll stand by her now. I fear 'tis little help we'll get from the rest of the village. We were never a close people as is. Lord Merin expected his villeins to care for themselves. What do ye want me to do?''

"Help your son clear the rushes and put in fresh ones. Then I need buckets of water. The room must be cleaned and washed with lye. All the blankets must be washed in strong soap and the animals removed to another barn. Then—"

Cyrus's hand on her shoulder stopped the list of directions. His anguished sigh made her turn. Coming down the path from the village, a thin line of people walked with leadened steps toward her. First in line was the woman who had questioned her about Cadel. In her arms she carried two young children, a boy and a girl. Soft whimpers and the children's restless movements explained the mother's distress.

Behind her, husbands helped wives, wives supported the tall bodies of their husbands, and more mothers hugged sick children to their breasts.

Arry slapped his hand over his mouth. "My God, 'tis a plague upon us."

"Get to work," Gwendolyn ordered. "I've seen this fever before. Death is by no means certain, though 'twill take a fight to overcome it. Are you man enough to battle for your family?"

"'Tis the first sober moment I've had in years. And to think 'tis due to a little bird like you." Holding his gut, he added, "Though 'tis quite a peck you managed to deliver."

The giant waved the approaching villagers into his home. "Aye, Lady Wren, I'll fight. We'll all fight. I'm thinkin' you're more than ye let on. A warrior we ken follow and win with."

Gwendolyn swallowed hard and looked at the still faces of the people around her. Now was not the time to play the cripple or the imbecile. Time was the enemy. The days ahead would be filled with the sounds of ill children and parents. And with the sounds of mourning.

Chapter Eight

The narrow walkway on the outer wall barely allowed Falke and Ozbern to walk in tandem. At the sentry posts, neither man gave way, forcing the guard to come to attention and step back or risk being knocked over the high wall. Falke did not bother to engage in conversation with his friend, for his mind was back at the pool with his night angel.

With Titus and his men nursing wine-soaked heads, Falke had time to recall each sensuous detail of his adventure last night.

The wood-sweet smell of her skin haunted him. Each perfect curve of her body was scorched in his mind. Desire rippled in his loins as he recalled the feel of her young, lithe body. Overhead, the morning sun seemed harsh, making him long for the cool silver light of the moon and his angel's hair. Night had always beckoned with lonely arms, but now the moonlight tempted him with the slender limbs of Artemis. How could such a vision send terror through a ruffian like Titus?

''What's happening in the village?'' Ozbern pulled up short and pointed toward the huts.

Crossing his arms over his chest, Falke tucked away his memories, then concentrated on the activity in the village. A bonfire burned in the center green. Peasants trudged back and forth from the huts to the fire, carrying bundles and casting them into the flames. Even from this distance, Falke could sense the urgency. Something or someone had put spurs to his villeins.

'''ello, the castle.'' From near the barbican, a voice boomed. ''Have the lord come speak with me.''

''Nobles don't take orders from smithies,'' the marshal shouted. ''Enter and make petition same as any man.''

''Can't.'' The voice shouted back, anger in his tone. ''Tell Lord Falke that Lady Wren is with me.''

''She's suppose to be with Alric,'' Falke hissed as he and Ozbern raced toward the central tower.

''She is. Or was,'' Ozbern answered breathlessly as they climbed the tower stairs.

At the top, Falke shoved aside the startled marshal and peered down. A giant of a man stood below. Leather apron and bulging arm muscles marked him as the blacksmith. ''A woman-beater and drunk.'' His angel's warning took on new meaning as Falke spotted the short, plump shape standing next to the man—Lady Wren. One blow from the smithy could crush her skull.

"I swear I saw her in the chapel." Ozbern shook his head in disbelief.

"Free the woman, blacksmith." Falke yanked the spear from the marshal and took aim on the big man's heart.

"Nay." Lady Wren stepped forward and placed a protective hand across the smithy's chest. Falke still had a straight shot at the man's heart, directly over her head. "We cannot enter the castle. Nor may any of you leave."

Ozbern threw his hands in the air. "Now we are laid to siege by a girl and a commoner?"

"Aye, Sir Ozbern." Lady Wren lifted her head and shook away the tangles covering her face. Determination tilted her pointed chin. "Mistedge is at siege, but not from us, but by pestilence." She spoke without her stammer, and apprehension crept up Falke's spine. It must be dire indeed for Lady Wren to give up her ruse.

"'Tis a fever, milord." The blacksmith pointed his thick finger at Falke's weapon. "And ye'll not win this battle with sticks and such."

"Most of the children are affected. This fever spreads fast, takes many." Lady Wren spoke slowly, but Falke sensed 'twas not due to playacting, but from dread.

Fever! Another turn from his usually good fortune. Was his night apparition really an angel? Had he switched his luck from good to bad with a stolen kiss? The idea caused his throat to dry and his heart to pound. Nay, her lips were real, the softness of her skin not a mirage. If she was a villager, then her life could be in danger.

The walkway became crowded with men and servants. Tension and panic wove through the gathering crowd. As heads popped up along the wall, Lady Wren stepped behind the bulky smith.

The giant leaned down to listen as she whispered in his ear. Straightening, he shouted, "'Twould seem the village is the only place stricken. If we are kept apart, mayhap this plague will go no farther."

There was no other choice. Falke could not risk the illness spreading throughout the keep. "Close the gate," he ordered.

"Nay, milord," a servant woman called in anquish. "Me son is out there, and me husband."

"Close the gate!" Falke spoke through clenched teeth. He gave the marshal a narrow-eyed stare.

The marshal sprang to life and shouted the order. Ropes creaked, then whirled as the soldiers manning the gate wheel lowered the iron grate. With a clang, the heavy bars sealed the castle from the outside world. Falke threw down his weapon, useless against this foe that would rob him of his home.

"There be a woman…" the smith continued, relaying what Lady Wren whispered to him. "…Darianne, she'll be knowin' what to send. Lower the supplies over the wall. For now, we be needin' blankets and a heap of strong soap."

"'Twill be done straightaway. Robert!" Falke called as he spotted the knight on the wall. "Get

Darianne—I've a hunch you'll find her in the chapel.
Fetch whatever the villagers will need.''

"I'll be back with a cart to haul the supplies."
The blacksmith smiled down at Lady Wren. "I'll be
taking the lady back to the village now."

"Nay," Falke shouted.

Lady Wren paused, but did not speak. When she
lifted her face, Falke saw no fear in her azure stare.
Instead, he saw a resolve akin to that of a warrior
entering battle. Whatever lay beneath the surface of
this woman, 'twas not cowardice.

"Do what you must. Anything you need will be
given to you. And Lady Wren?" Falke suspected
who the village healer must be. "God's blessing be
on you. I wish you well in your task."

She nodded, then shuffled away with the big man,
resuming her crippled step. Panic at the threat of illness had blinded most inhabitants of the castle to her
momentary slips of speech. With luck, she might still
keep her masquerade a secret. But what did he know
of good fortune? 'Twould seem his had finally run
dry.

"Ozbern, see that a sentry is stationed at the road
and tell him Lord Falke will have his head if one
man, woman or child carries this fever within the
castle."

Falke and Ozbern pushed past the men on the wall
and made for the stairs. At the bottom, Falke headed
for the arch separating the inner and outer yards.
"I'll see to sealing the inner bailey tunnels. You take
the outer."

"Aye." Ozbern turned on his heel, then asked, "Falke, how could Lady Wren escape the castle so easily? And why was she in the village? Despite the whispers, 'twas plain the smithy took his orders from her."

"I don't think either of us have really seen that girl. I don't even think she knows who she is herself." Falke spoke more to himself than to his friend as they parted to prepare Mistedge for siege.

"What's all the wallerin' about, love?" the young wench called from the pile of fresh hay.

"'Tis your da and...that woman from the castle—Lady Wren, they call her. The sight of 'er is enough to scare ye sober. And I think that's just what she's done to your da." The soldier readjusted his breeches as he peered out of the barn window.

"They ain't found us, have they?" His companion sat up, her long hair partially covering her naked breasts.

"Nay." The soldier's gaze rested on the girl's nipples. A hardening in his loins caused him to lick his lips. "Nesta, your folks ain't gonna find us here in the hayloft." He kissed her swollen lips and his hands clamped on to her soft mounds.

"Elined!" She giggled and halfheartedly brushed him away. "We just finished and ye want to go again?"

He resumed fondling her chest and lowered her to the fluffy straw. "I can't help it, love." He kissed each nipple. "I am so hot, I think I'm on fire." He shed his breeches once more.

"Aye, hot I am." Sweat slickened Nesta's skin, and her face flushed with heat. "Won't they miss ye at the barracks?"

"Me brother'll cover for me. Don't worry." The throbbing in his groin suddenly joined with a steady, painful beat in his head. His climax came and went, but the pounding in his head remained.

"That's enough for today." Nesta rubbed her temple and rolled away. "I gotta see about me mum." She swayed slightly when she stood and climbed down the ladder from the loft to the main floor.

Elined took his time putting his breeches back in order. The crashing pain in his head wouldn't relent. Once back inside the bailey walls, he could get a good cold draft of ale and find some corner to catch a nap. Then he'd join his brother and friends for some games of chance. He lumbered down the ladder and made his way back inside the walls of Mistedge by use of an escape tunnel.

"Brother!" A large hand came down on Elined's back. "Where have you been?"

Elined turned and faced his younger brother's scornful gaze. "Just out havin' fun, Fergus."

"Were you in the village? Tell me the truth, Elined. Lord Falke's put the whole area off-limits because of fever. Were you there with that girl again?"

Fergus was always so narrow-minded about right and wrong. If Elinid told the truth, Fergus might report him and then he would be stuck in that village. He had smelled and seen the results of plague before. The ghastly stench and nightmares had haunted him for months. Not again.

"I was gamin' with some of the guards on the outer wall. I haven't seen Nesta for two days."

His brother narrowed his eyes and pursed his lips. "Thank God. Mind you, keep away from that wench until the fever's passed. You look dead on your feet. Go into the guardroom and take a rest. I'll take your watch on the outer wall."

"My thanks, Fergus." Elined clasped his brother on the shoulder and sauntered back to the soldiers' dormitory. Three guards were drinking and gambling in a corner. Elined joined them and took a long swill of ale from their jug. The pounding in his head intensified. He rolled onto a pallet and loosened his tunic. Heat radiated from his body. His joints ached each time he moved. Sleep overtook him in a wave of intense fatigue.

Falke stood on the inner bailey wall, his mind seething with questions but no answers. He watched Ozbern stride across the outer courtyard to the guardsmen's dormitory. His friend would choose several men to quarter off the village and see to the tunnels.

Isolating the village was a hard move, but necessary. Fevers spread like wildfires, and protecting the castle would ensure aid to the crofters. Lady Wren understood that; she had requested the order. So why was he riddled with guilt?

Falke surveyed the outer courtyard. The yard was full of soldiers, some wrestling on the exercise field, most loitering, unconcerned about an enemy attack. Falke didn't blame them. They were all waiting until lordship of the keep was firmly established before they showed allegiance. If the men sided with him and he lost, their lives would be forfeit. The danger to Mistedge lay within its walls, not from outside.

"Falke, come to the wall."

The sound of Ozbern's concerned voice warned Falke his bad luck had not changed. He started for the stairs.

"Nay, Falke, do not open the inner gate."

A tremor of real fear gripped him as Ozbern's voice called out with urgency and foreboding.

"Ozbern?" Falke knew the answer to his unspoken question even before he saw the slumped figure of a young soldier being carried from the dormitory.

"He's sick with the fever. I'm having him taken to the village. Seems he has a wench who'll lift her skirts for him. He got more than he bargained for the last time."

The full impact of his friend's words hit him. Ozbern was stranded outside. Falke was alone inside the keep with Alric, Robert, and a castle full of vassals who wished him ill.

His friend's dark head shook back and forth. "Falke, you know what you must do."

"Aye, though 'tis hard, my friend." Before issu-

ing the command that would separate him from his
comrade, Falke said, "We will speak each day. You
will come to the wall to gather supplies." The words
conveyed Falke's hidden fears—that Ozbern could
well fall ill himself.

"Close the inner gate." Bitterness made Falke's
tone harsh and unrelenting. Men who had been loaf-
ing before ran toward the arch as the heavy gate fell.

The splintery sound of the thick bar sliding across
the doorway brought cries of outrage from the outer
courtyard. The shouts and curses drew noblemen and
castle servants from inside the keep.

"What's going on?" Laron demanded. "The servants are in a panic."

"The gate is down. Are we prisoners?" Mistedge's most senior vassal, Lord Baldwin, queried.

"Aye." Falke pointed to the village and the dark
smoke against the crystal-blue sky. The universal
purge of disease silenced the men. "A fever has
struck the village. Sir Ozbern has found a soldier in
the guardroom with the illness. Hopefully, the fever's
not spread within the keep proper as yet."

"As usual, you're too late to be of any real help
to those people," Laron snapped. "They'll die in
droves."

"Not I!" Ferris pushed aside the knights and faced
Falke. "I'm leaving, whether Titus or anyone else
from Cravenmore can sit a horse or not."

"You'll go nowhere." Falke stalked the smaller
man. Looming over Ferris, Falke spoke slowly,
clearly, his tone iced with ominous certainty. "You

may leave this keep, but not these lands. I'll kill you myself before I allow you to spread this ague about the countryside. Besides, your lady cousin is in the village.''

"So your damnable luck prevails." Ferris curled his lips in a sarcastic smile. "She dies from fever and you escape marriage."

Laron's face twisted into a smug grin. "Come, Ferris, let us inform Titus of his niece's peril. And of Sir Falke's negligence in protecting her. And his people."

Falke slammed his fist into his palm as the two knights left. The sympathetic gazes that passed between the nobles and Ferris made Falke want to gag. Not one of them cared whether Lady Wren lived or died; they only wanted to hedge their bets should Laron wrest power from Falke.

Separating himself from the nobles, the servants and his few remaining loyal men, Falke watched the black smoke. The dark cloud mushroomed in shape and moved with ominous fingers toward the castle of Mistedge.

Chapter Nine

From beneath the tattered war tent, a knight begged for comfort. "Lady Wren!" he croaked.

Gwendolyn looped a strand of hair behind her ear and eased the crick in her neck before turning toward the canopy that served as an infirmary. She lifted a wooden bowl to the man's lips and waited patiently as he sipped the strong tea. Leaning back, he rested, and his hand patted hers in thanks.

"Lady Wren, ken ye check this tea and see if'n 'tis strong enough?" A village woman wiped her face with the edge of her apron and waved Gwendolyn toward the black kettle near the bonfire.

"Mummy, I'm so hot," a child wailed from a cot nearby.

Her composure worn as thin as the rag she called a gown and Gwendolyn fought down the wave of panic that threatened to derail her. The past week had seen the fever spread throughout the village and the outer bailey of the castle. As yet the inner keep remained protected, along with the keep's inhabitants. Her uncle and the Cravenmoor nobles remained tightly sealed within the safety of the high walls.

And that served her well. With men, women, soldiers and children falling ill, Gwendolyn had been forced to shed all vestiges of her playacting. Panic had subsided after Gwendolyn began issuing instructions and organizing work crews. Now, after a week of caring for the fevered, the serfs were too tired to worry.

"Lucas, fresh water, please," Gwendolyn ordered as she swiped a cloth from a stack of clean laundry, then joined the child and mother. The boy hurried to obey, then trotted off to aid another.

Sprinkling lavender seed into the water, Gwendolyn soaked the cloth, then wrung it damp. Softening her tone, she instructed the woman, "Blot this on your daughter's head to cool the fever and ease her headache."

"Aye, Lady Wren." The child's cries lessened to a distressed mewing as her mother mimicked Gwendolyn's actions.

Standing, Gwendolyn surveyed the bustling serfs. No matter their age, if they were able to stand, she had put them to work. Children stripped medicinal leaves from twigs for brewing, old men and women collected kindling, the able-bodied washed linens, prepared tea or stitched death shrouds. And still chores remained to be done.

"Arry, fetch some clean linen and change the bed-

ding on these cots.'' Gwendolyn pointed toward the
sweat-soaked bed clothes of several soldiers.

"Aye, Lady Wren.'' The titan jumped to complete
the task. He twisted the ear of a boy snuggled up on
a stack of blankets. "Get up, ye lazy good for nothing. If Lady Wren don't rest, then ye don't rest.''

A hidden smile tugged at Gwendolyn's lips. 'Twas
said the reformed were the hardest to live with, she
thought. And Arry was certainly proving the point.
Even after burying his daughter, Nesta, in the common grave, he had returned to work. His newfound
sanctity served as a model for the rest of the village.

With Arry overseeing the laundry, Gwendolyn
made for the bonfire to check her medicinal tea. The
moss-colored liquid simmered in a great iron kettle.
Pillows of steam rose, scenting the area with borage,
bay, burnet and lovage.

Gwendolyn stirred the concoction with a heavy la-
dle, noting the color and thickness. "Aye, 'tis strong
enough, Anwen. Cut it with a bit of honey for the
little ones. 'Twill make the taste easier, though not
by much.''

The young woman nodded. "The smell is bad
enough, but the taste!'' She shuddered and scrunched
up her mouth. "'Twas lucky I came down with the
fever only for a few days. I had to hold my nose to
force it down.''

"And we'll do the same to those soldiers if they
refuse again.'' Gwendolyn crossed her arms and
moved to the canopy where most of the infirm lay.

Rows of sick people lay on makeshift cots and

straw pallets. Tired relatives waved away the insects swarming over the ill. Up and down the rows, women gave the caretakers bowls of tea and clean water to force down the fevered patients' throats.

A painful sorrow struck Gwendolyn in the heart. So many had died already, and the death count still climbed. She lowered her head and covered her mouth with her hand. Tears stung her eyes along with dejection. How could she hope to save these people? Yet even as she asked herself the question, she began to walk up and down the rows, checking on each patient.

Her inquiries were met with warmth and hope. To each she offered a bit of praise or instruction. Just a few moments of tenderness meant the world to these people so near death. For some, 'twas all the kindness they had ever experienced in their short lives.

Like Falke had offered her. Nay! She could not afford the luxury of thinking of him and the bits of tenderness he had shown her. A gentle hand upon her shoulder in the great hall. Kindness in his tone when he spoke to her and Cyrus. And the taste of desire as his lips touched her mouth. *Stop this!* She chastised herself as the memory of his musky smell caused strange emotions to flutter in the pit of her stomach.

"Lady Wren, come quick!"

She turned to see Lucas pointing toward his father. Arry carried Ozbern toward the sick ward, the knight barely able to hold his head upright.

"Lucas, be quick and clear a bed." Gwendolyn

rushed to meet the blacksmith. One touch of Ozbern's forehead and she knew the pestilence had found another victim.

"Ken ye save 'im?" Arry asked with real concern.

The knight's hard work and soft humor had endeared him to all the peasants. And to Gwendolyn, too. Never once had he questioned her actions or orders, and he had taken over the visits to the castle's inner wall, thereby enabling Gwendolyn to keep out of Titus and Ferris's sight. And Falke's. The lord of Mistedge remained in safety, while his people, and now his friend, fought for their lives.

"I will do my best," she answered.

She owed the knight much. It had been Ozbern who had shamed the soldiers and kept them from storming the inner keep in panic. And it had been he who had lifted their spirits with stories of his and Falke's escapades. Though in every tale 'twas Falke who saved the day, the serfs' allegiance rested with Ozbern. The villagers still did not trust Sir Falke, who remained within the inner keep, away from the danger of the illness.

"Lay him here," she ordered Arry as they reached the tent. With care, the blacksmith placed his charge on the makeshift bed.

"Lady...Wren." Ozbern clutched her sleeve. "You...go to the gate." His arm dropped, his strength sapped by the effort.

"Hush. You must rest," she murmured consolingly.

"Nay." Ozbern shook his head and coughed.

"Alone...Falke's alone. Laron...Ferris want to take Mistedge." Ozbern drew a deep, rattling breath. "Falke needs this place. Promise me you'll go." His eyes opened wide and he made to rise from his bed.

"I'll send Arry." 'Twas one thing to show a bit of her true self in the village, quite another to flaunt it under Ferris's nose. To call out at the castle wall and converse with the staff would reveal too much.

"Must be you." Ozbern pulled himself to a sitting position, blinking his eyes into focus. "More than you seem. Like Falke. He needs to know." With effort Ozbern swung his legs to the ground.

"I will go," she promised. Anything to get him to rest. From behind her, she heard Cyrus snort his disapproval. Ignoring her foster father, Gwendolyn pushed the fainting knight back down. "I'll go, Sir Ozbern. Rest easy." At a wave of her hand, a chipped wooden bowl of thick green tea filled her palm, handed her by a villager. "Drink this." As usual, the words were a command and not a request.

"Lucas, fetch me two donkeys for carrying supplies from the castle. Blodyn," Gwendolyn called to a woman stirring a cauldron of dirty linen, "have we need of more lye?"

"Aye, Lady Wren, we will by the morrow if you insist on fresh linen for each."

"Then 'tis more lye I'll get. Each time those sheets are drenched in sweat they're to be changed and washed with hot water and strong soap."

"If Lady Wren says 'tis to be, then 'twill be." Blodyn nodded toward the women stringing the cloth to dry. No complaints came forth; all were too tired to do more than just comply.

Cyrus stepped in front of Gwendolyn, his brows wrinkled and his lips set with determination. "Any one of us can fetch supplies. It need not be you."

"I promised."

Gwendolyn hid the true reason for her desire to go to the castle wall. Ozbern's words pricked at her conscience. Lord Falke's easy laugh and quick wit did not portray a man alone in the world. Nor did he seem particularly interested in Mistedge. To her knowledge, he had never even visited the peasant village. He seemed to spend his time charming the women, infuriating the vassals and gaming with his men.

Yet she had ofttimes observed that Falke's cerulean eyes did not reflect the roguish smile on his full lips. Even when Lady Ivette flirted outrageously with him, his gaze would be on the knights behind her or nearby. In the depth of his stare, Gwendolyn detected a hidden center. And if she was not an expert on hiding one's soul, who was?

"This is trouble, lass," Cyrus warned. "You've been fortunate thus far that Titus has not found you out. Best take Arry with you to do your talking."

"If 'twould make you feel better."

"The only way I'm going to feel at ease is if you don't go." Gwendolyn opened her mouth to protest, but Cyrus placed his fingertips over her mouth. "But I know 'tis a useless wish."

"Lady Wren, I've found the donkeys." Lucas

rushed toward her, the two flea-ravaged beasts in tow.

"Good work. Now get your father and we'll make our way to the castle gate."

"Is he here yet?" Falke climbed the wall steps two at a time. The wooden stair creaked from the hard stamp of his feet. His eyes scanned the muddy expanse that lay between the gatehouse and the first cottage. The bright silk of the yellow tent near the woods caused his heart to quicken with dread. The old war shelter served the dying, now from illness instead of battle.

"Nay, milord. Sir Ozbern's not been to the gate today." The young squire stood tall and snapped to attention, almost smacking himself in the face with his lance.

Cursing under his breath, Falke tried not to vent his frustration on the lad. God's Wounds, he wanted no part of Mistedge or Laron's treachery. 'Twould be better to roam the country as a mercenary than to lose Ozbern. No land or keep was worth his friend's life. Falke itched to leave the confines of castle. Over two-thirds of Mistedge's army lay under the canopy in the village. Whatever mischief Laron might think up, he could not plan a siege with so many ill, nor would an army invade when plague ran rampant. For now, Falke's only fear was for his friend.

"Milord, someone approaches." The sandy-haired squire dropped his lance in excitement. "Aye, 'tis a tall man, the smithy I think. And there's a boy and an old woman.'' The squire blushed and he gave Falke a half smile. ''Sorry, milord, 'tis your betrothed with them.''

''No one else?'' Pushing aside the bony lad, Falke held his breath as his gaze sought the approaching group. Air escaped his lungs in a sharp blast. No Ozbern. Falke rubbed his forehead with his fingertips. The tightness in his throat matched the clenching of his jaw.

''Is Lord Falke about?'' The blacksmith's voice resounded like a call of doom across the empty yard.

''Aye, I am here.'' Swallowing his grief, Falke lifted his head and waved.

His betrothed shuffled from one foot to another. She kept her head down and her words barely reached him. ''Sir Ozbern bade me come.''

A clatter on the stairs halted her message. A contingent of knights climbed up the wooden ladder and joined Falke on the narrow walkway. The men fanned out on either side of him. Laron and Ferris stood at his elbow, grim smiles on their faces.

''Go on, woman, how goes it in the village? Has the fever run its course yet?'' Laron demanded.

If a person could be transformed Falke would swear he witnessed it in the grass below. Instead of a caterpiller to a beautiful butterfly, the woman before him reversed the process. Gwendolyn's plump form seemed to become squatter and more misshapen before his eyes. Her chin dropped to her chest and the mass of bog-colored hair tumbled over her face. She whispered something to the smithy and the boy.

"Milord, we still have new sick coming in. Your friend fell ill today along with ten more. We be need'n more lye, borage, lovage and food. And Lady Wren wants to be talk'n with her woman, Darianne. Fetch her to the wall." Arry let out a long breath from the unaccustomed speech.

"Fetch her?" Ferris threw back his head and laughed. "Who do you think you are speaking to, man? We are knights, not common servants."

Falke noted the sudden stillness of the woman below. Her fists shoved into the folds of her skirts. Her toe twisted into the hard-packed ground and a feeling of déjà vu swept through him.

Now was not the time for hunches or intuition. Ozbern needed aid and needed it now. Falke ignored the ripple of discomfort that ran down his spine and ordered, "Find the woman she seeks." His gaze pierced the nervous squire's, and Falke took a few menacing steps. The lad tumbled down the stairs to fulfill the command.

"She'll be here soon." Falke had to ask the next question although he was afraid of the answer. "Ozbern? How does he fare?"

"The same as the others, burning with fever. Some made it through, some didn't." Arry tilted his large head at Gwendolyn. "She be the one to know. She's been shoving tea and medicine down everyone's throat."

"Then they are doomed for sure," Ferris said with a laugh.

Lady Wren was tending the ill? Falke felt relief

and apprehension. He knew well her expertise at tending her horse, but what of communicating with the superstitious peasants? If the villagers had turned to Lady Wren for guidance, then the situation must be dire indeed.

Lady Wren spoke, her words barely discernible, yet Falke detected a trace of fortitude and strength. "I'll do my best, though there's many in the same lot as he." She lifted her head and shaded her eyes from the blaring sun. "Your friend is dear to many in the village." These words sounded stronger and contained a hint of censure toward Falke.

"My thanks." Falke hid the bolt of anguish that struck him. Ozbern's life rested in the hands of this strange girl below and villagers who detested their lord. What hope did his friend have?

He pushed his way through the crowd on the walkway and stairs. Questions rang out. Cousins, wives, children, husbands, parents—all wanted reports on their loved ones. Arry's booming roar answered back with short answers. A prayer of thanksgiving or mourning accompanied each response.

Falke slapped the hilt of his sword. "Would that I could save Ozbern's life with this blade as he has saved mine." Worry and frustration gnawed at his soul.

He had stayed behind the inner walls because he had promised Ozbern to try and win the vassals to him, but Falke could remain idle no longer. Let the lords and ladies think their lord abandoned them. Let

Laron plot at will. Falke would go to his friend and offer what aid he could.

Stripping off his embroidered tunic, he grabbed a plain wool tunic from the line and used a piece of twisted rope to cinch it at his waist. Dressed as a laborer, he headed for the castle gate.

"Falke, where are you going?" Ivette's voice sounded brittle and strained as she strode to keep up with him.

"Out." He lengthened his stride toward the portal.

"I just heard about poor Ozbern," Alric interjected slipping between Falke and Ivette. Robert marched behind.

Falke kept his stare on Lady Wren standing just outside the inner gate. As she spoke with Darianne, her stammering, rasping voice fueled his purpose. Aye, the girl had more wits than she let on, but not enough to entrust Ozbern's life to.

"What are you going to do?" Robert asked the question as though he already knew the answer.

"Ozbern needs my help. I'm going to help him." Falke kept up his deliberate push toward the gate.

"You can't go out there." Alric placed his hand on his commander's shoulder. "'Twill do Ozbern no good if you fall ill also. And think of Laron. He'll be preaching treason in your own hall."

"Mistedge and Laron can go to Hades. I'll not leave Ozbern out there alone." Falke's tone sliced the air with deadly anger. The younger knight pulled back his hand, his face flushed.

"Are you going to throw away everything?"

Ivette's normally sultry voice cracked with disbelief. "The answer to our problem is this fever. With any luck, that wretched girl will die from it." Her blue-black eyes narrowed and she pointed one slender finger at his gut. "Stay in here where 'tis safe, and bide your time. If you don't, Laron will turn those knights against you, and as soon as this fever passes, they will overthrow you. Think of your duty to Mistedge." The ring of her words grated on Falke's ears. 'Twas an order, not a request.

He mentally commanded his fists to uncurl. Making an abrupt turn, Falke kept silent while he headed for the gate. Standing in front of the iron bars that sealed him from the ravages of the fever, he kept his gaze on the weary group in the outer courtyard. Closer to them, he could see the heavy cloak of fatigue each wore. Lines near his eyes and mouth softened the blacksmith's features. The boy had been whittled away to nothing more than bones and skin.

And the girl-woman, Lady Wren. Her hand trembled as she held the reins of the donkeys, and she leaned against one skinny beast for support.

"Open the gate," Falke shouted to the guardsman at the gearwheel.

"Milord, you're going out...there?" The guard pulled himself up taller, straightened his shoulders.

"Aye."

Falke's answer echoed in the whispered gossip of the nearby men and women. In the blink of an eye, Mistedge's nobles joined them.

"What are you trying to pull now, Falke?" Laron

quizzed from the walkway. Like a swarm of bees, the knights left the wall and made their way toward him.

"I'm going to the village." Falke silenced the protests with a curt wave of his hand. Although he spoke to all, he faced Laron and Ferris.

Ferris sneered, "I bet a gold coin he's planning to disappear and leave the rest of us to fend for ourselves."

Falke's fist shot out like an arrow from a crossbow. The hard crack of his knuckles against Ferris's jawbone was pleasurable pain. The arrogant knight flew backward and into the arms of several of Falke's vassals. In unison, they spread their arms and let the knight fall.

Surprised, Falke lifted his eyebrows. "Sir Baldwin—" he shot Laron a calculated gaze "—I leave you in charge in my absence."

The gray-bearded knight puffed out his chest and spoke in a gravelly voice. "You can count on me, Lord Falke. I admire a man of action." He gave a quick nod of his head in Ferris's direction. "He was out of line. No one insults a lord—or temporary lord—of Mistedge." Then nodding toward the village, he added, "There needs to be some direction out there."

Pointing to the gearwheel, Falke repeated, "Open the gate." Without hesitation, the soldier put his back into turning the wheel. The gate lifted, protesting the movement with earsplitting screeches. The noise drew the attention of the group in the outer bailey.

As the iron gate creaked upward, Lady Wren moved farther and farther away.

Just before leaving the safety of the inner keep, Falke turned, grabbed Sir Baldwin by the arm and gave him a firm handshake. The elder man said in a loud voice, "Go with God, Lord Falke. I look forward to your return."

Releasing the knight's arm, Falke took a deep breath and stepped beyond the gatehouse walls. For a moment, the high stone archway shadowed him and chilled his skin. Blood raced through his veins and nervous energy made him question his decision.

Then footsteps other than his own echoed on the worn cobblestones. Before he could turn, Robert and Alric were at his side, along with the young guard from the gearwheel.

"My brother's down there." The guard spoke with affection. "He's taken care of me most of my life. I reckon 'tis time for me to return the boon."

Falke gave a sidelong glance at his friends. Alric slapped him on the back. "Ozbern's our friend, too. And so are you. Count us in."

A tremendous sense of responsibility settled on Falke's shoulders. Was he leading them to folly, perhaps to their deaths? He should push them away, prevent them from making the same mistake as he. Yet even as he opened his mouth to dismiss them, they rushed forward to gather the supplies and greet Lady Wren.

"Do you know what you've done?" Lady Wren asked serenely as Falke joined the troupe.

"We've come to help." Falke noticed she kept her head bent. He could see the crooked part of her oily hair and the line of white hairs at her crown.

"Then perhaps," she sighed under her breath, "there's hope for you yet." Then she gave a tug on the reins and led the laden donkeys off.

Chapter Ten

After a week in the village, Falke had grown accustomed to the sweat sting in his eyes, but not the indignity he suffered. He pushed the heavy wooden paddle about in the iron kettle, his mind festering with self-righteous anger. Hot sudsy water sloshed over the sides, soaking his leather breeches and his bare chest. Lumps of rags and blankets slowly agitated in the soapy water. Laundry! The lord of Mistedge was reduced to washerwoman.

"Milord, those be clean enough now." Blodwyn shelved a willow basket on her hip. "Lift 'em 'ere and I'll hang 'em on the line to dry." The square-jawed woman gave him an appraising stare. "There's more to be fetched by the tent."

Taking orders from a serf. If Laron and the knights within the keep saw him thus engaged, after their bout of laughter, they'd be more than happy to replace Falke as lord. Biting his tongue, he used the paddle to lift out the heavy, sopping blankets. He plopped the load into Blodywn's basket, then set off for the tent, still nursing his bruised pride.

His self-righteous anger slowly cooled as he marched toward the sick ward. All around him the ill lay on pallets, tended by what were left of the healthy villagers. A week seemed like a lifetime to Falke now. Death greeted the village daily. The old and the young were the favored guests. And now beneath the tent, Robert lay next to Ozbern, both stricken with the plague.

"Lady Wren, we've five more soldiers ill." A village woman nearly cried as she gave the news.

"Crowd these beds together." Rising to her feet next to a patient, Lady Wren pointed to an area already nearly carpeted with pallets. The news of more ill did not break her composure. Unruffled, she issued a series of orders. "We will need more tea brewed. And fresh water."

Without question or complaint, her requests were carried out by a group of gray-faced serfs, themselves on the brink of fever or just recovered. Falke wished his own vassals would attend his orders as these serfs did Lady Wren's.

"And tell the laundress we have need of more linen," Lady Wren added.

"The laundress…is here," Falke snorted.

"L-Lord Falke," she stammered. Her eyes, barely visible through her hair, met his, then quickly dropped. "I—I did not notice you. You have no shirt on."

"'Tis in the laundry," he replied. *Did not notice*

him, my eye. If there was one thing Falke had learned this past week, aside from not washing the bright reds with the whites, 'twas that Lady Wren was totally aware of all that transpired in the village. She was no simpleton. In fact, she dispatched workers with the precision of a battle commander. Women to brew the medicinal tea. Men to fetch and carry supplies. Children to fold and change linens. Falke to do laundry.

Bent on removing himself from the degrading work, he gave her a charismatic bow. Falke half grimaced, half smiled in an attempt to woo the lady to his thinking. "Point me in the direction of your soiled whites, mildewed wools and grimy garbs. Unless there's something else you'd have me do?"

Not even a grin. His smile was perfect, his delivery flawless, and yet he was unable to beguile Lady Wren any better than the woman he had met at the pond. He gritted his teeth in defeat. "I'll get the laundry."

She arched one brow and studied him for a few moments. Searching his face, as though intent on discovering some hidden truth, she replied, "Lord Falke, if laundry is not to your liking, there's other work to be done."

The look on her face bore him no goodwill. Glancing to the side, he noticed several women emptying chamber pots. Nay, she'd not dare! Falke straightened, considered the solemn-faced woman and knew she would.

"I would not think to supersede your orders, Lady

Wren.'' Although he spoke with sarcasm, a good bit
of truth underlay his words. This lady had the wit
and focus of a mercenary. She fought to win, though
her enemy be death itself. None in the village or
outer bailey spoke her title without respect and awe.
Including him.

For the sake of these people, Lady Wren had shed
all pretense, and in doing so, put her life in danger.
Not only from the fever, but also from Titus. Should
her uncle discover how he'd been made the fool,
Lady Wren's life would be forfeit. In truth, Falke
could not help but admire the woman.

Sighing, she pursed her lips and pointed to the far
end of the tent. ''Very well, the soiled linens are
there. They should be easy to spot now that they are
all pink.'' She dismissed him by turning away from
him. ''Arry, I need more borage, and where is the
lavender?'' Her list of requests flowed as she in-
spected the area made ready for the sick.

Falke trudged toward the mountain of dirty cloth.
What did the woman want from him? He fulfilled
every chore she instructed, no matter how menial.
Yet still he sensed she wanted more. But what? And
why did it matter to him if he did disappoint her?
He had long ago grown callous to others' disillu-
sionment with him. Lady Wren touched cords in his
soul that he thought long severed.

Falke paused near a bucket of cool well water and
took a sip. The liquid parched his dry throat, as Lady
Wren quenched his dry soul. He let his head hang as
he dropped the gourd back into the wooden bucket.

Aye, she did just that, he admitted. With unexhausting energy, she bathed fevered bodies, cajoled children to drink her awful-tasting brew, and shoved the same foul tea down the throats of complaining soldiers.

As she revived the spirits and hopes of the serfs, she had somehow rekindled Falke's cynical soul. She acted not from duty or fear of what others might think of her, but because she cared. And Falke found that to be one weapon against which he had no defense.

And then there was Ozbern. If he lived, Falke owed Lady Wren a boon he could never repay. And this week had taught Falke another fact. He could not marry Lady Wren. He respected her too much to have her suffer a loveless marriage as his mother had. Despite his restlessness and limited sleep, Falke's dreams were still haunted by his ''night angel.'' If she called, he would gladly fall into her arms.

Just the memory of the woman sent hot lust to his groin. Without a cold bath to ease his thickening, Falke settled for a dipperful of water over his head. 'Twas a poor substitute, but the shock of the cool water on his bare chest helped him to push aside thoughts of the mysterious woman.

His hair still dripping, Falke decided to check on his friends before gathering the wash. He walked over to Ozbern's bedside. The knight's dark hair lay plastered to his scalp. Dark smudges beneath his eyes marked his pale face. In the pallet next to him lay Robert.

Falke should never have allowed young Robert out of the inner bailey. The boy was newly knighted, so full of life, and now, because he'd followed Falke, he might die.

In the back of his mind, he saw and heard his father, Bernard de Chretian—his tone full of disgust and disappointment, his aristocratic nose down-turned, a deep frown carved on his lips. Aye, his father would condemn his son's actions, from Falke's refusal to marry Lady Wren to leaving the inner keep. As usual, Falke had lived down to his father's opinion.

Taking a rag from a gourd of water, Falke rang out the excess and placed the cool cloth against Ozbern's forehead. At least he could help his friend in this small way.

"You're dripping all over me," a voice croaked.

Falke almost tipped the entire bowl of water over on his friend's chest. "Ozbern? You're awake?"

"Aye." Ozbern smacked his chapped lips together. "I'd prefer a bit of water in me rather than on me."

The sound of his friend's voice sent a lance of joy straight through Falke's heart. This had to be a good sign. Ozbern must be recovering.

"Lucas," Falke shouted with urgency. "Fetch fresh water and Lady Wren." Cradling Ozbern's head on his arm, Falke waved his free hand with impatience until the lad filled it with a leaking gourd. Gently, he tilted the vessel to Ozbern's lips. The liquid disappeared in slow, loud gulps.

"'Tis good to have you back among the living, my friend," Falke declared.

"'Tis good to be back," Ozbern replied. "But why are you here? Laron? Mistedge?"

"Is not nearly as dear to me as you are." Falke clasped his second's forearm, emotion making any more speech impossible.

"Lucas said you wanted me." Lady Wren spoke from near his side.

Falke looked up into a rare glimpse of Lady Wren's face. Her sapphire eyes could not veil her fatigue. Thick lashes cast shadows on the high cheekbones and finely chiseled features. White streaked her dark hair, appearing, it seemed, almost overnight. For a moment, with her face framed with lighter strands, she reminded him of his night angel.

Aware of his scrutiny, she knelt at Ozbern's side. Falke lost the foolish image. How could a few stray tresses make him forget her mass of tangled, mud-colored hair or her plump form? Lady Wren was an angel—but of mercy, not his unknown temptress.

"He's awake. Ozbern woke up." Falke choked out the words from around the lump in his throat. He didn't know where the sudden emotion in his chest rose from—Ozbern's recovery or the depths of Lady Wren's lapis eyes.

"Welcome back, Sir Ozbern." Her long fingers eased down his cheek and prodded the skin below the jawline.

Her hands were an odd mixture of age and youth—strong and nimble like a child's, knicked and callused like an old servant's. As she moved them in her examination, Falke could detect only gentleness.

"A few days rest and he'll be back to his old self," she pronounced.

A slanted smile tugged at Falke's mouth. "Are you sure, Lady Wren? I was hoping to get something better than the old Ozbern from all this tender care. Do you mean to tell me he's going to go back to his usual overbearing self?"

"I'm afraid so." It was slight, but the edge of her mouth turned up as she spoke.

Blessed Saints! She smiled. An infusion of pride puffed Falke's chest. He had made Lady Wren smile! That was an accomplishment. And he hadn't even been trying. Falke rubbed his hand over his mouth to hide his grin. Between Lady Wren's smile and Ozbern's recovery, he felt downright giddy.

Lady Wren drew her mouth into a tight line, as though sensing his humor. She rose, lost her balance and reached into the air to steady herself. Jumping to his feet, Falke attempted to right her. Taking her large girth into consideration, he gave a hefty shove and she landed on her hip, dazed.

"I'm sorry. Truly, I meant you no harm." Falke apologized as he jumped over Ozbern to help her to her feet.

She waved away his attempt to aid her. "I can manage. Go back to your work." Huffing, she drew herself to her knees, then lumbered to her feet.

Amazed at her dismissal, Falke barked, "I'll stay here with Ozbern and Robert."

The peaceful blue of her irises darkened to the color of a stormy sky. Yet with all the emotions raging in her gaze, the placid features of her face remained unchanged. "I thought you were lord of Mistedge," she challenged.

"I am."

"Then each and every man, woman and child is your concern. As each is mine."

"How can you care for so many?"

"How can you care for so few?" No sarcasm tainted her words.

Frustration seized Falke with a stranglehold. He wanted to ram the words down her throat, but the truth of her statement could not be ignored. As lord, he was responsible for all of Mistedge, and for the first time he felt the weight of every inhabitant on his shoulders. From simpleton to physician to seer, the woman before him unveiled a new layer at the most unexpected of times.

It hurt to abandon his friends to the hands of strangers, but there were better ways he could help them. "Very well, I'll go back to the laundry."

"If that's what you think is best." She spoke through clenched teeth. Her tone implied in some way he had shirked his duties.

Her head barely reached his shoulder, but she had managed to ruffle Falke's temper. "Woman, you cannot mean to scold me. I've chopped wood, fetched water and lugged dirty linens. Christ's wounds, I've done laundry!"

Ozbern scrunched his eyes closed and murmured, "And I missed such a sight."

Falke shot to his feet as the lady backed away. "I am lord of Mistedge. Do not forget it." Her head lifted and she scurried from the tent.

"By heaven, the woman has no right to talk to me that way." He paced up and down beside his friend's cot. "I'm the head here whether anyone likes it or not, and I'll be damned if some brown bird of a girl is going to condescend to me. I'm Lord Falke of Mistedge." He slammed his fist into the palm of his hand.

A painful chuckle escaped Ozbern's lips. "Forsooth, Falke, I believe Lady Wren has done what I failed to do."

"What?" Confusion tempered the anger in Falke's chest. "Drive me completely daft?"

Ozbern gave a tired sigh and closed his eyes. "That, and have you accept your role as lord here. Somehow she's made you *want* Mistedge." A snore trailed his last comment.

The little trickster! Falke felt his mouth drop open as he slapped his forehead. How had Lady Wren managed to transform Mistedge to more than just a piece of land for him? But he knew the answer already. By chopping wood, fetching water, and aye, doing laundry. From the most menial of tasks he had learned the greatest lesson—that a keep was not composed of stone walls and castles, but of its people.

No longer were the serfs nameless workers. There was the laundress, Blodwyn, with her military stance.

And Lucas, nervous, young and eager to learn. Arry, the blacksmith, newly sober, devoted to Lady Wren and strong as an ox. The list went on, from the reeve to the newest babe, born just yesterday, a gift of life in a time of death.

Falke left the canopy and strode down the dirt path after his betrothed to thank her. He found her standing between two unplowed fields. Grass and wildflowers swayed in the gentle breeze. He caught the rich scent of fertile earth that seemed to come as much from her as from the ground.

Staring at the fields, she spoke to the wind instead of Falke. "'Tis March and the fields are not planted."

"And what would you have these men do—rise from their sickbeds to plow the fields?" Falke wondered at Lady Wren's sudden insensitivity. She had opened his heart to the villagers' plight, yet now she seemed to have closed hers. These people could not be expected to till the land in their condition.

Her toe ground a dirt clod into the dry earth. Her hands shoved deep into the slits of her dun-colored tunic. "Nay, Lord Falke, I do not expect the weak to do the work."

"Then who? Only a handful of villagers are well and you need them to help you."

"Aye, 'tis true." Exasperation steamed from her short body.

Falke could feel the waves of frustration she emitted. "Christ's blood, woman, just get it off your chest and be done with it."

"Fine." The last thread of restraint broke. "Are you a blind man? These fields must be planted and soon. I'll not save these people now only to hear they starved come the winter."

"First the fever, then the fields," Falke advised.

Her hand flew from the recesses of her tunic and pointed one long finger at him. Despite her stature, she commanded all of his attention. Her head flew up and she seared him with a look of pure anger. "If the villagers can't plow the fields, then that castle of knights and lords surely can."

Her eyes opened wide in shock at her own candor. She gulped, then panic erased all emotion from her face. In fear, she tried to run from him.

"Hold on." Falke reached out to stop her, but he found empty air. Lady Wren had gauged him, just as she did Titus. Did she do the same to every man? Judge how far away to stand to avoid a strike or a kick? Pity tempered Falke's anger as his long legs rapidly caught up with her.

"Stop, Lady," he commanded.

Immediately, she crumbled to the ground and curled into a tight knot, her hand covering her face, her muscles tensed for an expectant blow.

"Stand, Lady Wren."

Gwendolyn took a deep breath and complied. 'Twas her own fault for acting the way she had, reprimanding Falke for neglecting the fields. What was she thinking? Cyrus had taught her to hide her emotions better than this. She was lucky it was Falke and not Titus or Ferris. Had she lost her temper with them, 'twould be more than a beating she'd be receiving.

"I'm ready, Lord Falke."

Afternoon sunlight glistened on Falke's darkly tanned chest. Sweat gleamed on the ripples of his abdomen. A trickle of moisture meandered down his bare chest and disappeared beneath the wide leather belt at his hips. Fury darkened his blue eyes. He stood before her, an Apollo with golden hair and skin, and she knew how she must appear to him. Drab. Dull. Ugly.

He stood so close to her she could smell the heady, musky scent of his body mingled with a trace of lye. The coarse wool fabric of her kirtle hid her trembling fingers. She closed her eyes and waited.

His hand cradled her chin. She stiffened for the blow. Then softly, gently, he forced her chin up, and with the other hand brushed the hair from face.

"Mark me, Lady Wren, from this day, speak as you will with me and have no fear." She opened her eyes and stared into the brilliant crystal blue of his gaze. His tone hypnotized her with its soothing sound. "I will never lay a hand upon you in anger. On this you have my word."

"The word of a knight with no honor?" She bit her lower lip and cursed her impudence.

He leaned closer, his full mouth just a thread's width from her own. "My word as a friend, and in this I am always faithful. Just ask Ozbern." He sealed the contract with a kiss.

Heat radiated from the point of their joining, and

Gwendolyn felt the rigidness ease from her stance. A wild churning spun in her gut and she clung to him, afraid to release him for fear she would faint. Afraid to touch him, for fear she would make a fool of herself and reveal the intensity of desire that washed over her. Too quickly, he severed their connection. She took a deep breath and savored the taste of him that lingered on her lips.

"Friends, milady?"

How could she speak when her heart was beating as fast as a kestrel's wings? She nodded and kept her silence.

Falke took her hand and led her to a mossy rock. Seating her on the stone as if it was a throne, he pointed toward the castle. "I know you're bright enough to realize Laron wants Mistedge. If my vassals see me plowing fields like a common laborer...well, 'twill be all the easier for Laron to overthrow me."

"But Lord Falke, the people will support you. This week they've seen you're willing to put your life on the line for them."

"Aye, which is the irony of the situation." Falke leaned back against the rock. His muscled thighs grazed Gwendolyn's leg. Strange, wonderful sensations danced along the point of contact.

"Lady Wren," he continued, "when first I entered this village, I cared not whether I kept this place or not. I would have plowed those fields just to thumb my nose at the crew within. But now I do want it."

"Then fight for it."

"I am trying." Anger seeped back into his tone.

Frightened, Gwendolyn shrank back, but Falke's ire faded before her eyes. He patted her hand and smiled. "Remember, do not fear me."

"I don't," she whispered. Then again, she repeated, "I don't." And she didn't. Aside from Cyrus, Falke was the only other man who had ever gained her confidence.

"Good, because I value your friendship, milady. I will have sore need of it when the fever breaks. Laron will be at my throat. And I cannot lose this place." Loneliness softened his voice.

"You won't." Gwendolyn rested one hand on Falke's shoulder. She could feel the heat of his bare skin, and a warmth began to build in her heart. "Why do you have such faith in me, when my own father never did?"

"I see things." Gwendolyn tried to explain her unquestioning belief in him. "My days have not been filled with sewing, dancing or music. I have spent my time hiding from Titus and his lot. It's given me an eye to observation."

Falke stared at her, and Gwendolyn held her breath, thinking he could really see her, minus the hair dye and padding around her hips.

"Go on," he urged, and Gwendolyn thought he might add, "my night angel," but he did not.

"I have listened in the castle, to both your friends and foes. But I did not know your ilk until you left the inner bailey. Lord Falke, I think you know not the definition of honor. For you are an honorable man.''

"There you are wrong, sweet lady." Falke shook his great mane of golden hair. "For my father taught each of his seven sons the code of chivalry, and what sacrifices must be made in the name of it."

Bitterness hardened his face, making him seem remote and cold. "My father gave up the woman he loved, who he adored, because she had been raped, just before their wedding. Honor would not allow him to have a woman tainted, though the sin was none of her own fault. His refusal meant the poor girl was wed to her rapist—her family feared she might bear a child from the act, and God forbid they share that shame. My father was given a choice of another family's daughter, which he took, though he barely knew her name."

Intensity shook his voice. "I spit on any doctrine that sentenced my mother to a loveless marriage. She deserved better. As do you."

Slowly, Gwendolyn climbed down from her perch. Falke had more honor than even she had guessed. He acted from the heart. And his heart would never allow him to marry her. Not unless he loved her. "What if I were beautiful—"

"'Twould make no difference." He held her hand and gave her a sad smile. "I will not marry you just to keep Mistedge. I would not see you waste away as my mother did. Nor will I let Titus take you back to that hell. Rest assured of that."

"My thanks, Lord Falke." She took a long, shuddering breath and swallowed her fear. Titus would never abandon her to Falke unless a hefty sum of money greased his palm, and the coffers of Mistedge would be lean this year. Falke could not afford to pay off Titus, nor could Mistedge stand ready to fight. She would have to leave here, to save the villagers and Falke. Unless he married her.

Nor could she reveal her true form, for although he might lust after her as she appeared at the pond, he did not love her. And he would never love Lady Wren. To keep Titus in the dark, she must keep Falke that way as well.

"And Lady Wren..." Falke's gentle voice jerked Gwendolyn from her sad conclusions. He leaned forward so that she was forced to meet his gaze. "I want you to know that to me you are beautiful. You have a spirit and soul so lovely that no mirror can do them justice."

His words were sweet torture, and Gwendolyn could endure no more. "Excuse me, I must return to tending the ill."

"Lady Wren, wait, I will escort you—"

"Nay, I have work that needs be done." Pointing to the fields, she spoke from her heart, unafraid. "And you have work to do. Do not fear the opinion of those knights within. Nobility rests in a man's actions, not in his birth. You need only look to my uncle to see the truth I speak. Plow the fields, save the people, and Mistedge will be yours."

And never mine to share with you. She left him leaning against the rock, staring at the fields.

Tired, worried and frazzled, Gwendolyn eased the crick in her back as she stood. Hours under the hot afternoon sun had melted her composure. She wanted to sit down and cry, but she hadn't the time. New patients continued to be carried in from the outer bailey and village. If there were just some sign that the end of the plague was near! Anything to bolster her flagging hopes.

"Well, what is that rogue up to now?" Blodwyn's voice interrupted Gwendolyn's dismal thoughts. She glanced about and saw a crowd of serfs standing at the edge of the tent.

"'E's a tryin' to put the yoke on me oxen." A hunched-over man pursed his lips. "'E's goin' to plow by 'eself."

Rushing forward, Gwendolyn pushed her way to the front of the gawking crowd. In the field, Falke fought a losing battle with a team of quarrelsome livestock. Over and over he tried to force the contrary animals into the harness. Finally, he succeeded in capturing the animals and moved them toward the field.

"My God." Alric snaked his way to Gwendolyn's side. "Has Falke gone mad?"

"Nay." With pride, she corrected him. Raising her voice so that it would carry, she added, "Lord Falke is seeing to the needs of his people."

"Laron and Ferris must be having a good laugh."

Alric spat out the words. "Falke has no idea how to plow a field. He looks like a fool out there alone."

Lifting her head, she gave the arrogant young knight an angry glare. "He is your lord, is he not?"

"Of course."

"Then why aren't you helping him?"

"You want me...to go down there...and plow a field?" Alric voice sang with disbelief and indignation.

"Nay," Gwendolyn replied in a solemn, quiet tone, "I want you to go down there and plow and plant all the fields."

The knight turned and came face-to-face with the spent villagers. Their drooping shoulders and gray-white faces proved the people's exhaustion. They had no more to give. What remained of their small supply of energy was needed to fight off the fever and tend to the ill.

"Falke and I will never live this down. Knights working like field hands...!" Alric muttered as he looked at the few crooked rows that his lord had managed to dredge from the dirt. Waving his hand in the air, he trotted down the path and called, "Falke, wait up. I'll help you."

"Now, that Sir Falke be a nobleman with vision," Blodwyn commented to another woman.

"Aye, and a man not afraid of hard work." The elderly man nodded his white head in reverence. "I was a thinkin' the man was too caught up in 'e's own affairs to be thinkin' about us. 'Pears I might be mistaken."

A general mood of acceptance engulfed the crowd. Gwendolyn could not help but rejoice. Falke had gained the people's trust and loyalty, but would the knights in the castle understand the sacrifices Falke was willing to make for Mistedge? From her eavesdropping, she had surmised that Falke's more senior vassals sought a leader with more than just a title. They sought a man who put Mistedge first, a man they could depend on.

"Lady Wren," the old villager called out to her, "if ye ken spare me, I have a mind to go down there and show those boys a thing or two about farming."

Gwendolyn glanced down at the now unmoving oxen and the two knights tugging on the yoke. "Pray do so, Durin." In her heart she prayed that Sir Falke would show his vassals a thing or two about being a lord.

"What a disgrace." Laron paced back and forth along the narrow walkway of the inner wall. "Imagine, the lord of Mistedge plowing a field."

The assembled lords and ladies shook their heads and *tsked* in censure. Sir Baldwin peered over the wall at the men trying to budge the stubborn oxen. A wry smile crossed his grizzled face. "And he's doing a pretty poor job of it." Waving to a few elderly lords, he gave them a wink. "I think we underrated the lad, my friends."

"Underrated!" Laron sputtered. "He's shaming us all."

"I hate to admit it, but you're right, Laron." Sir

Baldwin's smile faded and his eyes darkened to black glass. "Lord Falke is out there alone, seeing to it that the villagers are cared for and our bellies will be full come the cold dark days of winter. Tell me, Laron, did you expect to dine on your fine words and fancy dress come December? Nay? Then 'tis best a farther-seeing man is our lord or there would be many a rumbling belly come the winter."

Facing the knights and ladies of the keep, Sir Baldwin continued his lecture. "I'd be joining him now, but his orders to me were to stay and guard the inner keep. And I obey my liege."

A quiet whisper spread among the nobles. Finally, a clean-faced youth stepped forward. "I'm ready to join Lord Falke." With hesitant steps, four more knights joined him.

Sir Baldwin's gaze fastened on the two men guiding the reluctant oxen. "Gentlemen," he called out to his friends gathered near, "I have hope that Mist-edge has truly found her lord."

Chapter Eleven

Falke stomped across the broken fields, scattering the hens pecking for bugs in the furrows. Morning dew released the rich aroma of the tilled soil. Three days and only one field plowed. Those ignorant, stubborn, arrogant oafs were more of a hindrance than a help. And this time he wasn't talking about the oxen. Nay, the knights of Mistedge were more disagreeable than the smelly beasts.

Five able-bodied knights, plus Falke and Alric, should be able to turn more than one measly field. That is, if the Mistedge knights would take Falke's direction. The knights ignored his, the old farmer's and each other's advice. Each man went his own way, and nothing was accomplished.

"Salutations, my friend," Ozbern called as Falke approached the canopy. "Pray, do not take this as a criticism, but I have never seen seven men work so hard and achieve so little."

Falke gave his friend a tired smile. "Would that I

could bind those knights to me as Lady Wren has the villagers. With a snap of her fingers, she has a battalion of men, women and children to do her bidding, without complaint, without question.''

"Aye, 'tis true enough." Ozbern pointed to the mountain of folded laundry near his pallet. "Even I, newly risen from my sickbed, have been put to work folding laundry." He gestured toward the village park, where Lady Wren, surrounded by her eager helpers, ministered to the ill. "Go and ask her advice."

Falke shrugged at the irony of the situation. "And to think we judged her a simpleton."

"Instead we find her a loyal soul, brave, strong, intelligent." Ozbern pondered his words, then added, "She would be an excellent chatelaine for Mistedge."

"Do not suggest it." Falke rose and placed his hand on Ozbern's shoulder. "I will not wed her. But I have promised to protect her from Titus, and I will."

"'Twould be easier if you married her. Titus will not give her up, nor can you count on Mistedge's support should Titus lay siege. And in King Henry's court, you'd be in the wrong."

"Ozbern, you recover too quickly. As usual, you point out all the flaws in my plans."

"And as usual, you will no doubt find a way around them." He clasped Falke's arm and struggled to his feet. "Go, seek out Lady Wren, while I seek out the garderobe."

Falke left his friend and wove his way among the pallets toward his betrothed. A cloudless blue sky heralded a hot spring day ahead, one that should be spent sowing and not plowing. Each sunrise brought Mistedge closer to winter starvation with the delay in planting. But Falke's serfs had no thoughts of that now.

A few peasants slept on straw pallets, their night duty of tending the sick ended with the recent dawn. Others broke their fast with a simple fare of bread and cheese.

The thought occurred to Falke that he had yet to see Lady Wren sleep more than a few moments or stop to eat. Just as now, she seemed always on the move, overseeing all aspects of her patients' care. Yet in the weeks of the pestilence, she had not lost any of her bulk. Falke studied her as she paused to inspect a woman's basket of herbs.

Lady Wren captured her mass of white-streaked hair in one hand, drawing it away from her face while she examined the medicinal herbs. Smudges covered her face, but could not hide the sculpted quality of her cheekbones, the tilt of her nose or the delicate arch of her light brows. She released her hair, and the snarled strands fell back over her face.

She could be...passable if she washed up, did something about her hair, lost weight. A new wardrobe wouldn't hurt. Aye, Falke thought, with some help from Aunt Celestine, Lady Wren could find someone to marry her. Just not him.

"Come quick, milady. He's in bad shape." A

woman grabbed Lady Wren's hand and hauled her toward the outer bailey and the soldiers' sick quarters. Lady Wren scrambled to keep up, moving with surprising speed for a woman of her size and girth.

Falke followed, not sure why his neck was tingling and his instincts seemed to be laughing at him.

"Nesta, where be ye, lass?" The tormented cry ripped through Gwendolyn's heart as she entered the dark hall lined with fevered men.

"My brother's dyin', ain't 'e?" A young man standing near the pallet questioned her. Grief carved his features into stiff lines of sorrow.

"I'm sorry, Silas," Gwendolyn murmured. She could do nothing to save Elined.

"Nesta, that be ye?" Elined's hand shot out and latched onto Gwendolyn's wrist. In delirium, he placed her hand over his heart. Death tainted his hot dry breath.

"Is everything all right?" From behind her, a low baritone voice interrupted. Falke appeared at her side. His hand covered hers buried beneath the sweaty palm of her patient.

"Aye." She gulped and felt her blood racing at the image before her. The deep slit of his leather jerkin displayed the sculpted lines of his powerful chest. Real concern wrinkled his brows and created tiny crow's-feet at the corner of his eyes. A shiver ran down her spine and a peculiar current of emotion swirled in the pit of her stomach.

"Nesta, stay with me, love," the soldier croaked when Falke tried to free Gwendolyn's hand.

"Pray, Lady Wren, do this for him." Silas glanced down at his brother, his voice cracked from overpowering sorrow. "He can't rest till he speaks with Nesta, but she's gone. 'Tis the only thing causing him to linger, and we both know there's no hope for him."

"I know not what to say." Panic choked her like thick ivy, twining around her self-composure and crumbling her resolve. What did she know of words spoken between lovers?

"I'll be here with you." Falke's soothing voice calmed her frazzled nerves. "He needs you."

"Nesta?" The sick man struggled to roll upright.

Looking into the quiet blue of Falke's eyes, Gwendolyn took a deep breath, drew strength from his closeness, then crooned, "Aye, I'm here."

The dying man kissed the back of her hand. His lips felt like sand against her skin. He confessed, "I told me friends ye was just another bit a' skirt, but 'twas a lie. I want us to be wed proper like. Nesta, will ye have me?"

Bewildered, Gwendolyn cast about for an escape. A marriage proposal, the one thing that would save her from Titus, and for it to be from a dying man while Falke, the one man who could save her, looked on. She wanted to curl up and cry from the ache breaking her heart in two.

The acrid smell of the dying man's sweat-drenched body burned her nostrils, and the lump in her throat threatened to choke her. Her gaze finally settled on the glassy eyes of her patient. Gwendolyn could see the pain in his heart. The fog of indecision lifted and her action became clear. She could not abandon this man. Whatever he needed to ease his death she would give him.

With all the tenderness she wished for in her own bleak life, Gwendolyn kissed her patient. "I'd be proud to call you husband."

A peaceful smile graced the ill man's lips. Serenity smoothed the torment from his face. "Nesta, ye've made me a happy man." A deep sigh rattled in his chest, then the sound stopped.

Gwendolyn raised her head and listened for a heartbeat. Nothing. She felt remorse along with heavy guilt. Death had won another victory over her. Her fingers trembled as she closed his eyelids. Another she had failed.

"My thanks to you, Lady Wren." Silas rose from his knees and bowed toward her. "You allowed him to die with peace. I'll never forget your gift, milady." With stiff legs, he left them and walked toward the women sewing shrouds from cast-off cloth.

The fresh rushes snapped as Gwendolyn sank to the floor. She leaned her forehead against the bed frame and spoke her condemnation in a low whisper. "But I couldn't save him."

Falke watched her actions with bewilderment. No tears, no wails. Not even anger. Moments ago she had portrayed a dying man's lover, accepted his marriage proposal, and Falke knew how much that must have hurt her. 'Twas like a slap in her face. Even he, with his schooled detachment, had felt the sting. A dying man had done what Falke refused to—ask Lady Wren to wed him. Yet she withstood all with a stone face.

A violent tremor shuddered through her body. Despite her size, she appeared frail and vulnerable. Tucking in her chin, her hair covering most of her face, she rocked trancelike. Another tremor shook her.

"Lady Wren?" Falke feared she was having some type of fit.

She lifted her face and Falke sucked hard for air. Her almond-shaped eyes displayed her emotions like an expensive glass mirror—every torment clearly distinct and apparent for all to see, yet imprisoned inside.

Kneeling to be eye level with her, Falke brushed back the snarls and whispered, "Little Wren, go ahead and cry."

Instead of relief, fear blended with her despondency. "Nay, I'll not cry."

Falke pulled her into the nest of his arms. "'Twill make the grief easier if you don't hold it in so."

She struggled to free herself, almost frantic. He could feel the erratic flutter of her heart next to his chest. "Pray, let me go." A half sob caught in her voice.

"Cry!" Falke ordered. She would become sick if she kept all this sorrow inside.

"Nay, I cannot." She bit her lower lip. Her chin

wobbled slightly, her voice filled with wistful remorse. "I've forgotten how."

Forgotten! Falke's suspicious mind flared at the ridiculous notion. A woman who didn't cry? Preposterous. Every woman knew how to use a few tears and smiles to get her way. But then, how often did Lady Wren smile, or laugh? Either was a rare occurrence.

"Come now, do not jest with me, girl." He made his voice abrupt and harsh. "Everyone cries."

"'Tis too dangerous. Then Titus would know the things that hurt, the things that matter."

Titus! Falke should have suspected that devil lay at the core of his little wren's hurt. She expected a beating if she provoked anger, torture if she cried. What about laughter? Had Titus driven that simple joy from her life as well? Falke cradled her against his shoulder, rocking her like a frightened child. "With me, you can cry."

Lifting her head, she graced him with a rare eye-to-eye stare. Lost in the turquoise sea of her gaze, he prayed she would relent and allow him this simple measure of payment for all her aid.

Her lip trembled, and he nestled her against his chest with her head just under his chin. The smell of her, herbal and earthy, enveloped him. He wove his fingers with hers. "My poor little wren."

In silence, she leaned against him. He wished she could draw in his strength, his vitality. The tautness of her body abated. His heart rejoiced when a few tears moistened his chest. He sat there, holding this

strange woman, his betrothed, while she wept soundlessly.

Falke whispered, "I've caused you anger and I've
freed your tears, my little bird. But next 'tis your
laughter I'll hear. On this I state my word."

Unmindful of the knights waiting in the fields, or
the rustling of men placing the body in a shroud,
Falke held her. Brotherly affection seared him with
the desire to protect her. He would find her a husband
who would cherish her as she deserved. Someone
worthy of her.

"Lady Wren, where be ye? Arry's a lookin' for
ye." A pale-faced woman stumbled to a stop in front
of them. "Milord? Milady?"

"I was...we were..." Crimson colored her cheeks
and neck as she scrambled from his arms and to her
feet. "Show me where Arry is." She glanced back
at Falke, wiped the tears from her face and added,
"My thanks, milord."

A woman who thanked him for bringing her to
tears. Lady Wren never ceased to amaze him. He
watched her run away from him, his arms feeling the
emptiness, his heart feeling the same.

"Falke." Ozbern braced his back against a tree
and gave a weak wave.

Falke rushed to his friend's side and wrapped an
arm around his waist in support. "You push yourself
too fast."

"Aye, mayhap the garderobe was a bit far to venture." Ozbern half closed his eyes. "But Lady Wren
has given me orders to drink bucketfuls of that foul-

tasting tea and there is no naysaying the woman.''
He drew back and quirked a brow. ''I say, you've
stained your tunic. And that smell. 'Tis familiar…reminds me of a cool forest.''

Falke pulled at his leather jerkin. A dark muddy
blotch spread down his shirt from his shoulder to his
chest. Sniffing at it, he understood Ozbern's comment. Deep, rich aromas of spices and herbs assaulted him. An earthy perfume of the forest after a
rain. An aroma that seemed a part of him. Its famil-
iarity teased him, and then he knew it. 'Twas the
scent of Lady Wren.

Chapter Twelve

"Beans and dark bread! We toil all day in their fields and they fed us this slop." Sir Clement, the most belligerent of the Mistedge knights, threw down his wooden bowl in disgust. "I am a noble and as such expect to be fed properly."

Gwendolyn looked at the mutinous knights, their backs and faces burned red from the sun. The men looked ready to walk out and leave the villagers to fend for themselves. The warrior within each knight balked at the menial work. Somehow she must make them see that a war raged within this demesne and that when they lifted a plow or hoe, they did battle just the same as if they lifted a broadsword.

"Sir Falke." She pleaded with him for aid.

"'Tis your expertise, Lady Wren. I know no other that does it so well." Falke's golden eyebrows arched, a half smile crooking his lips. He was daring her to confront the group of knights. The very thought terrified her, but his supportive nod and nearness gave her courage. Very well, she'd not falter. The knights must stay. And deep inside, she knew Falke would protect her as he had this morning. When he had sheltered her in his arms, she had felt invincible and cherished—two emotions that had been rare in her life.

Fortified by Falke's nearness, she tapped her finger on her lower lip. "I see your point, Sir Clement. Pray, come and speak with today's cook so that the same mistake will not be made." Respect and reverence for the knights oozed from her voice.

"I'll see to it we are fed as our work deems fit." Sir Clement rose, readjusted his thick leather belt and rolled his shoulder muscles. The cheers of the other knights encouraged his bravado.

"Clement will tell them what for." Three of the knights, eager to see their leader put the commoners in their place, hustled to their feet and followed. As she escorted the gentlemen away, Falke gave her a sly smile and a wink. Her face burning and her pulse racing, she led the four knights to a modest hut.

Unlike Arry's home, the wattle-and-daub structure was tight and strong. A window and the open door allowed a breeze to enter. The strong smell of mint pervaded the air and mingled with the sounds of soft hymns.

The group of knights brushed past her and Sir Clement's voice boomed out, "Where is the cook?"

Gwendolyn pushed her way past the wall of tall men just as they realized where they were. The bluster faded from Sir Clement's face and he paled to a sickly white. All the pomposity of the group escaped in an audible gasp.

A thin woman sat on the floor holding the unnaturally still form of a toddler. "Here, sire." With a damp cloth, she rhythmically cooled the youngster's face and hands. All along the perimeter of the tiny room, other mothers did the same to their children. Of all the places in the village, Gwendolyn's heart ached the most in this small hut that served as the children's ward. Fear, anguish and grief hovered over the women, threatening to overcome them at any moment.

"I...I beg pardon." For once, Sir Clement and his crew were at a loss for words.

The child in the cook's arms thrashed weakly. "Hush, dearling." The cook brushed a tear from her face. Cradling her son, she rocked him softly while dribbling a few drops of water down his throat.

Looking up, the haggard woman asked, "Are you in need of me again, Lady Wren? It seems I've just had a blink of time with my boy." She kissed the child's head and placed him back on a straw pallet. "Ma will be back soon."

'Twas plain the sight moved the knights. Gwendolyn had no intention of letting them off so easily. This scene needed to flash in their mind every time the heat became too unbearable or the pull of the plow too painful. "As a matter of fact, 'twas Sir Clement who wished to speak with you. Seems the food was—"

"Excellent." Sir Clement found his voice and

gave Gwendolyn an apologetic glance. "I and these men—" he waved to the other knights "—wished to thank you for your wonderful repast. We know how precious your time with your babe is. That you gave up some of those moments to prepare our meal humbles us." He turned to leave, pushing his group of meeker knights out the door.

"Sir Clement?" The cook rose and clasped the knight's hand. "I wish a word with you." Gwendolyn held her breath, waiting for the noble's reaction.

A newfound mercy gentled the usual arrogance in the knight's eyes. "Pray, how can I be of service?"

"You already have." The cook's gaze swept around the room. "We women have always seen your kind as quick to take an insult or to grab a handsome village girl. Our crops and people got the worst of your battles and wars. But when I look out at that field and I see ye workin' the land so that we all ken eat this winter, then 'tis proud I am to say Sir Clement is a knight of Mistedge. Proud to say I'm from Mistedge. Thank you, thank you all." Tears glistened in the cook's eyes. She released her hold on the knight and settled next to her child once more.

Sir Clement cleared his throat, twice. He puffed out his chest and sniffed. "Dust." He sniffed again, gave each of the women a regal nod, then waved Gwendolyn forward and out the door.

"Could have warned me," he accused as he tried

to compose himself before rejoining Falke under the shade of the trees.

"Of what? Of life? Of death?" She stopped in the center of the green. "Sir Clement, this is Mistedge, not that closed group within those walls. This demesne has been in decline for years, not from lack of wealth but because of a lack of unity. Now is the time to stand together, not separate. Try to build instead of destroy."

"Lady Wren. Arry's come back with more supplies from the castle. We need ye to help parcel them out," Blodywn called from the road.

Gwendolyn watched the knights sit in the cool shade next to Falke. The episode had opened their eyes to what Mistedge needed in a lord. Sir Clement was willing to forge a friendship. Was Falke?

Sympathy for Sir Clement sneaked up on Falke. The braggart never missed a chance to make a snide remark or despair over Falke's leadership abilities. Now the bravado was wrung out of the man. But if Lady Wren had woven her magic, Clement would be a better man and perhaps would see her worth, and the knight would help Falke keep her out of Titus's hands.

"Hey, Clement, what of our meal?" one of the knights who'd remained behind querried. "When is that woman fixing us a real meal?"

"Shut up and eat." Sir Clement picked up his trencher and ate silently.

"But I thought—"

"Listen to the man." Falke silenced the heckler with a steely gaze. "Eat while you can. Then we return to work."

Sir Clement shot him a grateful glance. "My thanks."

"Lady Wren serves up many types of medicine, both for the body and the soul. Her tonics do not always have a sweet taste." Falke leaned against the trunk of the oak, then shot forward at the sting from his sunburn.

"And of us all, my good friend Falke has suffered quite a bit of Lady Wren's tonic for the soul." Ozbern cracked a good-natured grin. "I believe he is glad Clement bears the brunt of her lesson and not him for once."

"Ozbern, you are newly risen from your bed." Falke arched a brow. "Do not waste what strength you have on heedless prattle."

"Sir Ozbern, as a knight of Mistedge—" Sir Clement sat up straighter, his voice lifted so that all could hear "—I am always glad to do service for my lord." His gray eyes centered on Falke, letting him register the full impact of his words.

The underlying message did not elude Falke. A pledge of loyalty did not come as a small token to such a knight. Aware of the silent tension, he grasped the knight's hand and smiled. "And your lord is thankful for this and all services you render me." *One more protector for Lady Wren.*

"I ask one boon, milord. Pray keep me on the fair

side of Lady Wren. Her wounds do sting.'' Sir Clement squinted his eyes in an imagined injury.

''Aye, that they do,'' Ozbern agreed. ''She makes a man see his shortcomings.''

''Nay.'' Falke shook his head. '''Tis not the faults of the man she sees. That's why she's so hard to win against. Someone tears you down, 'tis only natural to fight back. Lady Wren sees the man you could be.'' *The man I'll never be.* '''Tis hard to win a joust when she can crack all your armor and leave you naked on the field.''

Sir Clement gave him a sage nod and pursed his lips. ''I see you've had more than one bout with the lady.''

Rising, Falke dusted off the back of his breeches and muttered, ''Aye, and lost every battle. Come, the noontime is over and the fields await.''

Without hesitation, the men rose at his word. In slow, deliberate steps, Falke felt the firming of his position as lord. And centered at each of his advances was the prodding hand of Lady Wren. When the fever invaded Mistedge, Falke had thought his luck had evaporated, but now he wondered. What he'd thought of as a disadvantage was fast turning into an asset.

But how far would he have to go to seal his future? Marriage to Lady Wren? Aye, he admired her and was genuinely fond of her. But love? Nay. His father had driven that emotion from Falke's heart. 'Twould take a miracle to drive it back. And didn't the lady deserve someone more worthy than him?

What did he know of leading a fief? Caring for serfs? Before, when Mistedge had just meant wealth and land, if he failed, 'twould have been little more than fulfilling his father's prophecy that Falke would never be more than a mercenary. But now that Mistedge meant its people and all their hopes and dreams, if Falke failed 'twould be a heavy burden. He would not have Lady Wren share that humiliation.

Nor could he forget his angel of the night. Thrice he had returned to the pool, searching for her, to no avail. The woman had disappeared. His discreet inquiries of the villagers proved to him that the woman had not existed before Titus's arrival. The old lecher's response to Falke's description of her made him even more curious. What hold did this woman have over Titus, and how could Falke use it to protect Lady Wren?

But a baser, more primitive motive pushed Falke to find the woman. Her beauty tempted him each night. Despite the fatigue of plowing and working in the fields, he found his dreams haunted by his night angel. And strangely, by Lady Wren. Each night, 'twas the same. The angel would come to him, they would embrace, kiss, make love, and then she would melt away. And standing in the shadows would be Lady Wren.

Bah! After twenty years was he finally developing a conscience? Was he feeling guilty for dreaming of one woman while engaged to another? What foolishness. Falke had made love to several women, all in one night. Married, widowed, as long as they were willing. All of them beautiful, he reminded himself. And not a one of them had pricked through to his heart.

But somehow, Lady Wren had.

It scared him right down to his garters.

Chapter Thirteen

Gwendolyn parted the tall reeds near the pond and scrutinized her reflection. White streaked her dark, tangled tresses, especially near her face. Along her crooked part, the lighter roots threatened to expose her.

The last time she had come to this spot to repair her disguise, Falke had found her. That encounter had prevented her from applying the dye correctly, and it had lasted only weeks instead of months. With Falke busy plowing the fields and Cyrus running interference for her in the village, this time there would be no interruptions.

Gwendolyn stripped off her patched, ragged gown and belt of pockets stuffed with herbs. A faint breeze penetrated her thin linen shift as, kneeling by the pond, she combed vinegar wine through her hair to remove the old color. With relish, she scrubbed her face and washed away the last vestiges of her masquerade.

In a few hours, she would once again be drab, ugly Lady Wren, but inside, she would never be the same. Before coming to Mistedge, she had only dreamed of what she might be missing. Now she knew. A devil-may-care, charming, infuriating knight, Falke de Chretian.

Weariness, both physical and mental, seeped into her bones as she selected herbs to make the dye. The disease in the village taxed her endurance, but Falke's sheltering arms had breached her innermost walls.

Crushing the withered herbs between two flat stones, she found their pungent odor tickled her nose. Just as she had freed the leaves' perfume, Falke had freed her emotions, using a gentle touch and soothing words as his mortar and pestle. Yesterday, cradled in his arms, she could not deny her heart's painful truth. She had fallen in love with Falke de Chretian.

And to show just how dangerous her plight had become, her heart whispered an even more cutting truth—she didn't want him to love her, Gwendolyn. She longed to have him pledge his heart to the woman who worked at his side day by day, who encouraged him, believed in him—Lady Wren.

What irony! Jealous of herself! And for naught. Falke would never wed her, either as his night angel or as Lady Wren. He would not be forced into marrying Lady Wren, nor would he marry his angel and risk losing his lands to Laron's treachery.

To tell him or not? Could she trust Falke's love if

he married her for her beauty? Was it wrong to hope for more than lust to bind a man to her?

But what of Titus? Once she returned to the castle and the villagers talked, he would know she had deceived him about her wits. Would he think to question her looks as well?

Pouring the crumbled herbs into a small wooden bowl, she added water and stirred the murky mixture. 'Twas like seeing her future, dark and shadowy.

Running wet fingers through her long hair, she dipped a limp curl into the bowl, massaging the muddy color into her hair. She ordered herself to forget the tenderness in Falke's indigo gaze as he'd comforted her, the feel of his lips upon hers as he'd sealed his oath of friendship. 'Twas Lady Wren she must become and remain until Titus could no longer harm her. Or Falke learned that a woman was more than the curves of her body.

"By the saints!"

The sound cut the silence of the forest and stabbed her heart. The curse drove away her despair and replaced it with panic. Like resisting hands, the wild rose brambles just a few measures away from her shook, littering the forest floor with pink, red and white petals. From within came a steady stream of damning oaths.

Jumping to her feet she ran a few paces, then stopped. Where could she run? The village? Nay, not as she was, with her hair stripped of dye. The dye! Heavens, she couldn't become Lady Wren without it. Her gown. Her belt of herbs. Frantic to escape, yet unable to run without her camouflage, she raced back to retrieve the precious mixture and her belongings.

The lapse was her undoing.

The brambles parted and Falke pushed his way into the clearing. Rose petals stuck in his shoulder-length hair. A look of surprise, then panic creased the handsome planes of his face. "Angel, wait," he pleaded as he tugged his arm free of the thorns.

His plea halted her, though she wished it did not. "Just a few moments," she begged her conscience. "Just a stolen moment with the man I love."

"With the man *I* love," countered her mind in the soft, hesitant voice of Lady Wren.

Like a trainer with a skittish filly, Falke approached, his hands outstretched, his voice low and soothing. "Do not fear me."

A mad, bubbly lightness overcame her as she met his laughing eyes, and soft sunlight sprinkled his honey-colored hair. It made her feel daring, willing to take any risk to be with him.

"I'm not afraid of you," she answered truthfully.

Falke hesitated, both from his surprise at her response and her tone. 'Twas so like Lady Wren's, a mixture of breathless wonder and gratitude. His angel studied him through a thick fringe of dark lashes, her lower lip puckered in concentration.

"Pray, tell me your name." Expectation nearly choked him as he spoke.

"Angel will do." She withheld her name, but

Falke had already christened her as his. This beauty would not escape him again.

Heat fanned from his groin and stabbed at his chest. Christ's blood, but she was more beautiful than he remembered. Sunlight created a halo as it reflected off her unbound, waist-length hair. As she moved, the tresses flowed like liquid silver along her graceful neck and curled down her shoulders. One strand, the end stained by mud, clung to the valley between her full breasts. The tip curled demurely, drawing his attention to the outline of her nipple beneath her thin linen shift.

Primal lust flared and Falke doubted Hades could withstand such heat. Arousal silkened his tones as he sought to flatter the woman. "I have searched for you often since last we met."

"You have?" Censure and surprise made her eyes widen. "I would think you too busy plowing the fields to waste time on such pursuits."

"The oxen tore the yoke leathers, so I thought to while away the time here in hopes of finding you. The search for perfect beauty is always just." Arming himself with his charming smile, he approached her and reached for her hand.

She very purposefully drew both hands behind her back and cocked one brow. "I thought you had learned to cease your flattery by now."

"And pray, who would teach me such a lesson?"

"Lady Wren."

The name was like a bucket of cold water on his passion. Aye, Lady Wren would snort in disdain if he tried to woo her with pretty words and a charming smile. His suspicions flamed as his ardor simmered. This beautiful woman knew Mistedge well, while no one there seemed to know of her existence.

"Lady Wren has taught me the use of plain speech." Falke crossed his arms over his chest and stared down at the petite woman. "So I will use such with you. How is it you know so much of the happenings in the village, yet have never set foot there? And most importantly, why do you scare a devil like Titus into fleeing?"

Her head dropped, and Falke noticed one bare toe peeking from under the hem of her gown. Unease twined around his heart. Angel was like a song that ran over and over in his head, yet he could not recall the words. Or a tantalizing dish prepared with a spice he could not identify. And most disconcerting of all, he felt that his well-honed instincts were again... teasing at him.

Angel raised her head and looked upward, as though reading a script in the heavens. "I am the...mistress of one of your vassals. He hid me here in the woods so that I would be near but he need not have to share me with others."

"Which lord?" Falke demanded as he mentally prayed, *Let it not be Laron.*

"I will not say, for fear of him and for him." Then her eyes softened and a smile curved her lush lips. "But rest assured, Lord Falke, my lord is true to you and your claim to Mistedge."

"You protect this man, even though he left you to fend for yourself in this plague?"

"He could not venture out and expose himself. And I have kept myself away from the village for my safety and his, though Lady Wren found me. 'Tis she that keeps me abreast of the happenings at Mistedge."

"Why would Lady Wren not tell me of meeting you?"

"I begged her not to, and she felt you had better things to do than search the woods for me."

That sounded like his Lady Wren. Work first, pleasure last. Falke rubbed his chin, coming to terms with the fact that his innocent angel was the mistress of one of his lords, a loyal one at that if she was to be believed. Yet one mystery remained. The most important to him and Lady Wren.

"And Titus? I saw fear in his eyes when I described you," he stated.

"Lady Wren told me I looked very much like her mother, Isolde." Angel lifted her gaze and met his. Hatred honed their depths to so fine an edge that Falke felt their sting. "Titus fears Isolde's wrath from beyond the grave. At least this is what Lady Wren has told me. When you described me, Titus must have thought I was a ghost. Would that I were, and could scare the evil from his heart."

The intensity of her hatred made Falke question her story. "Lady Wren has just cause for her loathing. What sin has Titus done you?"

"I hate all men that would use a woman so. Titus

lusted after Isolde's beauty and when he could not posses it, he allowed her to die.'' Angel gave her chin a defiant tilt. ''A woman's beauty does not lie within the vessel, but within the spirit. Should a man ever learn to love that essence, he would possess a love beyond all.''

Ferocity marked each word, and Falke knew them to be from the heart. His cousin Roen and his wife, Lenora, possessed a union that knew no limits or boundaries. And his mother had held such a love for his father. Bernard de Chretian's rejection of his wife's priceless offering had destroyed her. Nay, Falke would never risk such heartache and loss.

His angel possessed no great weapon over Titus, and thus he could not use her to save Lady Wren. Nor would he marry his betrothed and sentence her to the life his mother had. She deserved so much better.

A terrible fatigue settled over him. What use was he as a lord? His people were dying, his fields lay in half-plowed, crooked rows, and he could not save one lone woman. A woman who moved his soul in ways that frightened and intrigued him. Bah! He was useless.

Ignoring the ravishing vision before him, Falke dropped to the mossy ground and slumped against the trunk of a willow. Since he'd kissed her, his life had shifted into a nightmare. His only solace was Lady Wren's gentle half smile and sharp wit.

''Milord? Are you ill?'' Angel knelt at his side, her palm testing his forehead for fever. Concern created a tiny V between her silvery brows. Again a bolt shot of unease lanced through Falke and made him brush away her hand in frustration. Why did her simple movements trigger his heart so?

"Heartsick, nothing more." The admission passed his lips as he gave her a wry smile. Lady Wren, the pestilence, the villagers, Laron, Ozbern and Robert's illness. All weighed heavily on Falke at this moment.

He stroked her cheek with tenderness. "You warned me your kiss would take away my luck, and so it seems it did. If I thought your kiss would cure all that ails the village, I would demand another."

"And I would give it." Her voice dropped with disappointment as she added, "I am but flesh and blood."

And what a delightful arrangement of flesh she was. Her body intoxicated him with its nearness, as though her very skin was a wine, and Falke longed to savor its bouquet. Desire drove him to boldness, yet when he gazed at her face 'twas the concern in her eyes that stirred emotions deep within him. Emotions that overpowered all his roguish instincts.

He spoke without guile, without studied effect, and voiced his inner thoughts. "And if I asked, as a man of flesh and blood, weary of battling disease, plowing fields, and awash in betrayal, would you grant me the boon of a kiss?"

Lust Gwendolyn recognized and could ignore. But the wistful tremor in Falke's voice betrayed more. He needed comfort from the visions of death in the village and the threat of betrayal from within the castle walls. Comfort that he had so willingly given to Lady Wren. Gwendolyn could not deny him.

"Aye, milord. I would willingly give you a kiss." And much more.

She steadied herself for the crushing bruise of his mouth on hers and then closed her eyes. She waited. Nothing happened. She opened one eye.

His face hovered over her own, his lips just a breath away from hers. "I fear your lord has mishandled you." His lips met her own, gentle, searching, imploring. With a whisperlike caress, his mouth explored the outline of her upper lip. Each touch took away her breath, and her fear.

"Did that lord of yours ever do this?" Falke nibbled the corner of her full mouth, then traced the line of her neck with his fingertip. Her pulse quickened at his touch.

"Nay." She sighed as delicious heat meandered down her neck and dipped between her breasts.

"I thought not."

Gwendolyn smiled at the pride in his voice. And the knowledge that he wanted her to feel this pleasure intensified all the exotic sensations speeding through her body.

Coupling was no mystery to her. The Cravenmoor knights took women whenever they wished, in the great hall, the solar, even during meals. A few slobbery kisses, two or three grunts, and most had finished in blink of an eye. Pain had contorted the women's faces, and a look of relief accompanied the last thrust. Never had Gwendolyn imagined a man's touch could be so wanted, so desired, and never had she thought the act could be so…deliciously…slow.

His breath at the hollow of her neck sent a shiver of delight along her spine. A rough, callused hand cradled her head, supporting the weight of her thick hair. The other combed through her damp strands, making bare toes curl as his strong, long fingers caressed her neck, collarbone, then the contours of her breast, finally resting near the stiff peak.

Her back arched as though pleading, begging, demanding the mound be captured. As though sensing that desire, Falke complied, but with his mouth. Lightning quick sensations pulsated through her. Hot, driving, needful.

The thin shift that she wore suddenly became too thick, too hot to bear against her sensitive skin. Her fingers itched to touch him, yet she lacked the boldness. The best her timidity would allow was to wrap her arms around his neck and let her fingers play with the silky, flaxen hair. Purring, she nestled closer while breathing in his essence of sweat, passion and maleness.

Hard, smooth muscles along his chest met the soft mounds of hers. The contrast made her want to explore the difference between his body and her own. Pushing past her shyness, she slipped her hands beneath his tunic and traced his sculpted back. His groan of pleasure dissolved her bashfulness and replaced it with wanton curiosity.

Moving before she lost the courage, Gwendolyn dipped her fingertips below the waistband of his woolen breeches. His muscles clenched, sending a delightful jab to the apex between her legs. An ache began to build, radiating upward, toward her breasts, her fingertips and down her back.

"Angel," Falke growled, as he tore his lips from the valley of her breasts. "Go no further lest you are willing to give me all." Want burned in his eyes, straight through her to the core of her soul.

A year more with Titus. Long, bleak days. She could fill them with wishful thoughts, or memories of Falke, here and now. Of his touch. His kiss. 'Twas a simple decision.

"I am yours to take, my lord."

"Angel, you do me in," he said with a chuckle as she pushed him to his back with a gentle shove.

Gwendolyn laughed, at him, at life, at the thrill of power that he was allowing her. Bold with want, heady with love and drunk from his musky scent, she shed her inhibitions. The laces of his tunic were gone, leaving a deep wide valley of tanned skin for her to touch, taste and nip. With impish laziness, she trailed kisses down his neck, then flicked her tongue across his exposed nipple.

His response tickled her. She'd had no idea a man could react the same as a woman. The skin tightened; his groan came from deep inside his throat. She thought of the sweet ache that emanated from between her thighs. Did Falke feel the same heat there? To further test, she slid her hand slid down his flat chest, along his hips, then rested on the shaft.

"Angel, your lord taught you too well how to

please.'' Falke spoke through clenched teeth. His manhood dug into her palm. Stabbing heat radiated from the point of contact. Reason, caution, desecration evaporated from her mind like a morning mist.

Urgency overtook her. She needed....something, something that her body knew Falke possessed. Straddling him, she let the weight of her hair tilt her chin up, and concentrated on the ever-building fire located at the juncture between her legs and his manhood.

Instinctively, she rocked, begging, ''Falke, pray, ease this need.''

''I am ever willing to champion a lady,'' he whispered in her ear as he lowered her to the ground. His lips never hurried as they traversed the contour of her shoulders. The tie of her shift had loosened. Or had Falke untied it with his teeth? She couldn't seem to remember, only that each inch her shift dropped allowed him more skin to touch, kiss and massage.

He ignored her insistent pleas to end this torture. Had she thought his unhurried pace a blessing? Now she cursed it. She barely noticed when one hand slid beneath her gown; Falke's breath across her sensitive breasts consumed all her attention. Embers that had smoldered in the pit of her stomach flared into incredible heat as his hand cupped her womanhood.

''Falke!'' She meant to scream his name, but instead spoke with a deep, husky voice. With cursed slowness, one finger entered her, and she shuddered from the thrill and ecstasy.

Passion urged Falke to take this woman, lust

tempted him to ravage her, but he could not. Pleasure held her in rapture. Hypnotized by the emotions flickering across her face, he reveled in her delight. With her eyes closed, her body soft and giving, she tilted back her head, giving herself freely to passion's joy.

Her lord had never shown her such enjoyment, such delight. Somehow, he would find a way to free her from her selfish master, and then spend nights instructing her on the art of lovemaking.

Liquid heat bathed his hand as tiny shudders trembled across her bare skin. Her breasts peaked and a rosy glow flushed her alabaster skin. Now was the time. His excruciating wait would be over.

"I need more." Angel opened her eyes wide, the irises dark with a woman's desire.

"And you will get more," Falke promised as he lowered himself over her. Still exercising a self-control he never knew he possessed, he entered the tight sheath of her womanhood. Basked in the pull of the tight glove of warmth that encircled him. Entered bit by bit, letting her grow accustomed to his size. Marveled at the smoothness of her as he slid deeper, deeper, deeper.

It was all too much for Gwendolyn to comprehend. Too many sensations. The forest breeze that danced across her exposed breasts. The currents of ecstasy that curled along her inner thighs as he lowered himself into her. But most of all, she was aware of the indescribable pain of need that kept growing as he filled her with his shaft.

"God's wounds, woman." Falke's slow transgression halted abruptly. "You are a maiden."

"Aye." Gwendolyn sighed, still engrossed in the play of emotions traveling through her. Spine-tingling tremors racked her body, and still she felt the need for more. Greedy for satisfaction, she wrapped her legs around his hips and arched forward. "Now, Falke, now."

Once given the power of choice, Gwendolyn had no intention of releasing it. 'Twas her decision, hers alone. And she would have Falke, all of him. A tilt of her pelvis, then she clenched her legs and pushed.

"Nay, I thought you were a fallen wo—"

'Twas no use arguing, nor turning back. The barrier separating Falke from Angel's core broke with her thrust, and he tumbled deep into her. Though maiden, her body instinctively began the rhythmic dance of lovemaking, and Falke found he could not deny her.

A moan began her travel to fulfillment. Her fingers gripped his shoulders, urging him deeper, closer to the edge of control. He ceased to be. Instead, he felt himself joining with her, he and she becoming one.

If passion had a face, 'twould be Angel's. Her fairy-silver hair fanned about her, the light breeze carrying strands to his face, their touch a caress. Each of his plunges brought her breasts to within kissing range, a challenge Falke could not ignore.

As he fell into her, her eyes opened. Clear, sapphire eyes that shone with awe, pleasure and rapture. She rose to meet each thrust with anticipation and exhilaration. Then she laughed—a great joyous sound that seemed to surprise her.

"Laughing, are you?" Falke rotated his hips slowly, enjoying her slight gasp. "A man does not wish to hear his woman giggle as he makes love to her."

"Really? 'Tis this ache I feel. Like my body is becoming air, and I am rising on the clouds." Guilt clouded her eyes and Falke instantly regretted his banter.

"Laugh all you wish, my angel." He gripped her softly curved backside and brought her forward as he thrust. "While I travel with you to the heavens." Want dictated the pace. The thrust. The quickening.

Comprehension left her. Caution deserted her. She met Falke's gaze, darkened to midnight from his lovemaking. His hot, pulsating shaft reached deep within her. She trembled from the sheer pleasure. How could she explain this gift he bestowed on her? A life spent guarding her feelings. And now, Gwendolyn could release. Let them fly free.

And she was flying, higher and higher. Faster and faster. She felt herself rise above the soft mossy ground, her soul reaching to merge with Falke's. Her blood pounded. She couldn't get enough breath. Still Falke drove deeper, faster.

The whirlwind grew within her, fueled by Falke's exquisite dance, twisting Gwendolyn into an explosive ball of want, desire and passion. And then she exploded. Great waves of bliss undulated through her and she groaned in pleasure.

Her fulfillment was Falke's undoing. He could not withdraw, only join in her completion. With a mighty plunge, he released his hot seed, clutching her to him as she racked his back with her fingertips. Time ceased as he emptied his loins within her waiting womb, joining as he had with no other woman.

Sated, exhausted and still transfixed by the intensity of their lovemaking, Falke laid his head on her breasts. Inside her, he could feel the spasms of her fulfillment ebbing. And his desire reawakening.

'Twould be cruel to have the woman again after so thorough a joining. With regret, he withdrew and lay beside her.

"Nay!" She protested feebly and lifted her heavy lids.

"Aye." Falke smiled at the rosy glow across the skin and the deep even breaths of her naked chest. He kissed her shoulder, then slipped up the edges of her gown. "You must rest."

Like a kitten, she curled up next to him, her body molding to his. "I'm not tired. I'm…wonderful."

"Aye, that you are." Falke wrapped his arms around her, pulling her even closer, thinking she was correct in both statements. Later, after she napped, he would ask about her lies. Mistress? With her maidenhead intact? Yet he found it hard to be cross with her. The knowledge that he alone knew her as a man gave him great satisfaction.

Chuckling, he intertwined his fingers with her own and kissed each blunt-nailed fingertip. Her callused hands showed the signs of hard work and strength. Nestling her head under his chin, he wondered just how long he should let her rest before he could justify another round of foreplay. As he felt his manhood quicken, Falke knew the wait would seem like centuries.

Gwendolyn fought to reach wakefulness. Something was skipping along her hip, reaching under her gown, playing in the down between her legs. A recognizable warmth crept up her limbs and lodged at the pit of her stomach.

"Falke!" She turned and smiled as she met his mischievous gaze. She could feel the strength of his desire pressing against her shift. His hand sheltered the triangle of her womanhood.

"Twice we've made love and now you wish it again?"

"A thousand days and nights would not be enough with you."

His hand traveled along her inside thigh, making her skin spark with anticipation. How could she deny this man who had opened the gates of her soul? Had let her feel for the first time the tremendous waves of passion?

"But alas, I fear I must return to the village. The sun has already crested—"

"What?" Gwendolyn stumbled to her feet, searching for some break in the leaves. Panic seized her as she spotted the golden disk in the western sky. She had missed the midday meal. What would Cyrus think? How could she explain away her absence for the entire morning and afternoon?

Gathering up her belongings, she wrapped her recognizable old gown beneath her belt of pockets. "I must leave. Now."

"Wait, Angel." Falke jumped to his feet, searching for his breeches, boots and tunic as he spoke. "Come with me to the village—"

"Nay, I cannot." Gwendolyn spotted the bowl of hair dye and snatched it up. Perhaps she could find some copse of trees and reapply her disguise. Her hair was dry, but a fast application would stay for a few weeks at least.

Falke pulled up his breeches and gave her an indulgent smile. "Have no fear, Angel." He pulled on one boot. "And no excuses. I took your maidenhead." The bravado in his voice grated on Gwendolyn's ears. A man *would* crow about taking a woman's virginity.

Giving her a wink, Falke added, "So there is no lord to keep you from me. There is nothing to separate us. I will have those thousand days and nights to love you."

"Nothing stands in our way?" Pray God, let him see the error of his ways. Let him see he misspoke and let tenderness rule his heart instead of lust.

"Nothing. I will find you a place in the village. The work is hard, but the nights will be worth—"

Stunned at his audacity, Gwendolyn sputtered, "You expect me to just accept you bringing a mistress in right under my—" All the tender feelings for the golden giant scuffling for his clothes dissipated. "My friend's nose."

He didn't care about her. Or rather, Lady Wren, Gwendolyn corrected. Oh, he wanted his angel, lusted after her, but the woman he should cherish above all others he didn't concern himself with, not even wondering whether this would hurt her.

"Of whom do you speak?" Confusion wrinkled his brow as he grunted to get on his tight leather boot.

"Lady Wren," Gwendolyn fumed. "Your fiancée. Remember, the woman who aided you? At her own peril, I might add. The woman who saved your sorry hide by treating the sick, helped you gain your knights' approval. And you would return these favors by parading a mistress right under her nose? Spurning and embarrassing her in front of the peasants? Have you no heart? No thought of loyalty?"

Fueled by anger, her heart slashed with hurt, she unleashed all her fury. "I'll not put my faith in your cheap vows and promises." She released one last blow. "Your father was right not to expect much from you. It saved him the heartache I now feel."

Tears glistened in her eyes, and again Falke felt

the same sense of déjà vu; as though he had seen her just this way before. He reached out to give comfort.

Turning her back to him, she glided away, blending in with the forest, disappearing as the underbrush concealed her. Sinking to the ground, he rubbed his fingertips over his eyes, worried that there might be tears. Every word she'd spoken cut him to the quick with its truth.

He always seemed to fail the ones he loved. Mother, Ozbern, Angel—and most of all, Lady Wren.

Chapter Fourteen

Gwendolyn wiped away the perspiration on her cheek, then returned to stirring the enormous vat of laundry. The bright sun, along with the fire under the kettle, made the air stifling. Few came her way, avoiding the heat and the chance she might ask them to relieve her.

But she wouldn't. The laundry was the chore Falke detested most, and the least likely place for him to visit. For the past week, since their afternoon of lovemaking, she had managed to avoid him. And if he sought her out, there were plenty of reasons to explain away her absence. Ill to tend, soap to make, huts to repair, women to instruct in herbal medicine. Anything that would keep her away from Falke's presence.

But this hour, midday, was the worst. Falke and his men would leave the fields for their meal. Even now she could hear their easy laughter and banter as they approached. Villagers called out joyful salutations and the knights returned each greeting by name.

Though she should rejoice at the bond now forged between the warriors and serfs, only selfish thoughts filled her. Did Falke ever think of the mealtime he'd spent gorging himself on her kisses and lovemaking? Did he realize how much he had hurt her?

'Twas all that Gwendolyn could think of. Gooseflesh prickled along her skin as she recalled the sensual touch of his hands on her body. Like a bellow, Falke's full, masculine laughter carried across the village, flaming the embers of want she struggled to extinguish.

Gwendolyn clutched the paddle, leaning her forehead against the work-worn surface. Her fervent pace had not even gifted her with dreamless sleep. When fatigue forced her eyes shut, she was still haunted by him, reliving those sweet hours, and the terrible heartache caused by his callow soul.

A mistress right under her own nose! It made little difference that the woman was herself. Falke didn't know that. And thank goodness he didn't.

What if he chose to announce to the world that she was no longer a virgin? 'Twould be her word against his that 'twas he who'd deflowered her. He could give her back to Titus as soiled, and thereby free himself of a forced marriage to retain his land. Unmarried and devoid of any masquerade, she would be without protection against her uncle.

"Gwendolyn!"

The sharp call brought her back to attention. Cyrus had his arm around her waist, while Blodywn tugged the hem of Gwendolyn's gown back from the flames.

"Milady, ye near fell right into the fire." The laundress unclasped Gwendolyn's hands from the wooden paddle. "Ye need to sleep."

"I am fine, only careless," Gwendolyn argued. Sleep would bring dreams of Falke. The drudgery of work occupied her agitated mind and kept her from confessing all just to have one more kiss.

Cyrus, his arm still around her waist, guided her toward the canopy. "There are plenty of vacant beds. Take a few moments and nap."

"Nay!" Her curt tone hurt even Gwendolyn's ears. Contrite, she explained, "There's much to do."

"And many to help." Cyrus studied her, an anxious frown on his craggy face. "You've been working yourself ragged since you disappeared last week." Rubbing her hair, he showed her the stain on his thumb and fingers. "And still you've not got the dye right."

Of their own accord, her eyes were drawn to the group of warriors. Cyrus turned, following her gaze, his mouth drawn into a thin line. "Lord Falke was missing for a time that day, also. The two of you haven't spoken ten words to each other since. Did you have an argument? Did he see you coloring your hair?"

Sighing, Gwendolyn admitted only a small fraction of what had transpired between her and the lord of Mistedge. "He does not know who or what I really am, Cyrus." Summoning up all her foster parents' training, she withheld her sorrow and tears as she revealed her true pain. "I think he never will."

* * *

Falke and the small group of knights collapsed at the far end of the village, where the cool shade of the woods offered a respite from the noon sun.

Ozbern pulled his sticky linen shirt from his chest, smelled his armpits, then screwed up his nose in distaste. "Stars! I need a bath."

"We all need a bath," Falke commented. "A blind man could not tell us from those field beasts."

"Aye, that he could. We are more agreeable." Sir Clement rolled his eyes in despair. "How those field hands can get those oxen to move is beyond me."

"Robert had one step on his foot. He broke three toes," a young knight said.

"Oh, Robert deserves it. He's almost as bad-tempered as the cattle are."

"I take exception to that." Falke's young friend, still weak from his recent illness, called from beneath the shade of an elm tree. "And when I'm up to it, I'll see you for that comment. Right now, 'tis too damn hot and I'm too damn tired."

Falke enjoyed the sounds of camaraderie from his vassals and knights. The quiet animosity of Mistedge's knights had warmed to tentative friendship and regard.

These men, more accustomed to the feel of a weapon in hand, were breaking their backs to make the fields ready to sow. Villagers and soldiers who were healthy enough, were already planting seeds for the harvesttime crops. If the weather held, and summer offered no drought and winter came late, then Mistedge had a fighting chance.

For Falke, this past week had enabled him to sow the seeds of respect in his vassals. Laron would not be able to turn these men against him easily. Yet one woman held the power to do so—Lady Wren. She had only to hint that Falke had insulted her, and the newly forged loyalty between him and the vassals would sever. Falke had their service; she had their love and respect.

'Twas plain she knew of his affair with Angel. Why else was she avoiding him? Every day more serfs joined him in the field, and under the canopy, more and more empty beds appeared, which meant there were more and more helpful hands. Yet, Lady Wren could not spare even a few moments to speak with him.

At first he had tried to waylay her and explain away his sin. But he had forgotten how quickly she could disappear in a crowd. Each of his attempts failed. Finally he relented. If she didn't want to see him, he'd not force his attentions on her, no matter how much her absence pained him.

And that was the true surprise. He rubbed his chest, a vain attempt to massage away the hurt stabbing his heart. All of Angel's beauty and passion could not mend him. Their hours of lovemaking seemed nothing more than a regretful memory, one he would rectify if he could. Mayhap a good marriage to one of Falke's lords? Anything that would convince her to intercede and help him heal the rift with Lady Wren.

What he longed for was the opportunity to bring one half smile to Lady Wren's somber mouth. He missed her scolding, aye, and even her lectures. But most of all, he longed for her belief in him.

He had not known how precious a jewel she offered him until it was gone. Faith, shining in her eyes, had pushed him to fight for Mistedge. Hope, radiant in her smile, had given him strength. Even now, as his men waited for the women to bring the food, Falke found himself searching the group for a glimpse of the one person who'd taught him to believe in himself. The void in his heart grew larger as he saw she was not with them.

"Water, Milord?" Blodwyn handed a gourd to Falke. Her forearm bulged from the weight of the water bucket in her other hand. Other villagers were offering water to the rest of the weary men.

Taking the vessel, Falke let the cold spring water trickle down his throat, then poured the rest over his head.

"That looks delightful." Ozbern took the gourd from Falke's hand and dipped it into the wooden bucket. He scooped out a cup of water and splashed it over his own sweat-stained tunic. Soon the other knights and workers were doing the same.

"My thanks for the refreshment." Falke snickered as a few knights grabbed water buckets and dumped them over Sir Clement's head.

"Milord, I need to speak to ye about Lady Wren."

The serf woman had his full attention now. "What's wrong? Is she ill?" Crushing bands of icy fear wove around his heart.

"Nay, milord. She's not got the fever—yet. But I'm afeared for her." The woman glanced about at the now quiet group of men.

"Pray, tell us your fear, dear gentlewoman." Sir Clement stopped his antics. "The lady Wren's welfare is of concern to us all."

"Aye, she's a queer one," Robert commented. Falke shot him a black look. The young man faltered on with an explanation. "I mean no disrespect. If not for her, I'd not be here now, dripping wet, bone tired and glad of it. 'Tis just, well, she's hard to figure out." A mottled red blush spread along Robert's neck and face.

"I know the truth of your words, Robert." Falke motioned toward the villein woman. "Come, tell us your fears."

Taking a deep breath, the woman clasped her thick, stubby fingers together in prayer. "'Tis been over a week since that soldier died, the last death in the village. And nearly a month since any new have fallen to the fever."

Falke rose in one swift movement. "My God, that means—"

"The fever has run its course," Ozbern finished. Looks of startled wonderment, then joyful reprieve gave new vigor to the men.

"Aye, Milord Falke," Blodwyn agreed. "But that don't mean nothin' to Lady Wren. She ain't slept nor ate proper during this entire scourge. She shan't last much longer.''

The loud celebration faded to silent concern.

Again in command of the knights' attention, the servant warned, ''Me and her man, Cyrus, just caught her as she fell asleep at the wash fire. That rag of a gown was this close—'' the woman held her fingers a splinter width apart ''—to the fire. 'Tis only a matter of time afore she hurts herself.''

''Order her back to the castle,'' Robert suggested. ''There she can rest in luxury and peace.''

''Peace?'' Falke snorted. ''You think she would get any rest from the likes of those behind the stone walls?'' He stabbed his finger toward the dark gray outline Mistedge. ''We know her, we owe her, we…care for her. Not them.''

'''Tis true, they'd be back to poking fun at her the moment she returned. Some of us must accompany her.'' Ozbern lifted one brow and gave Falke a hard look.

''Order her back?'' The aged knight, Cyrus, dumped a load of dirty linen on the ground. Shaking his head, he muttered, ''She can't leave. The ghosts of the past won't let her.''

Exasperation made Falke clip each word. He'd not fail her in this small regard. ''By God, if I order her to leave, she will leave.''

''You don't understand, Sir Falke. Chains bind the girl to the sick, each and every link forged by the evil hand of Titus. A chain all my wife's and my love cannot undo.'' Cyrus's face became more wrinkled, older and haunted.

''Murdering her father 'twas bad enough. But her mother....'' As he combed his arthritic hand through his still-thick gray hair, the older man's voice became harsh. ''Titus made her mother suffer for three days in pain, unaided by any physician or medicine. Three days of Gwendolyn hearing her mother's cries echo in the halls of Cravenmoor, with no place to blot out those heart-wrenching calls for mercy.''

His eyes glistened with unshed tears, so like his foster daughter. ''Gwendolyn sees in the sick and hurt her mother. And unlike Titus, she cannot stand by and see them suffer. And I must protect her from danger, both from Titus and her memories.''

''Sir Cyrus,'' Falke said, calling the old man by his long-ago title, ''rest assured, Lady Wren will be protected. From herself, as well as from those who would do her harm. You no longer stand alone in this mission. I stand by your side.''

''As do I.'' Ozbern stood next to Falke. One by one the rest of the knights formed a circle around Cyrus.

The old man's voice wavered as he spoke. ''My thanks. But the castle offers dangers as well as a reprieve for my lady. Titus will know by now that Gwendolyn tricked him about her wits. And about a few other things he's bound to discover soon.''

''Such as?'' Falke queried.

''She's been fixing the books. Making her promised dowry appear not so profitable. She figured Titus—''

"Would never let her leave if it meant losing a sizable sum," Falke finished. He chuckled as he shook his head. "I'll wager she gave the lands enough of a profit that Titus kept her alive, yet not so much that he'd risk war over losing them."

"Aye, you know my lady well."

"'Twould be what I would do."

Appreciation shone in Cyrus's eyes, bringing a flash of hope to his dour face. "I have a feeling you've got a handle on some other plot, or you'd not have posted the sentries when we were in the castle."

The old man still had the senses of a fighter. There was no use hiding the danger. "Titus offered to have Gwendolyn murdered, and spare me a marriage," Falke explained. "Ferris gave Laron the same offer, framing me for the murder."

"She can't go back in there." Sir Clement struck his fist on his palm. "The Cravenmoor knights don't stand a chance against us, but Laron is another story. The man is sly. We won't know what lords he might have already swayed."

'Twould be just a matter of time before Titus or Ferris reached her. And if Titus learned the truth of Gwendolyn's holdings, then he'd whisk her away, keep her imprisoned in Cravenmoor, and she would never escape his cruel domain.

There seemed to be but one way to protect the woman. And as the idea tumbled around in Falke's head, it didn't seem so disagreeable. In fact, the emp-

tiness in his heart lightened. Every instinct hummed
with accord. There was respect, at least on his part,
and with time, he would earn Lady Wren's good
graces again. After all, was he not known for his
charm? And genuine fondness—that she could not
have forgotten so quickly. And he needed her, for
she made him a better man than he'd ever thought
he could be.

'Twas true, she deserved better, but no other could
cloak her from Titus's evil. Nor would Falke tolerate
another man trying to do so.

"We need to protect her just long enough for her
strength to return. A few days." He clasped Ozbern
on the shoulder. "Then neither Titus nor Laron will
be able to harm her."

"Do you have a safe haven for her?" Ozbern
asked.

"Aye, that I do."

"Where?"

"In Mistedge." Suddenly, an emotion so pure
filled his heart that Falke found it hard to speak. Placing his hand over his chest, he added, "As my lady
wife." Quieting the cheering men, Falke added, "If
she'll have me."

Chapter Fifteen

Cyrus cupped his hands together, gave Lady Wren a boost up into the saddle, then stepped clear of the precocious animal.

"'Tis not safe for her to be on the beast," Falke muttered. Anxiety roughened his voice to a harsh whisper. He clenched his teeth when the horse laid back its ears in obvious distress.

Cyrus shook his head and led Falke toward the waiting knights. "Greatheart is as gentle as a lamb with the girl. Rest assured the stallion will return her safely to Mistedge. Then 'tis your place to do the same."

"Come, we have no time to tarry." Lady Wren gave her entourage a weary chiding. "Sir Alric said the missive called for our help. The fever has spread within the castle walls." Alric grimaced at Falke, obviously not comfortable with his part of the plot.

Dark circles called attention to the paleness of Lady Wren's face. Sitting astride her great beast, she wavered back and forth, the stallion swaying gently beneath her. Falke felt little guilt at the ruse he played upon her. Besides, 'twas the old man's idea—have her return to the castle under the pretext of helping more ill, though 'twas she who needed rest.

Before departing, Falke whispered a final reminder to the assembled knights. "Let no tongues wag. Should Titus or Ferris learn I plan to marry the lady, they will rush to complete their schemes. 'Tis imperative that Lady Wren has a chance to regain her strength." *And that I have time to plead my case.*

Falke pulled himself up into his saddle, his heart heavy with the truth. He had thought lying with Angel would be a trip to heaven. Instead he found himself in a hell of his own making—a world without Lady Wren's friendship. Nor would charm and sweet words win back her affection. Nor could he openly woo her, for to do so would warn Titus, Laron and Ferris of his intentions.

Shaking his head at his mental debate, Falke waited as his friends Ozbern, Alric and Robert mounted their steeds. Behind him, five other knights joined their ranks.

Lady Wren clucked her tongue against her teeth. The stallion moved out at a fast walk. The men trailed behind, eating the warhorse's dust.

Grit coated Falke's mouth, dust covered his woolen tunic and leather boots, and fear clenched his heart. Ahead, Lady Wren swayed on her mount's broad back, the reins slack in her hands. Should the animal bolt, she would be thrown. Yet if he tried to approach the warhorse, the cantankerous beast might kick. Falke had no choice but to watch, his heart in his throat, as the destrier clip-clopped along. The castle gate looked miles away instead of yards.

"Saint Christopher!" Robert exclaimed.

Just a few yards from the gate, Lady Wren slumped forward. The stallion, Greatheart, stopped dead in the trail, completely free to throw off his unconscious rider and gallop away.

"Hold!" Falke gave the order and waited to see what the stallion would do next. Snorting, the creature turned his head slowly and leveled Falke with an impatient stare.

"Keep your horses back, we don't want to spook the animal." Falke gave the command, then slid from his mount. Throwing his reins to Robert, he ordered, "Take my stallion, I'm going to try and lead her horse in."

He made a wide arc around Greatheart, making sure the animal could spot him. Taking a position a few steps in front of the horse, he stopped. "Come, Greatheart." He spoke a command, not a croon. This animal bore scars and battle marks. As a lord's mount, he was accustomed to barked commands, not gentle words.

The horse's ears perked and swiveled toward him. Falke took a few steps, not looking around. A second hesitation, then the steady sound of hooves against the hard-packed earth resounded behind him. On foot, he led his troupe through the outer bailey to the inner gates of Mistedge.

Falke could make out the shapes of spectators along the inner wall. When he came to the towering wooden-and-iron portal, he ordered, "Open the gate, Lord Falke has returned. The fever has passed." No creak of an opening gate answered.

Laron's voice called out from the marshal's tower. "What word do we have that you speak the truth? The wench there looks sick enough."

"The word of your lord." Falke bit out his reply. Drawing his sword, he let the long blade glint in the morning sunlight.

In unison, the men behind him drew their own blades—eight broadswords against a castle full of men. But the display proved a point. Falke did not stand alone.

With a creak, the gate budged from its stationary position and grudgingly lifted to allow the group to enter.

Walking into the inner courtyard, Falke was astounded at the filth and litter strewn about. Scraps of food and animal waste created a stench more toxic than the smell of dying bodies. While those in the village had sweated to clean and detoxify their surroundings, the castle folk had fallen into slovenly ways.

"What has gone on here? Where is Sir Baldwin?" The skin at the back of Falke's neck prickled with his sixth sense.

"Fell down the stairs last week. Broke his leg."
Laron hastened down the stairs, followed by Ferris
and Ivette. A nasty smile carved Laron's face into a
caricature of remorse. "I'm in charge."

"Were in charge," Falke corrected, then turned
his attention to Gwendolyn. Her body lay draped
over the side of the mount. The curious crowd en-
croached on the space between himself and the stallion.

"Get away!" Falke pushed aside the nobles, taking no heed of their offended complaints. His knights
dismounted and created a barrier between the castle
folk and Lady Wren.

He tried to wake her from her comalike sleep.
"Lady Gwendolyn? Gwen...Lady Wren?" The
name caused her to rouse from the deep slumber.

"I am here. Tea...blankets...I am coming." She
reached for some imaginary vessel, then fell from the
saddle into his waiting arms, her bulk seeming to be
no more than a bundle of rags.

"Falke, are you mad? You've brought the fever to
us." Ivette stepped away as he neared, placing her
dainty embroidered handkerchief over her mouth.

"Move aside, woman. I have no time for you."
Falke noted the narrowing of Ivette's eyes and the
hard pout on her lips. Cold beauty portrayed the heart
within, stonelike and uncaring. He gripped his tattered bundle tightly, afraid he might lose the warmth
found within, Lady Wren. Suddenly, she became the
most precious bundle of rags he had ever possessed.

Robert ran up the steps and threw open the door. Falke swept inside, issuing orders with a look that would tolerate no laxity. "Bring water and peppermint tea to—" He took one look at the long flight of steps leading to her cell-like accommodation. "Bring them to my chambers, immediately."

Falke climbed the steps to the first-floor gallery and kicked open his door. His lady slept on, totally unaware of her surroundings. Tenderly, he placed her head on his pillow and laid her on the majestic bed. Grabbing a corner of the velvet coverlet, she rolled on her side, rubbing the satin edging against her face. Falke looped the other end over her and tucked the corners down, afraid that in her sleep she might roll off.

"My child—where is she?" Darianne toddled into the room, pushing aside the young men clustered around the bed.

"She's tired, exhausted, worked to the bone." Guilt cut a swath of emotion through him.

Why hadn't he seen the extent of her fatigue? She could well have died because of his neglect, and he had vowed to protect her from her uncle and cousin. A disgusted mental voice, sounding so like his father's, nagged inside his head. *You can't save her from herself, much less another warrior.*

Nodding, Darianne caressed Gwendolyn's cheek. "Aye, 'tis always this way with her. She gives all she has and holds nothing back for herself."

"She should learn to be more selfish." Falke

wanted his words to be gruff, but they came out wistful and soft.

A rosy-cheeked servant girl burst into the room with a tankard of tea and a bucket of steaming water. "'Ere ye are, milord." The girl bobbed a curtsy and dropped the wooden pail.

"Go up to Lady Wren's room and bring down all her things. To this room." Falke shot the girl a cold glance, daring her to shun the duty. Wide-eyed, the girl dipped another curtsy and scurried out the door.

Nervousness twitched the older woman's mouth. "That's not necessary, Lord Falke. We are fine in the room we have."

"Nay, Wife. 'Twill be all right." Cyrus hushed her misgivings. "Lord Falke will see to Gwendolyn's needs."

"As will all of Mistedge." Falke let his gaze fall on the knights hanging back near the door. They stood taller and prouder under his stare. "Lady Darianne, there will be a servant posted outside this door for your convenience. Anything that you or your lady should need, send the servant after it. You are to want for nothing. Understand?"

"Aye, Milord Falke." Darianne whispered the words, her eyes wide with amazement.

"I will send in the servant girl to help you undress your lady."

"Nay, milord." Darianne clutched her husband's sleeve. "I can see to her myself."

"But surely you would want some aid in…undressing her. It would be a chore with the woman unconscious.''

''My wife can see to her needs, Sir Falke.'' Cyrus patted his wife's hand.

''Very well. I'll leave you to administer to your charge.'' Falke marched from the room, Robert and Ozbern following him. Closing the door, he spoke to Sir Clement. ''See that one of us is always nearby.''

''Aye, milord. I'll trust none save those that rode with us from the village.''

''Good. We must be on our guard.'' Falke shook the knight's hand and felt his own responsibility grow. These men followed him now and he was accountable for what befell them because of that loyalty. Surprisingly, he did not chafe under the added weight. It settled well on his shoulders and with his pride. Christ's blood, there he went again with the most uncharacteristic thoughts. Where had these almost honorable ideas come from?

A twitch of truth answered his question. Lady Wren. Stars, but she had gotten under his skin. And more, the truth-telling voice nudged him to admit. Somehow that misshapen little body with the sapphire eyes had slipped into his heart. Like a battered puppy, Falke reasoned with himself and stomped off, not wanting to hear his inner voice any longer.

''Look at what happened from carrying that creature.'' Jabbing his shoulder with her long, pointed fingernail, Ivette sneered, ''Look at this filth on your shirt. 'Tis ruined. And if you don't mind your ways, you will be, too.''

Looking down, Falke saw an unsightly brown stain on his shoulder. The aroma of cool forest greens perfumed the air. Lady Wren. He rubbed the spot with his fingers in slow circles. 'Twas not grime; he had seen her too often in the village scrubbing her hands and arms to think she would tolerate dirt on her person. Yet 'twas the second time he had held her, and the second time the stain had appeared. What in the devil caused it?

Falke flipped his dagger point into the wooden trestle table, pulled it free and then flipped it again. He stared at the staircase leading up to his chambers. For two days he had waited for word on Gwendolyn's health. Every day came the same message: ''She sleeps.''

Ozbern leaned back in his chair and rested his foot against the time-worn table. He swirled the last swallow of warm amber wine in the heavy bronze goblet.

''The gown you commissioned for Lady Wren is quite lovely. The color exactly matches her eyes.'' Ozbern drained the goblet, set it on the trestle table and let his foot drop to the floor. ''As you ordered, it will be completed by the morrow. 'Twill make a lovely wedding dress.''

Standing, Falke paced the length of the table, his eyes darting to the staircase at every turn. ''I want that gown perfect. If the women should need more time—''

'''Tis not the seamstress that dawdles, 'tis you.''

''Me!'' Falke turned on his second and balked. ''We must go careful here. Only the fear that the lady may have the fever has kept Titus from gathering his wastrel lot and departing, with Lady Wren.''

''You haven't visited her once since we returned.''

''She needs her rest.''

''You're afraid to ask her, aren't you?'' Ozbern leaned forward, a sly smile on his lips. ''You're afraid she'll refuse to wed you.''

''Nay.'' Falke flipped his hand elegantly. ''Lady Wren? Refuse me?'' Then with quiet emphasis, he added, ''She has no choice but to wed me.''

''And is that how you want her to make her decision? You or Titus?''

''She cares about me.'' Falke slumped into a high-backed chair and draped his legs over the sides. ''At least she did.''

''Ah, now we have it.'' Ozbern poured two goblets of wine from the jug and pushed one toward his friend. ''Did you think I would not notice how she was never at your side those last days? What happened?''

''I was a fool.'' Falke gulped the wine, letting the tart liquid burn his throat. ''That woman I saw before in the woods—well, I found her again.''

''Your angel?''

"Aye, and if her kiss brought me misfortune, lying with her brought me heartache."

"You made love to the woman?"

"Nay, not lovemaking." Falke sat up straight in the chair. "Well, at the time mayhap…but on reflection… Nay, I'll not deny it. I made love to the woman and asked her to return to the village, as my mistress, in full knowledge that Angel knew Lady Wren."

"And you believe this Angel told Lady Wren of the tryst?"

"Aye. Though for some reason, 'twas not the tryst that riled Angel so, but my request that she return to the village as my mistress, right under Lady Wren's nose."

"Discretion, my friend, has always been your strong suit. How is it this woman made you forget lessons learned long ago?"

Falke relaxed his neck and tapped his head on the high back of the chair. "Is it possible to love two women at the same time?"

"Rumor has it that you already have." Ozbern gave Falke a salute with his wine goblet.

Falke threw up his hands in exasperation. "My body lusts for Angel, for her beauty is without comparison. The passion we kindled in those few hours has not dampened." He struck his chest with his fist. "Yet my heart longs for Lady Wren. I would lay down my very life if she would grant me one of her smiles."

Ozbern stared at his goblet, turning the dull metal to catch the sunlight from the high window. "There are many women that stir a man's desires. And in your case, I do stress many. But, Falke, how many women have entered your heart?"

"Only one other, my mother." Falke poured his goblet full and drained it. "At first I resisted marriage, for I would not be dictated to. Then I resisted in order to spare Lady Wren, for I would not have her suffer a marriage of unrequited love as had my mother." Pouring himself another drink and gulping it down, he spoke the bitter truth. "Now, my friend, I fear 'tis I that will suffer my mother's fate. Ozbern, I do believe I've fallen in love with Lady Wren."

Chapter Sixteen

"Just how long do you intend to hide in this room?" Darianne pulled back the thick curtains surrounding the rope bed. Sunlight flooded Gwendolyn's dark, secure cocoon.

Blinking her eyes, she argued, "I'm not hiding." She burrowed beneath the mountain of pillows stacked on the bed and inhaled the masculine scent of the linens. Though Falke hadn't slept in the room in over two months, his essence still lingered on the sheets of his bed.

An ache started in the pit of her stomach, though she knew 'twas not food that could curb it, only Falke's kiss. Since making love to him, her body had developed a ravenous hunger for his touch and caress. 'Twas a famine her traitorous body would have to learn to deal with. There would be no appeasement.

"If 'tis not hiding, then 'tis sulking," Darianne suggested.

"I am most certainly not sulking." Gwendolyn bolted upright, outraged fixed on her face, while the truth pricked at her heart. She had awakened yesterday, her limbs heavy with fatigue and her soul weighted from Falke's betrayal.

"Falke de Chretian cares for no one, save himself," she declared.

Lust ruled his loins and he cared not a whit for her feelings. Had he thought of loyal Lady Wren at all while he was making love to his angel of the woods? Gwendolyn doubted he thought of anything but ravishing a beauty. Well, he hadn't really ravished her, she had been more than willing, but he hadn't thought to naysay the union, either.

Falling back onto the goose down pillows, she watched a few stray feathers puff into the air. Like her hopes and dreams, the white down drifted toward the open window and disappeared.

"Sir Falke insisted you take his chambers." Darianne swept her arm to encompass the large room. "I've had a servant to wait on me hand and foot. And he's stationed a guard to keep Titus from you."

A guard? 'Twould be harder to sneak out now that Falke and most of the knights knew she had two good legs. Nor could Gwendolyn count on Darianne's help. 'Twould seem Sir Falke had charmed his way into her cautious good graces.

As if to prove her point, Darianne continued with her litany of Falke's good works. "And he's ordered Lucas to tend to Greatheart in the stable."

"Nay, Greatheart will trample the lad."

"'Twould seem the horse and Lord Falke have come to an understanding.'' Darianne beamed as she lauded the errant knight. "Greatheart obeys him as he did your father. And Sir Falke has put an end to Greatheart's tantrums. Lucas is safe.''

Deserted! Even by her one true friend. Gwendolyn took little consolation from her horse's change of heart. Even faithful Greatheart fell beneath Falke's appeal.

"And—'' Darianne's voice grew smug "—Lady Ivette's been asked to leave Mistedge, along with her brother.'' Almost crowing, she added in a hushed voice, "Lord Falke intends to wed you. He told Cyrus so himself, but 'tis a secret. Should Titus know, he would whisk you away before the ceremony.''

Gwendolyn threw herself across the coverlet, despair and anguish deepening her voice. "Oh, what am I to do?''

"Saint's be praised! Rejoice, child.'' Darianne came to her side and tried to comb back the tangled snarls.

"He...he means to marry me!'' The words came out in great sobs. Falke meant to sentence her to a loveless marriage, cementing his hold on Mistedge and subjecting his wife to a parade of mistresses.

"From the sound of your voice, 'twould seem you're in misery.'' Darianne's confusion wrinkled her brow.

"I am, 'tis horrible news.''

"Horrible?'' Darianne echoed.

"Aye, horrible.'' Stronger sobs took command

and Gwendolyn let the full brunt of her sorrow seep into a pillow.

"But why? I know at first we feared Sir Falke was not an honorable man, but Cyrus has told me the man's changed."

"Mayhap on the surface Falke gives honor lip service, but cut deep, and he's not changed at all."

Gathering strength from her self-righteous anger, Gwendolyn bounced from the bed and paced the long room. "He lusted for and seduced a woman, then had the impudence to request she return with him to the village."

Darianne sputtered at the news, but Gwendolyn gave her foster mother no time to comment. Like a rock building speed down a mountain, an avalanche of Falke's crimes tumbled from her lips.

"He was *so* beguiling. 'I've searched for you.' 'I'm so alone.'" Rolling her eyes, she added, "'…a kiss to bring back my luck.' My eye. 'Twas not his luck that drove him, but his lust."

Twirling around to face Darianne, she pronounced Falke's greatest crime. "Under my very nose he would parade his paramour. After all we've been through, after all of our talks. After the day he held me when that soldier died. When he kissed me, I thought I meant something to him. Something more than Mistedge. I thought he cared about me."

"I can see how you would feel betrayed, but how came you to know so much of this private encounter?" Suspicion lifted Darianne's gray brows in a high arch.

Would it be best to relate the truth bit by bit or just jump in with the most startling news first? One look at Darianne's stare, and Gwendolyn decided to take the plunge.

"The woman in the woods that he seduced…'twas me."

"You! And Falke! Have lain together?" Darianne took three deep breaths. Then three more. "You're the woman Falke asked to be his mistress?"

"Well, not me exactly. Not Lady Wren."

Plopping down onto an upholstered ottoman, Darianne rubbed her temples. "Pray, child, have pity on this old woman. Did you or did you not give your virginity to this man?"

Heat flamed across Gwendolyn's cheeks as she nodded. "Aye, I did. But he thinks he made love to his angel of the forest. Falke has no idea she and Lady Wren are one in the same."

"Giving yourself to a man before marriage! By your blessed mother, how could you?"

Kneeling at her side, Gwendolyn leaned her head against Darianne's skirt. "Something happened here—" she placed her palm over her heart "—when he looked at me." She stared at the pure gold beam of light that spilled in from the high arched window. "His hair glowed in the sunshine. His eyes were so blue, like a calm sea in summer. And his voice, 'twas so sad and lonely. I wanted to comfort him.

"I know 'twas wrong," she confessed, "but I just wanted the chance to be—"

"What you are, a beautiful, young girl." Darianne

gave her a quick, fierce hug. An understanding smile softened the lines of reproach in her kind face. "And you love him. I can see it in your eyes and hear it in your voice."

"Aye." 'Twas no use denying it. Even after all the disappointment, love still filled the most sacred place in her heart. "He's arrogant and self-centered and full of pride, and loves to tease me. But he can be tender, and merciful, and kind, and humble. And I love him. But as Lady Wren, I have no hope to gain his heart. Though I had trust that his friendship was mine. That he held Lady Wren in regard. And that is what made me weak."

"But I was wrong." Gwendolyn huffed as she added, "He thought nothing of bringing another woman into my home as his mistress. He's only marrying Lady Wren to gain control of Mistedge, and mayhap out of some misplaced friendship. I want him to marry me—"

"Because he loves the woman you are—Lady Wren. Not the vision of his angel." Darianne completed the explanation.

"You understand?"

"Of course, child." Darianne patted Gwendolyn's hand. "You love Sir Falke with all his faults and want that love returned in kind. But wed him you must, for without the protection of marriage, Titus can order you back to Cravenmoor. And he is not pleased to learn you are no idiot and have duped him all these years."

"I am doomed to torture, either by Titus's cruel

hand or Falke's careless heart." Gwendolyn slumped against her foster mother's knee. "Is it so rare for a man to love a woman for who she is?"

"Aye, my child." Darianne stroked Gwendolyn's hair. "'Tis why it is a prize every woman longs for."

"I'll slit the nag's throat and feed the wench the pieces." Titus removed his dagger and approached the stall door. His grin widened as Greatheart's nostrils flared, as though sensing his doom.

Ferris knocked his father's hand aside. "Kill the beast now, and Falke will have reason to delay our departure. We must get away from Mistedge before Falke weds Gwendolyn."

His fingers whitened around the hilt, but Titus managed to see reason. He growled low, the anger within him boiling like a thick stew. "You still believe Falke de Chretian intends to marry her? 'Tis true she's no idiot, but she's still a pig."

"He intends to marry her. He has no choice." Ferris leaned against a stall and heard an animal scurry to the far side. "The peasants and the soldiers owe Gwendolyn their lives. If Falke should send her packing, all of Mistedge would rise up in arms against him."

"So we take her, and leave behind enough evidence to point to Falke." Titus grinned, his tombstone teeth forming an eerie smile. "And when we get back to Cravenmoor, I'll teach her, Cyrus and his wife the cost of playing me for a fool."

"And what of the curse?" Ferris narrowed his

eyes and gave Titus a sly smile. "Isolde's ghost has been seen at Cravenmoor and even here at Mist-edge."

Cold slithered around Titus's spine and put fear into his heart. "I won't draw her blood. But by hell's gates she will learn the cost of lying to me."

Ferris pushed away from the stall door. "Give her to me. I will take delight in discovering all her little secrets." Beads of sweat formed along his forehead and he licked his lips as he muttered, "And I will finally put to rest Isolde's ghost."

"Gwendolyn is yours." Titus clasped his bastard son's hand in agreement. If Ferris could put Isolde's vengeful spirit back in the grave, Gwendolyn was a small price to pay. And if Isolde's ghost claimed Ferris in revenge, 'twas a small loss, and Titus would still have Gwendolyn to torture—without drawing blood.

"We will need help to get Gwendolyn beyond the castle walls."

"We have allies, Titus." Ferris turned his father toward the stable door. "Come, let me show you how we will escape."

Lucas peered out of the knothole from inside Greatheart's stall. Carefully he crept to the door, pressed his ear against the rough wood and waited. Nothing, only the sounds of the horses shuffling in their stalls. Light-headed from holding his breath, he slowly released the pent-up air and eased open the gate.

At the stable door, he looked about, trying to spot

Ferris or Titus. They had disappeared into the crowded yard. Ahead of Lucas, a platoon of soldiers drilled, hiding the rest of the exercise field. Cattle, their sides no longer showing rib marks, milled about in the inner bailey while their herder flirted with a young girl. Villagers, knights and soldiers hustled about with daily chores, their friendly exchanges mixing with the cacophony of animal brays, calls and complaints. With the plague finally over, Mistedge was a fief reborn. A sense of festivity filled the bailey. People sang. Children played. And danger schemed to destroy it all.

Lucas sprinted across the yard, determined to find Lord Falke and save their lady Wren.

Chapter Seventeen

Not a single ray of moonlight cut the night as Gwendolyn shuffled across the great hall. The bulky wrap around her waist returned Lady Wren's girth and made her less able to maneuver around the sleeping knights and servants. At least she no longer had to limp; that truth was well known throughout the castle, and to Titus.

"Come, my lady." Lucas tugged her gown, pulling her toward the chapel. "I was told to tell ye to hurry."

Without benefit of a torch, Gwendolyn relied on Lucas to guide her down the cold stone stairway. 'Twas only the need of her medical knowledge that pulled Gwendolyn from the safety and security of Falke's chamber. Careful that her footsteps would not echo, she followed Lucas past the marble altar. At the door to the priest's room, the boy hesitated.

"Are you sure the girl is giving birth here?" Gwendolyn placed her ear against the thick door, anxious because of the silence and location. Was the priest needed for a baptism or last rites?

The boy swept the church with a worried glance, pausing at the gilded image of the Christ Child before answering in a rushed monotone. "I was told to tell ye that Darianne needed your help with a birthing in the priest's room."

The birthing must be difficult for Darianne to send for her and for Cyrus to give his consent. Even the guard at her door had agreed to remain behind, giving any spying eyes the idea that Gwendolyn remained within. She pushed open the door, dreading to discover she was too late. If mother and child had died, 'twould explain the eerie silence.

Inside the small chamber, darkness retreated. Candles burned from every cranny, casting soft amber light. Men-at-arms stood along the side wall. She recognized Ozbern, Robert, Alric and Sir Clement—all dressed in their finest, their broadswords at their waist. And the priest, his sleepy-eyed look a sure sign he had been pulled from his bed, waited at the dais. 'Twas strange company to sit by the side of a pregnant serving woman.

"Lucas?" She turned to the boy for an explanation, but he scampered past her to stand next to Ozbern.

"I didn't lie," he announced to the priest. "I said I was *told* to tell her to come, and so I was. That's no sin, is it?"

"Worry not, lad." In the midst of the glow, a deep

baritone reverberated. "You did as your liege ordered."

Needles of apprehension pricked along Gwendolyn's spine. 'Twas Falke's voice, firm with authority and purpose. It took no strong mind to realize she had been duped. And that Darianne and Cyrus had been in on it as well. She could postpone no longer. At last she must confront the knight who had stolen her heart.

Light embraced him as he strode toward her, his hair the exact same shade as the candlelight. His velvet tunic absorbed the illumination, changing in hue from cinnamon to rust, bringing attention to the muscles that flexed and moved beneath. He placed one foot on the bottom stair and rested his hand on the rail, almost touching her own.

"Lord Falke." She squeaked his name, took a deep breath and straightened. Her position on the steps brought her gaze level with his full, sensuous mouth. She licked her lips slowly, recalling the soft caress of that mouth on hers.

Nay, 'twas not me he kissed, but another. Gwendolyn ordered her wanton memories away and commanded her heart to stand firm against him. Clearing her throat, she retreat one calculated step, lifting her eye-to-eye with her adversary.

She pointed toward the assembled knights and priest. "You need a company of armed men to hear your confession?"

A glimmer of amusement lit Falke's azure eyes. "'Tis good to hear your reproach again, my lady.

I've missed it.'' Leaning forward, he whispered for her ears only, ''And I've missed you.''

Flattery, 'tis nothing more than mindless flattery. Gwendolyn reminded herself of his sins while her heart raced and the skin tingled where his breath had touched.

He pointed toward his friends and allies. ''I have a contingent of men to take you to an abbey for sanctuary.'' He hesitated, then added, ''Or to hear our wedding vows.''

'Twas no shock, not after Darianne had warned her of his intent. After all, their marriage secured Mistedge for Falke.

''I have a choice?'' she scoffed. Taking her to an abbey would give Titus the right to bring King Henry's justice down on Falke's head. He would forfeit Mistedge and perhaps his very life.

''Aye, Lady Wren, that you do. I pray you will hear me out before you choose.'' He rested her hand on his own and led her down the steps. His gaze never left her face. Remorse softened the sparks of vitality within his dark blue gaze.

Seating her on a wooden pew, Falke knelt on bended knee next to her. The heat from his body seeped through the thin material of Gwendolyn's gown. His calf brushed hers and delicious warmth swirled in the pit of her stomach. No matter his sins, her body refused to forget the ecstasy he had introduced her to.

''I had hoped to have days to woo you back and win your forgiveness, but I find I have no time.''

Falke cocked his head toward Lucas. "The boy overheard Titus and Ferris in the stable. They are even now hatching a plan to take you from Mistedge. With help from within. 'Tis no secret Laron is being watched. Titus must have an ally we do not know about."

"Aye, my lady." Ozbern ruffled the boy's hair. "Lucas has done well to warn us of the danger. But we can not watch everyone, all the time. We must act fast to protect you."

Falke reached up and brushed a strand of hair from Gwendolyn's face. His fingers lingered on the curve of her cheek. "I could not bear for you to return to that hell."

"But marriage? To me? I thought you desired someone else." She could have bitten her tongue for questioning him further. If she tried hard, very hard, mayhap she could convince herself that he really did care about her, about drab, ugly Lady Wren. Happiness built on make-believe was better than no happiness at all.

"I thought so, too." Falke's candor drove a blade into her heart. "But I was wrong. Lady Wren is the only woman in my heart."

"But not in your bed." Her wounded pride would not be soothed by pretty words. Nor would her doubts remain silent. If she could only be sure his words were true.

Shame shadowed Falke's handsome face, but he did not turn away from her. Nor did his voice become a whisper. He confessed loudly enough for all his friends and Gwendolyn to hear. "I...wronged you...greatly. And the thought that *I* brought you sorrow gives me pain, for I swore to myself to bring you only smiles, and laughter, and aye, a bit of anger." He gave her a halfhearted smile, one that was just a bit crooked, showed just a hint of dimple, but reached deep inside his eyes.

"How can I explain my actions?" He took her hand in his and gently caressed the back with his thumb. "I cannot. Only to say that the woman I met in the forest, she..." Falke puckered his lips in concentration. "She was like an elusive memory. The way she moved, the turn of her phrase, they all reminded me..." He leaned his head to one side, one brow arched in surprise. "She reminded me of you."

"Me?" Gwendolyn pasted an incredulous look on her face and her heart pounded—this time not because of Falke's physical nearness, but at the truth in his assessment.

"Aye." Falke wrinkled his brow and studied her like a monk trying to decipher a Greek passage. "Her toe—she rubbed it in the dirt, just as you do. And she always let her hair fall in her face...." He reached forward, tracing the line of her cheekbone with his fingertip.

Panic twisted her gut and Gwendolyn jumped to her feet. "Surely, Lord Falke, you could never confuse Angel with me."

She pulled her hand from his and hugged herself, both to hide her hands from him, and to conceal their trembling. Retreating, she drew closer to the knights and turned her back to Falke's all-too-sharp eyes.

"Never." One stride and he was at her side, his hands resting on her shoulders. His chest rose and fell, brushing the length of her spine, letting her know how close he was, reminding her of how close he had been to her naked skin.

"Marry me, Lady Wren. I love you."

"My lady." Ozbern cleared his throat and cast the assembled knights a cautious glance. "The night grows long. Morning will be upon us. We have little time if we are to take you to the abbey. Arry and Cyrus wait in the stable with Greatheart and supplies, should you decide to leave."

"And Darianne waits in my chamber with the gown I ordered made for you. A wedding gift." Falke lowered his eyes and gave her a regal bow. "Whatever you choose, I will honor."

Gwendolyn took a long, shuddering breath. To her left waited Ozbern and the knights, ready to put their lives in danger to guarantee her safety. To her right stood Falke, the man she loved—but could she trust him? What would happen when he learned the truth about her appearance? Would he cherish her or possess her? Would he love her or use her? Could she risk these men's lives and all of Mistedge because of her selfish wish to be loved for who she was and not because of what she looked like?

"Faith is a delicate chain." Gwendolyn closed her eyes and prayed her heart led her in the right direction. "And if it breaks, 'tis difficult to mend, but not impossible."

Let him love me. Pray, let him cherish Lady Wren with the same passion he had for his angel in the woods. Opening her eyes, she met Falke's gaze, a glimmer of hope shining in its depths. "Aye, Lord Falke, I will marry you."

"Good choice, my lady," Robert and Alric chimed together.

"The night is lessening," Ozbern reminded them. "Clement, go to the stable and tell Cyrus and Arry the news. Lady Wren, I fear we cannot wait to collect Darianne and Cyrus to witness the vows."

"I understand. Let us be done with it."

"Hold." Falke widened his stance and pointed his finger at the tip of Gwendolyn's nose. "I'll not have you marry me out of pity. You'll do it because you want me, because you care about me, or you'll not do it all."

"Pity?" Disbelief made her jaw drop.

"Aye, I've bared my soul to you. On bended knee, no less. I clearly told you I loved you. And I have never told any woman, save my mother, that."

"Never?"

"Never. And I'll not marry a woman who can't say she loves me." Falke folded his arms, and stared down his nose at her.

Gwendolyn shifted back and forth. When she spotted the toe of her slipper grinding the floor rushes into dust, she quickly stopped.

"You do love me, of course." Falke attempted to

supply her with an answer, though a quiver of doubt lessened the arrogance of the statement.

"Did you think your prattle won me over? That flattery would turn my heart? Or the gift of a gown?" Gwendolyn hid her smile. *Aye, I think he does love me.* The knowledge made her smile widen. With pride she announced, "I am not an empty-headed imbecile. Nor am I so shallow as to be bribed."

Falke's nervous stiffness lessened, and he wrapped his arm around her shoulder and crowed. "Nay, you are a witty, generous woman who loves me."

"Aye, that I am." She placed her hand in his and turned to the priest. "Come now, I wish to marry the man I love."

In response, the priest yawned, opened his prayer book and began to recite the beginning litany of the marriage ceremony.

"Beg pardon, my lord and lady." Ozbern nodded toward the priest. "But time is short. Mayhap in a fortnight we might celebrate again, redo your vows, but we must make haste."

"Humph!" The priest opened his mouth, then gave the door to his bedchamber a longing stare. "The Lord will understand our need to shorten his ceremony."

"But not too short." Falke turned to her, bringing her hands to his mouth for a chaste kiss. "Lady Wren, I pledge before God, you and my friends to honor and love you. To protect you and cherish you. These hands have shown me strength. Shown me compassion. Shown me the way to open my own heart to others.'' He cupped her hands in his own. ''These hands hold my heart. They...''

''Falke? Are you all right?'' Gwendolyn asked as Falke's voice faded away, and he became mesmerized with her hands.

He stared at her chipped nails and ragged cuticles. Then he turned her hands over, running his fingers over the rough, hard calluses. His brows quirked into deep furrows. A dark grimace contorted his mouth. ''It cannot be.''

''What? Pray what ails you?'' Out of instinct, she pulled one hand free and placed it upon his forehead, testing for a fever.

He released a long, slow breath. His eyes narrowed into thin slits. ''And I was too blind to see until this very moment.''

Falke's gaze drilled into hers, and Gwendolyn felt bare beneath his scrutiny. What about her work-worn hands had caused Falke to turn so cold?

''What are you blathering about?'' Ozbern yanked Falke around to face him. ''Titus and Ferris could be here at any moment. Do you want them to take her?''

The mention of her uncle and cousin seemed like a splash of cold water on Falke's strange trance. He rubbed his lips as though wiping away bad wine. ''Titus! Curse that dog and his spawn.''

Regaining her hand, Falke spoke, his voice deep and curt with emotion. ''Titus will never hurt you again. You will never hide one smile, one tear, one angry word from the world again.'' Kissing her gently on the lips, he whispered, ''Remember always, 'twas Lady Wren I proposed to. And she that I love.''

''Come, finish this up.'' Falke's frown slowly changed from a halfhearted grin to a devastating smile that showed both his dimples. ''I believe I have a most interesting wedding night ahead of me.''

Confused, bewildered and overwhelmed, Gwendolyn stood next to him. Somehow in Falke's jumble of words, her belief in his love forged a new, stronger chain to link her heart with his. In a monologue of rushed, mumbled words, the priest married them, giving her life, wealth and future to Falke de Chretian.

With a shaking hand, she signed the marriage contract. Falke signed in turn with a flourish. Muffled by the priest's and knights' good wishes, Ozbern's wineless toast and Falke's presence, Gwendolyn's doubts on her marriage ebbed to the quiet recesses of her mind.

'Twas only as the group dispersed, determined not to allow Titus to know of the night's drama until the marriage was consummated, that her worries returned. Tonight ended all the charades. Tonight Falke would know all, and there would be no sanctuary to retreat to.

Gwendolyn entered Falke's chamber alone, grateful he had given her time to prepare before joining her. He had woken a servant and ordered a bath and tea sent to his room—no doubt an attempt to ease her worries about the marriage bed. 'Twas his nerves

Gwendolyn was concerned over. Especially when he discovered his Angel and Lady Wren were one and the same.

"You chose marriage." Darianne leaped from the curtained bed and rushed to her ward's side. "You're not angry with me, are you?"

"I was, but not anymore," Gwendolyn admitted. "I believe Falke truly cares for me, Lady Wren."

Her eyes shining with joy and unshed tears, Darianne led Gwendolyn to the bed. "Aye, that he does. Look at his gift."

"'Tis almost like Mother's." Gwendolyn pulled the gown to her, molding the curves to her own.

Folds of sapphire velvet covered her, the exact shade of her eyes. Silver lotus flower embroidery cuffed the neckline, hem and sleeves. A delicate silver and sapphire girdle encircled the waistline. 'Twas a beautiful dress, costly, and made in Lady Wren's wide, bulky size.

"'Tis simple to cut a gown down, but not to enlarge. Look at the seams—the velvet matches perfectly." Darianne brushed the rich fabric with her gnarled fingers. "This gown was commissioned with you in mind."

A sharp rap at the door gave Gwendolyn a moment to clear the lump from her throat. "'Tis the bath and tea Falke ordered for me. Pray, open the door for them, Darianne."

Folding the gown over her arm, she brushed the wonderful fabric against her cheek. What would Falke think when he saw her dressed in this gown, without the wrap of pockets around her waist, and the dye washed from her hair?

"You!"

Darianne's cry broke Gwendolyn's daydream. She caught a glimpse of her foster mother's prone shape on the floor and of Ivette dressed in servant's clothing. Then darkness descended as a coarse bag was thrown over her. Her arms still held Falke's gift. Her legs were tied, then she was trussed up on a man's shoulder like a sack of turnips.

"Follow me." Gwendolyn recognized Ivette's silky voice as she was carried from the room. "I'll get you out through the back entrance, then I'll make sure the old woman's taken care of."

"See that you do," Ferris cautioned. "She could cause us trouble."

Darianne! Gwendolyn squirmed, desperate to save her foster mother. Ferris's iron grip tightened. She tried to shout, but the thick bag muffled her screams.

A sharp rap to her head stopped Gwendolyn's struggles. In a clear, menacing voice, Ivette warned, "I mean to be the chatelaine of Mistedge. Nothing and no one will stop me. Not an old woman, a fat drudge or even Falke's newfound sense of honor."

"You'll get what you want," Ferris advised. "And we get what we want—our court jester back. We lose none of her lands, and there's the fee you're paying us."

"A hundred gold coins for what?" Ivette spat. "'Twas my servant who overheard Falke's order for the bath and tea. 'Twas I who distracted the guard so you could overtake him. 'Tis you that should be paying me.''

"With her gone, there will be an uproar," Ferris reasoned. "Falke will have to appease Laron's followers, and marriage to you will join the two factions. Falke will rejoice at not having to marry this sow."

They don't know we've already married. The realization hit Gwendolyn as cold night air sifted through the hot sack enveloping her. She heard the restless shuffling of horse hooves. The breath was knocked out of her as she was dumped over a saddle. Falke's gift, the velvet hopelessly crushed, cushioned her as her captors galloped away with her. *They don't know we're already married.*

Gwendolyn did not know if the fact would be her salvation or her death.

Chapter Eighteen

A monstrous black spider crawled across the wooden beam above Gwendolyn's head. She lay on a dirty straw pallet and watched the predator finish the last strands of the delicate web. The creature then backed to the center of the sticky creation, waiting for prey.

It took little imagination for Gwendolyn to picture her uncle in place of the spider. Like a fly caught in a web, she was helpless to escape Cravenmoor. And like the spider, Titus would take his time finishing her off.

She rose from the pallet, knowing that her tiny cell was exactly ten paces wide and long. Since her arrival two nights ago she had done nothing but pace and shiver, dreading Titus's punishment.

Though none yet knew of her beauty, all of Cravenmoor knew she was neither an idiot nor lame. Gwendolyn had no protection from Titus's retribution.

Gloom seeped into her bones, and she sought the one shred of hope she possessed. She dug her fingers deep into the straw and stroked the fine velvet of her wedding gown. She had managed to keep Falke's gift from Titus during the hard ride back to Cravenmoor by stuffing it under her wool shift. And since no one had bothered to bring her food or water since her imprisonment, she had been able to keep the exquisite gown for her own.

Wrinkles marred the azure cloth and the silver thread had pulled in places along the bodice, but during the frantic ride back to Cravenmoor, and the two days since they had arrived, the touch of soft fabric had bolstered Gwendolyn's courage. Falke would come for her. He loved her.

Yet there was doubt in her heart. If she died at Titus's hand, Falke would have fulfilled his duty, gained Mistedge and his freedom. "Pray, let his words of love be true." Gwendolyn slumped against the wall, her heart warring between trust and uncertainty.

The clatter of keys and raw language made her lift her head. "Titus wants you in the hall." The jailer snickered as he unlocked the door. Carefully, she arranged the straw over her gown, hiding the brilliant cloth.

Swinging the door wide, the jailer smiled, displaying teeth brown with decay. Gwendolyn rose, and from the corner of her eye she spotted the spiderweb. Tangled in the strands, a small beetle fought to free itself. 'Twas a hopeless struggle. As was hers.

* * *

"Bring the devil's spawn to me."

Titus's roar reverberated in Gwendolyn's ears as the jailer dragged her across Cravenmoor's great hall and threw her to the floor. The familiar stench of the rushes, rotten food and animal feces assaulted her. Decay and ruin made the air musty and stale. Gwendolyn slowly rose and lifted her chin in defiance.

Her uncle stood on the dais in front of the table, his pack of wolfhounds growling restlessly near his feet. His nobles flanked the hall, seated at trestle tables laden with food and drink. The smell of overcooked meat made Gwendolyn's stomach rumble. Luckily, no one heard her. Their jeers and insults drowned out her complaining stomach.

Titus wiped the ale from his beard with his bearlike hand and stood. "You conniving whore. Playing the castle simpleton and all the time stealing from me." He snapped his fingers and the steward rushed forward with the castle records. "Ferris looked over these." Titus pointed toward where his favorite bastard lounged near the hearth. "Seems there's been some rearranging of my wealth."

"Nay, Uncle, not your wealth. Mine." With no disguise to protect, Gwendolyn finally allowed herself to speak her mind and her heart. "Those properties are my dowry lands, and you have no right to them."

"Right?" Titus hooted. The knights and ladies joined in his mock humor. "I am your guardian. 'Tis to me the profits go. And if Ferris is correct, 'tis your lands that show most of my profit.''

"These shouldn't be your lands." Gwendolyn straighten and pointed her finger at where her uncle's heart should be. "Is Cain your patron saint that you would kill your own brother because you covet his wealth and his wife?"

Laughter evaporated in the hall, replaced with utter silence. Eyes stared at her and at her uncle's reddening face. Ferris jumped from the chair and approached his father, his hand on his dagger.

"Mistedge has spoiled you, girl. There's no one here to put on a show for you. No one here that is going to raise his sword to protect you." Titus sneered as he reached for a ham shank on the table. "'Tis time you learned your place."

He lowered the meat, letting the pack get the scent. Gwendolyn took a step back and glanced around the room. An animal gleam sharpened the nobles' stares, and Gwendolyn knew she was alone.

Tantalizing the wolfhounds with the ham shank, Titus chuckled. "Now that I know you've your wits about you, you're going to be much more entertaining." He swung the chuck of meat in a graceful arc and it landed right at her feet.

In a lightning flash, the pack raced after it. Six animals almost twice her size rushed at Gwendolyn. The lead dog hit her in the gut and she went down, her gown covering the shank. Shouts of encouragement to the dogs broke the hall's silence. Sharp teeth snapped at her ankles. Before, she had had to endure the humiliation and rely on Cyrus and Darianne, but no more. She had nothing to hide. And ten years of anger to draw on.

Gwendolyn fought back the gray bodies leaping around her. Frantically, she retrieved the shank, then, lifting it high, she rapped it across the lead dog's muzzle. His whimper startled the rest of pack long enough for Gwendolyn to regain her feet.

"You want this?" She raised the ham shank high, though barely over the dogs' heads. "Then go get it."

Gwendolyn repeated her uncle's act, but threw the ham amidst the Cravenmoor nobles. Six hounds immediately gave chase and crashed into the table, knocking over the chairs, men and women. For once, Cravenmoor's knights and ladies became the victims.

Facing her uncle and Ferris, Gwendolyn tossed back her tangled mane of hair and met their stares. She didn't conceal one drop of the hate and disgust that burned in her heart.

From behind her, she heard the sounds of growls, whimpers, snapping teeth, and men and women cursing, crying and whimpering. It gave Gwendolyn a warm sense of satisfaction. "Now that you know I have my wits about me, I'll be sure to be less entertaining. At least as long as I'm here."

Titus roared, "You're a fool. You think Chretian is coming to rescue you."

"He'll come."

"You are a simpleton." Titus stepped down from the dais and took sinister, methodical steps toward her. "Chretian was willing to pay me to take you away, to keep you away before you endeared yourself to the commoners. Right now he's probably drinking a toast to me for kidnapping you."

"You're wrong. Falke will come for me."

"Why—because you saved a few serfs? He was never going to marry you."

"Aye, he was and did."

"What?" The cry died in Titus's throat as his hand clenched the neck of her gown.

"Aye, Uncle. You did not kidnap your ward, but Lady Gwendolyn de Chretian. With the marriage vows spoken, the contract signed..." she paused, then added, "and the marriage bed consummated."

"Nay." Titus's denial arrived as his fist collided with Gwendolyn's cheek. The ragged edge of his ring tore at the tender skin near her lips. The taste of blood trickled into her mouth. She placed her hand over the wound and then pulled it away. Blood smeared her palm.

Ferris fretted, "Chretian can call on Henry for troops. We'll have the wrath of the king on our heads."

Titus stared at Gwendolyn's bloody mouth and hand, then gave a harsh whisper. "And Isolde's as well."

Chapter Nineteen

Falke stood at the opening of his war tent and stared at Cravenmoor's bleak walls. Imprisoned within the keep, Gwendolyn waited to be rescued.

Iron bars of pain squeezed his chest. In the back of his mind, he heard his father's condemnation, "My son, the failure." But a stronger voice gently chided away Falke's doubt. 'Twas Lady Wren's. And Falke knew this voice echoed from his heart.

Although he had discovered Darianne only a few minutes after the crime, it had taken the elderly woman some time to recover and name Titus's accomplice, Ivette. It had taken even longer to muscle through Laron and his allies to get to her and find out Titus's whereabouts. Longer still for Falke's loyal vassals to call for reinforcements. 'Twas nearly seven days now since his wedding and his wife's abduction.

Seven days for Titus to inflict pain and torture on Gwendolyn. Seven days in which Titus could discover her many secrets.

Falke crossed his arms and returned to the gathered knights inside his tent. His options were few, his time running out. "How long before we can expect the king's men?"

"Four to five days at least," Ozbern answered. Falke pivoted to face the knights assembled. Ozbern's face looked as bleak as Cravenmoor. "That's if Alric locates Henry in London. If the king is off on one of his hunting jaunts it may take that long just to find him."

"Call in Titus's messenger," Falke ordered. A foot soldier hurried off to obey. Falke disregarded the men's reminders that Titus could not be trusted.

From outside, the shuffle of feet signaled the arrival of Titus's man. He entered, a disheveled peasant too thin and elderly to do much manual labor. Dressed in a tunic too large and sagging stockings, the serf rubbed his neck, as though grateful 'twas still attached to his body.

The messenger bobbed his head to each noble, his eyes popping at the shiny armor and broadswords. "My lord," he gulped, gave Falke an even more pronounced bob of his head, and continued, "My thanks for the meal. And me head."

"I'll take your thanks for the meal. The other is uncalled for." *He must believe all lords are as cruel at Titus.* Falke widened his stance and dropped one hand to the hilt of his sword. "Now tell me, what does Titus offer?"

The serf gulped again, his pronounced Adam's apple bouncing up and down. He spoke in a rush. "Titus wishes to discuss terms for your wife's return. But with you only. Inside Cravenmoor. But the offer's only open for today."

"Titus knows Lady Wren is wed!" Ozbern rubbed his chin and questioned, "Are these good tidings?"

"Aye," Falke reassured his second. "Since we are wed, her dowry lands are lost to Titus. Should my wife die, he can only lose. Unless the king becomes involved."

"Hence the reason for Titus's haste," Ozbern reckoned.

"Aye. Should the king's troops arrive, Henry will demand an accounting. And Titus has no plea other than guilty."

"Then let us wait for the king's men," Sir Clement reasoned. "Surely with the knowledge that there is no hope of escape, Titus will surrender Lady Wren to us without endangering your life, my lord."

Falke gave his staunch ally a weak smile. "I fear I would save my own but forfeit Lady Wren's. My wife is the only one who can bear witness against Titus. 'Tis she alone who can testify that Titus took her against her will. With Lady Wren dead, we have only Darianne's word that my wife was kidnapped. Think you not Titus has already begun to rehearse a tale of how his ward begged him to take her away from Mistedge?

"I must meet with Titus," he added. "'tis our only hope of saving my lady."

Sir Clement stepped forward, a stubborn look of understanding on his craggy face. "You said Titus would gain no wealth should Lady Wren die, but if she should become a widow 'tis a different tale.''

The knight waited, letting his comrades grasp his logic.

''Then Lady Wren would inherit her widow's portion and Titus would become her guardian once again,'' Ozbern finished.

Falke could not deny the truth. To stall Titus meant his love's death. To save her life, Falke must forfeit his own.

''My lord?'' Titus's messenger cleared his throat nervously. ''Mayhap there's another way.''

In unison all turned their attention to the peasant. Falke leveled a hard stare in the man's direction. The serf stuttered, ''L-Lady Gwendolyn's held in the pantry. If I c-could set her free, there's a gap in the inner wall she could sneak through.'' His voice grew more stable and confident. ''Everyone at Cravenmoor knows of the hidden door in the outer wall. She could escape from the castle, and after that 'twould be up to you.''

The man's words gained Falke's interest. Aye, the plan might work. ''What would it take to give you the chance to free my lady?''

''I need most of the castle staff and nobles not lookin' my way.''

''And my arrival would do that, would it not?''

''Aye, 'tis the best I can think of,'' the messenger answered with frank honesty. ''Serfs wanta know what kinda man woulda married Lady Gwendolyn. Nobles wanta see what Titus is goin' to do to ye.

They'd fill the great hall, and wouldn't look twice at me goin' to the pantry.''

"I thought as much." God's wounds! Falke wanted to scream at the injustice of fate. To have given his heart to a woman such as Lady Wren and have his love returned was the greatest happiness he had ever known. But that joy was doomed to be short-lived. At least his death at Titus's hand would be his last gift to his beloved. Ozbern and his loyal vassals would bring Gwendolyn to safety.

Pointing to the serf, Falke commanded, "Show us on this map where the hidden gate is." The rail-thin man obeyed, pointing to an area dense with trees and underbrush. Perfect for his allies to hide in.

"Ozbern, you will take a few men and wait there for Lady Wren. When you have her, take her to the nunnery my aunt resides in. Titus cannot breach the walls of such a sacred place."

"Falke, you don't mean to ride into that cesspool?" Ozbern waved his hand with contempt toward the serf. "We can't trust this man. Why would he help his lord's enemies?"

A fire of anger glinted in the old peasant's eyes. "Lord William's me lord. Not that devil Titus." He rubbed his gnarled fingers together. "Time past, Mistedge and Cravenmoor visited often. Me only child, a sweet, gentle daughter, married a man of Mistedge. And if she's still livin', I hear 'tis 'cause the lady cured them."

"Aye, Lady Wren did work to end our plague." The memories of Lady Wren ministering to the sick brought fresh pain to Falke's heart. How he loved that woman—her bossy voice, her gentle hands, her loving heart. "If your child lives, you owe my lady. Pray, what is your daughter's name? I will tell you if she lives."

"'Tis tellin' the type of lord ye are to know the common folks' names." The messenger folded his hands in prayer and asked, "Could ye tell me if my delicate Blodwyn still lives?"

"Blodwyn?" Falke chortled. "Aye, she lives."

"Then my prayers are answered."

"And with your information, so are mine."

Falke turned to Ozbern. "I put my wife's safe-keeping into your hands."

Surrender made his second's voice tight with emotion. "I am your man, Falke. What you command, I will do. Lady Wren will be safe from Titus."

Falke shook each knight's hand, felt the warmth of their camaraderie, the depth of their loyalty. It made him humble and outraged. His woman's love, a home, the loyalty of good men—what more could a man ask for? It had all been his, but for so short a time.

"Prepare our horses," Falke ordered, then turned to the servant. "If we enter the gates now, how soon can you free my wife?"

"Best time be right as you arrive. Most confusion."

"Ozbern, pick your men and make haste to the wall to await my wife. You—" Falke motioned to the serf "—what is your name?"

"John, sir."

"Then let us depart, John, but before we leave, one thing." Falke waved Sir Clement forward. "John, if you're lying to me, and you betray me, this man will hunt you down and kill you."

The muscular knight scowled, a trace of a growl emitting from his twisted mouth. "You can count on it, John."

Taking John's coarse woolen sleeve, Falke dragged the man outside to their mounts. The poor man's knees were shaking as a soldier threw him onto a swaybacked mare. Side by side, they rode out of the camp and across the field to the Cravenmoor drawbridge. As the door slowly lowered, Falke nudged John's mount with his own to gain the man's attention.

"When you see my wife, tell her I love her," Falke requested as the drawbridge thudded to the ground. "Tell her I love Lady Wren."

"Aye, my lord, I will."

Falke urged his mount over the wide-planked ramp and wished with all his heart that he could tell her himself just once more.

Chapter Twenty

Dozens of footsteps clomped across the timbers above Gwendolyn's head. Dust peppered her bowl of thin soup and brown bread. Rising from her pallet, she covered her meager meal with a sleeve to protect it. 'Twas little use. Another drumbeat of footsteps raced overhead. Debris sifted through the beams, seasoning the soup and dusting her hair. Another herd of footsteps sounded. Where was everyone going?

A bit of spying was needed. In the storage room that had become her cell, she had but one view of the outer room. She brushed away the soiled rushes near the door and lay flat. A small gap at the bottom of the wormy portal allowed her a glimpse of life beyond her cell. Neither candles nor torches lit the room, only rare patches of sunlight. 'Twas too early for the evening meal, yet she spied several pairs of bare and booted legs racing toward the stairs to the great hall. Whatever was taking place, not a person in Cravenmoor wanted to miss it.

Could Falke have come at last? Gwendolyn kneeled and pressed her ear to the thick door, willing herself to hear his voice. The only sounds she heard were muffled cries and hurried murmurs. If Falke had overtaken Cravenmoor, surely there'd be a clash of swords. So he had not come. Not yet. But he would. And again the doubt in her heart taunted her. Wouldn't Falke be glad to be free of her?

He loves me. He'll come. It makes no difference that he does not know I am his Angel. The sound of the lock turning broke her chant. Her belief in Falke soared as the door slowly creaked open. She could not speak nor move as a harsh whisper came from around the door. "Lady Gwendolyn, where be ye?"

Not Falke, but surely one of his men. "Here." She swung the door wide, convinced a man of Mistedge would greet her. Her joy withered as she recognized John, a Cravenmoor serf. Titus must have ordered her to be fetched upstairs. Whatever was taking place, she wanted no part of it.

"Come with me." John beckoned as he gave the pantry a swift survey. "We ain't much time."

"Where?" She had no love of her confining cell, but neither did she relish another episode with Titus. Her mouth still ached from her last encounter. Though the skin had healed, her mouth still felt bruised.

"I'll help ye through the inner wall, then you're on your own to the outer. There're Mistedge knights waitin' on the other side of the secret gate." John shifted his weight from foot to foot as his gaze kept drifting to the nearby stairs that led to the great hall.

Falke was here! Her heart rejoiced while at the same time scolding her for her doubt. Her uncertainty resurfaced, this time directed at John. The man had never crossed Titus in all the years she had known him.

"Why should I trust you?" she asked.

"'Cause me neck's at stake. If'n you ain't at the gate, that husband of yours has got a mean-faced knight sworn to kill me. The man's got a look that would frighten the devil himself. He struck me as the type to keep his word."

A mean-faced knight? It could be no other than Sir Clement. At least John must have spoken to Falke. She cast an appraising glance over her home for the last seven days. Windowless, dank and occupied by an assortment of insects and rodents, the chamber offered no incentive to stay.

What more torture could Titus inflict on her? If she did not take this chance, there might be no other. "All right then, let's go." But she'd not leave without her wedding dress. "First I need to get—"

A shout echoed down the stairs, followed by jeers and whistles. John grabbed her hand. "No time. I don't know how long he's gonna last." With that, he dragged her toward the back of the pantry and out the service door.

So that was what had the castle in a tither. Titus must be torturing some poor soul. As Gwendolyn raced after John, she prayed for the unfortunate man whose death offered her a chance of escape.

Late afternoon shadows hung over the castle. The summer heat on the stone wall sent vapors rising, blurring the image. John and Gwendolyn took advantage of the shadows at first, then discovered the inner bailey was all but deserted as peasants and fighting men alike herded themselves toward the castle. Adopting a swift walk, Gwendolyn held her breath as she crossed the open grass. No one looked at her twice. Everyone seemed to be fixated on reaching the castle.

John led her to the empty mews, where a few falcon feathers were all that remained of her father's hunting birds. Tugging at the underbrush, the serf revealed a gap in the wall. "Here ye be, lass. 'Twill be harder getting across the outer bailey. Soldiers are thick on the wall 'cause of Mistedge on the other side. Take these." He pulled a bundle of scarves from beneath his loose tunic. "Ye can wrap yourself in these and mayhap none will recognize ye."

With glee, she draped a scarf over her head and another across her shoulders. 'Twas a disguise she had used many times within these very walls.

John blinked his eyes twice. "Ye just might get away." He rubbed the chain of wrinkles around his weathered neck and smiled. "I just might keep me neck."

Gwendolyn poked her head through the gap. John was right—soldiers lined the wall, but their attention was riveted beyond the bailey. She had a chance. In only a few moments she would be returned to Falke. Turning back to John, she squeezed his hand and whispered, "My thanks."

The serf held her hand tightly, not releasing her. "One more thing—he said to tell ye he loved ye. That he loved Lady Wren." 'Twas the look in the old man's eye, the catch in his throat and the way he said "loved" instead of "loves' that made fear creep up her bones.

"John, who's in the hall with Titus?" Dread at his answer already filled her. Whose appearance would draw so many, nobles and commoners alike? The man who had outfoxed Titus and wed his ugly ward, Falke de Chretian.

"Just go." John pulled his hand from hers and attempted to push her through the gap.

"Nay!" Her voice rose and John pulled his hands back, quickly surveying the yard for any unwanted attention.

"I'll not leave him." Gwendolyn withdrew from the opening. Fear, stark and vivid, made her voice fierce and commanding. "I will not leave my husband."

"There's no hope for him. He wanted you safe. If not for your sake then for mine, go from here."

"I'll bring his men here. They can rescue Falke."

"He'll be dead by then."

"Then we must stall Titus until help arrives."

"We?" John gave her a resigned look. "There's nothing we can do. 'Twill be dark in a few hours."

"I'm not giving up." Gwendolyn's mind raced. How could she draw Titus's attention away from Falke long enough for his men to come to his aid? What could she do to put the fear of God into Titus, a man who knew only the devil? Ah, the devil. She could not bring the Almighty to Cravenmoor, but she could bring an image from hell here. One that would scatter peasants and nobles alike, and terrorize Titus.

"John, go to Falke's men. Tell them that I am holding Titus at bay, and Falke will be alive."

"There's not that many of them."

"As you said, 'twill be dark soon. A few men could open the main gate, after which, Falke's troops can invade."

"That mean-faced knight will cut me throat."

"Tell Sir Clement that if he does I'll box his ears. He'll know those words are mine. Now go." Gwendolyn switched places with the serf.

Yielding to her persistence, John shook his head and ducked through the wall, muttering about women not knowing what was good for them. She stuck her head through and watched the serf lope across the bailey until she was certain John would do his part. Now she must do hers.

Drawing the scarf over her head, Gwendolyn assumed her old woman stance. It took iron self-control to hobble back to the castle instead of running, but she could not afford to be discovered. 'Twas not only her life she would forfeit, but Falke's as well.

She opened the door to the pantry and listened. Only the echoed noise from the great hall sounded. The lower level was still deserted, which meant Falke must still be alive.

With cautious speed, she collected the items she needed—wine vinegar, water, soap and a length of twine. She retreated to her cell to complete her plan, and for the final item, her wedding dress. 'Twas time for Isolde to return from the dead.

Unwashed bodies, soured wine and blood polluted the air in the great hall. The center of attention, Falke wiped the blood from his mouth with his thumb. Knights and ladies crowded the trestle tables, the men cheering on Titus, the women staring at Falke with hungry lust in their eyes. Serfs lined the staircase and the lower floor. Everyone wanted a close look at Titus's latest victim. Falke meant for them to have a long look. Long enough for Gwendolyn to reach his men.

Gracing the crowd with his most charming smile, he spoke to Titus. ''I see your hospitality hasn't changed much.''

Titus lifted a tankard of ale to his mouth and drank deeply. Rivulets of brown liquid ran down his greasy beard. He patted his round stomach and asked, ''How else should I treat the man that robbed me?''

''How can you of accuse me of stealing what was

not yours?'' Falke deliberately baited Titus. ''My wife's dowry lands were given to her at birth. Poor planning on your part, Titus. Murdered your brother for a ruined castle and a few overworked fiefs. I guess your soul isn't worth much.''

A roar accompanied Titus's fist. The older man's blow penetrated deep into Falke's gut. He would have fallen except for two knights, who pushed him back up to receive another hit.

The air punched from his lungs, Falke fought to gain his breath. 'Twas typical Titus, a bully when he was surrounded by his henchmen. But alone, 'twas another story. Balling his hands into fists, Falke wished for one second of freedom. He'd deliver just one bone-crushing blow and knock Titus's decayed teeth right down his miserable throat.

Stripped of his weapons, with crossbows aimed at his heart, Falke could only endure Titus's blows. In the back of his mind, he pictured Lady Wren, sitting near the hearth at Mistedge. The pain dulled. He could withstand more.

''Chretian.'' Ferris approached, staring down his hawkish nose. '''Tis strange a man like you would marry Gwendolyn, no matter how rich the prize.'' A calculating gleam shone in his eyes and caused a trickle of worry down Falke's spine.

Ferris's voice became smooth and silky, yet his eyes drilled into Falke, studying the effect of his words. '''Twould seem you discovered and revealed Gwendolyn's many lies. I wonder how many more she still has? I'm going to enjoy stripping every last one from her."

Like a badger, Ferris's words nipped at Falke. *He knows about Gwendolyn. He knows her secret. God's wounds, let John get her to freedom and spare her.* Titus was cruel, but Ferris could be the devil himself.

"In fact—" Ferris's eyes narrowed as his smile grew tighter and thinner, "—I believe our Gwendolyn is like a walnut. Dull, brown, round." He plucked one from the table and held it aloft for all to see. Then he dropped it and slammed his boot heel onto the shell. Picking up the inner pieces, Ferris continued, "But like a nut, there is sweet meat inside. I look forward to breaking her shell and sampling the sweetness."

"Nay!" Falke reacted in fury. His fist slammed into Ferris's chin, sending him flying over the table. Goblets, trenchers and salt spilled over the floor, the nobles and the serfs.

Ferris meant to expose Gwendolyn and humiliate her. 'Twas a threat Falke could not and would not ignore. He leaped over the table, determined to silence the knight forever. His fist slammed into Ferris's face again and again. Blood spurted, covering Falke's wool tunic and Ferris's embroidered finery.

"I'll kill you," Falke promised as his hands clenched Ferris's throat.

The crash of a wine bottle ended his threat, and the image of Titus holding the broken bottle danced before Falke's dazed eyes. His hold on Ferris's throat loosened and the man escaped. A Cravenmoor knight drew his sword and rested it against Falke's neck.

"I grow tired of this play." Ferris cleared his throat and demanded, "Kill him."

"Aye," Titus agreed. "'Tis time for retribution."

"Aye, Titus." A woman's voice called eerily from the upper gallery. "'Tis time for retribution. Mine."

Titus slowly turned. His cry, full of anguish and terror, sent the room into flight. "Isolde! She's come to take me to hell."

Chapter Twenty-One

Screams, curses and prayers commingled in the great hall. Titus stood on the dais, his chest heaving and his flaccid cheeks white as old ash. Arrogance drained from his face, replaced by a fixed stare.

Peasants rapidly made the sign of the cross, then repeated the action over and over again. Nobles who had never entered the chapel fell to their knees in prayer, weapons dropped and forgotten. Jeers and insults froze on their lips. Their hypocrisy pleased Gwendolyn. It showed they believed Isolde had returned from the dead.

That belief was all that stood between Falke and death. Lying at Ferris's feet, her husband wearily lifted his head and stared at her. Sweat streaked his golden hair. Bruises marked his handsome face, a mixture of emotions flickering over his features. Surprise. Confusion. Anger. And, most startling of all, pride.

He pushed himself to one knee, and Gwendolyn

sucked in a breath. Blood stained the gaping side of his wool tunic. Casting an anxious glance at her cousin, Falke gave a forced shout to Ferris. "Find Gwendolyn. Get her to safety."

Falke believed as well? Did Falke not recognize her as his angel, the woman he'd made love to in the forest? Her frantic thoughts halted as bedlam erupted in the hall.

"'Tis Gwendolyn who has drawn the ghost."

"Isolde will take revenge on us all."

A frightened knight stood and pointed at Titus. "'Twas he that drew her blood, none of us. We should not pay for his sin."

"Aye, he is right. Isolde, take Titus but spare the rest of us," beseeched a lady. The threat of eternal damnation drove a wedge between Titus and his followers. 'Twas a wedge Gwendolyn intended to deepen.

A powerful brew of glee, fright and panic bubbled in the pit of her stomach. It made her knees weak, her hands shake and her mind sharp. She had to act fast before anyone noticed the "ghost" wore a wrinkled gown three sizes too large and a twine girdle to hold in the excess material.

"Flee, Cravenmoor," she warned, "or share Titus's punishment." An exodus began before she finished speaking. Chairs toppled. Trenchers of food fell to the floor. The hounds ran in frantic circles, gobbling up the spilled food and chasing the frightened people.

"Flee and I'll send you to hell myself," Ferris

countered, and the crowd paused, torn between the fear of hell and Ferris's sword.

He strutted forward, pausing just beneath where Gwendolyn stood. A predatory smile twisted her cousin's aristocratic features. His cocky attitude tore at her confidence.

Where were Falke's men? Faint shouts and screams floated through the window above the balcony. But did they generate from an invading force or fear of the supernatural? She gripped the decayed railing and hoped for a miracle.

Her cousin used his sword to point at her. "So, Isolde, you have come to claim Titus's soul?"

"Aye." Gwendolyn continued to play the specter in an attempted to regain control. "And those that follow him."

"Then come, claim me." Ferris mocked her with his eyes. "For I intend to claim Gwendolyn, and do not think my hand will be stayed by the words of a woman long dead."

The look in her cousin's eyes and the arrogance in his threat made Gwendolyn fear he knew more of her secrets than she'd realized. Her ruse was crumbling, as were her and Falke's chances of survival.

Damn John. Why hadn't the serf led Gwendolyn to safety? But Falke already knew the answer. Lady Wren was a force few could withstand. But he feared Ferris might be one of those few.

Pain lanced Falke's left side as he struggled to his

feet. With one hand he stanched the blood flow; with the other he grabbed an abandoned sword.

"So, Isolde, no ghostly tricks?" Ferris sneered as he sauntered toward the stairs. "Let us see your justice from beyond the grave." The dare hung in the air, and Falke could see the inkling of doubt in the nobles' faces.

And then he heard them take a collective breath. He turned toward the balcony, pride surging in his veins. Gwendolyn had risen to Ferris's taunt.

"Then so be it." Standing between the wall and the statue, she mimicked the effigy's stance. Arms outstretched, palms upward, she cast a shadow that engulfed the great hall. "My justice falls on all of Cravenmoor."

'Twas as though the statue had come to life. The same silver hair. The same azure dress. The same fine, delicate face. But Gwendolyn gave life to the cold features, making her more beautiful and more spectral. Yet Falke knew the woman was no ghost. She was flesh and blood. She was his wife.

A slight breeze lifted her platinum hair, creating a halo around her head. Even with his eyes blurred with blood, Falke recognized the gown he had given her for their wedding. And he detected the crude twine criss-crossing her chest to hold it on. With more light and a less guilty audience, her ruse would be seen through easily.

Gwendolyn leaned her head toward the window. "Already my minions invade. All within are doomed."

Panic grasped everyone except Ferris. His maniacal laughter echoed in the hall. Gwendolyn had no more bluffs, and in a matter of moments Ferris would strip her of her last protection.

Falke lifted his broadsword and challenged, "Here stands your judge, Ferris. Come meet me."

"With pleasure, Chretian. I have time enough to deal with my cousin."

Ferris raised his sword just as the door of the great hall burst open. As though the gates of hell had released its demons, fighting men spilled into the room. Blood thickened the air. The acrid smell of sweat cut the foul odors of the rushes, and the sounds of bones breaking and men dying filled the room. It took precious seconds for the Cravenmoor knights to realize the demons attacking were Mistedge soldiers.

The great hall turned into a battlefield. Falke spotted Ozbern and Clement within the melee. So this had been Gwendolyn's plan—to stall death until help arrived.

Men fought and fell beside him, but he had no thought of battle. First he needed to find Gwendolyn and get her to safety. Standing with his sword at the ready, Ferris blocked his way.

He tapped swords with Falke, a tease of the battle to come. A pleased smile creased his face as he glanced at the wound. "I'll have her, Chretian," he taunted as their swords clashed. "Again, and again, and again."

"She is my wife." Falke lunged, his broadsword missing Ferris's chest by a breath.

"She'll be your widow."

The raw pain in his side did not compare to the fear Ferris's words stirred in Falke's heart. Gwendolyn's life with Titus had been cruel; a life under Ferris's rule, stripped of all her protection, would be torture.

"You'll never have her," Falke declared. Even if this day Gwendolyn became his widow, he would take her enemy with him. Conviction brought a wash of strength to his weary muscles. The broadsword became lighter, his head cleared and the room settled into an uneasy tilt.

Ferris sliced upward. Falke countered the attack. They danced a battle waltz among fighting Mistedge and Cravenmoor knights. Combat reigned around them, then space cleared. Falke lunged with his sword. Ferris hacked downward. Their blades met with a clear metallic clang, and locked.

Falke's biceps bulged, burning from exertion. A mixture of sweat and blood trickled into his eyes.

"You're weakening, Chretian." Ferris pressed harder on his blade, driving the edge just a hair closer to Falke's neck.

"Nay, Ferris. I fight for the love of my life. I...will..." he drove his blade toward his enemy's chest "...not falter." Again he summoned burst of strength and brought his sword closer to Ferris's heart.

"Think again." Using his fingers like daggers, Ferris stabbed Falke's wound.

Lightning bolts of agony shot through Falke's side, splintering his control. Pain sparked through his muscles and bones, destroying his strength, leaving him weak and vulnerable. He fell to one knee, his fist to his chest, the other with a slack hold on his sword hilt.

"As you die, Chretian, think of me, having Gwendolyn." Ferris moved in for the kill, his sword point aimed at Falke's heart.

The image generated an explosion of power in Falke. As Ferris rushed forward, Falke thrust his sword deep into his enemy's gut. Surprise froze Ferris's face. His wrist bent. His sword dropped to the floor as he fell across Falke's chest, pinning him to the ground.

"Falke!" Ozbern and Clement appeared at his side, rolling his enemy's dead body away. Drenched in blood, Falke had but one thought, of Gwendolyn.

"The pantry is empty. We can't find Lady Wren." Ozbern swept the great hall with a glance. "Have you seen her?" Fighting raged about them, though 'twas plain that the Mistedge forces were the strongest.

Falke's stare pivoted to the stairs and his sense of victory evaporated. Using his comrades as crutches, he gained his feet. "The stairs. She's on the stairs."

Ozbern's and Clement's gazes passed over the beautiful woman standing on the balcony. "Where?"

Falke had no time to waste in explanation. One last enemy stalked his beloved. Titus.

* * *

Stuck between the wall, the railing and the effigy, Gwendolyn could see only the left side of the great hall. She leaned over the railing, then pulled back as the barrier gave a bit under her weight. Where was Falke? She had lost sight of him during his battle with Ferris when a wave of soldiers cascaded across the great hall. She couldn't see his tall frame anywhere.

Backing out of the tight opening, she kept her gaze on the great hall, hoping to catch sight of her husband.

"Banshee!"

The shout made her freeze. Slowly she turned around and faced a madman.

Her uncle stood at the top of the stairs. Insanity seared his face, turning it red and purple. His sword hand gripped the hilt until his knuckles turned white. The veins of his neck pulsated as he spoke. "You'll not feast on my soul, Isolde. I'll see you in hell first."

Gwendolyn stared at her mother's statue and again duplicated its stance, hoping to frighten Titus away. "Aye, that you will, Titus, for you will be at my side."

Her words only served to fuel his madness. Titus slashed his blade through the air, smiling as the metal sang. "I'll scatter the pieces of your body in so many places, you'll never find your way to me again."

The wood floor creak as he took heavy steps toward her, blocking her escape down the stairs or toward the door on the far wall.

Trapped, she took small steps backward until she hit the railing. No room for retreat, no room to advance. Her uncle's smile deepened as he approached. ''You can greet Satan back in hell.''

''Greet him yourself, Titus.'' She ducked between the effigy's raised arms, but scrunched against the railing on one side, could retreat no farther. The effigy pedestal trapped her on the other, and Titus loomed in front of her.

At least she would die in her mother's arms.

''Gwendolyn!''

She heard Falke's voice, caught a glimpse of steel flash beside her, then the crack of wood as the railing shattered. Her feet dangled in the air, and looking down, she saw the stone floor of the great hall rush toward her. Then she comprehended the iron grip on her wrist.

''I've got you, Gwendolyn,'' Falke grunted. Blood streaked his face. Sweat darkened his hair. Tears marred his tunic. He looked beautiful.

Clasping her free hand over his, she tried to suppress the nausea in the pit of her stomach, the dizziness in her head, and held on for dear life.

Using the pedestal for anchorage, Falke heaved her up and back onto the balcony. A weak smile crossed his lips as he gave her cheek a soft caress. ''I've been looking for you, Wife.''

Gripping his sword, Falke looked beyond her and ordered, ''Go, Gwendolyn—''

''Straight back to the devil.'' Titus loomed at them from the other side of the effigy. Instead of rounding the statue, he clamped onto the statue's upraised arm and pulled himself across. His foot stomped down next to Gwendolyn's. His sword arm arced in the air, aiming for her neck.

Then she heard the earsplitting sound of wood scraping wood. She looked up, and her mother's arms seemed to fall forward, ready to embrace her. She saw Titus's face turn from one of rage to stark terror, then watched as the statue of her mother tumbled forward, carrying Titus with it. His shrill scream echoed off the stone walls of the castle.

Her uncle thudded on the hard floor of the great hall, chilling the battle that still raged. He opened his eyes and gave a soundless shriek as the heavy effigy plummeted on top of him. The statue of her mother lay faceup, unbroken and unharmed. Titus lay beneath, crushed.

"Gwendolyn," Falke called to her, his voice breathless and ragged. "Help me up."

She laid his arm across her shoulders and aided him to rise. "You need a decoction of yarrow to prevent infection in that wound. And I must have needle and thread to tend that gash."

Walking beside her, Falke gave a weary chuckle. "'Tis good to hear my Lady Wren again."

Lady Wren! But 'twas not that garb she wore now. She halted midway down the steps. "You called me Gwendolyn," she accused. "You know me."

"Aye, would not a husband know his wife?" A rascal of a smile crossed his lips. "And we are indeed husband and wife, though I would prefer next time we consummate our vows in a soft bed instead of on forest moss.''

''How did you know?''

He pointed to where her toe tapped impatiently on the step. ''Little things told me. But 'twas at our wedding, when I took your hand, that I suddenly realized why my angel reminded me so much of you.''

He rubbed his thumb over her callused palms and added, ''I remembered seeing your hands that first night in Mistedge, tending your horse. Then afterwards tending the ill.'' Kissing her fingertips, he added, ''Did you think I would not recognize the hands that hold my heart?''

Pausing on the staircase, he kissed her with a tenderness that melted all her doubts, filling her with desire and love. Eagerly, she returned his ardor, pressing her body close, enjoying the long hard feel of him.

He whispered love words in her ear, his breath causing a rampage of tingles down her neck. He kissed her again, his tongue dueling with her own. Fueling her want. Making her ache for the feel of his naked body against her own. Desire rushing to—

''Falke!''

The voice ripped into her passion-induced trance.

Falke tore his mouth from hers. Dazed, she leaned against him and turned to see the outraged faces of Ozbern and Sir Clement.

''Cravenmoor has surrendered,'' Ozbern informed them with a disgusted look. ''But we cannot find *your wife*.''

"'I fear Lady Wren is not here.'' Sir Clement crossed his arms, an angry snarl on his handsome face. ''Already you have forgotten her tender ways and gentle guidance. An angel of mercy.''

''Nay, my friends, I have not forgotten Lady Wren, though I fear you have.'' Falke gave Gwendolyn a roguish smile and said, ''I don't recall your showing Sir Clement much mercy.''

Gazing up at her husband, letting her love and adoration shine in her eyes, Gwendolyn answered, ''I was much too lenient on him in the village. I should have had him doing the laundry instead of you.'' She gave her husband a tight squeeze.

''Ah.'' Falke bit his lower lip and place one hand at his side.

''Your wound!'' Gwendolyn motioned for the stunned knights to aid her husband. Lifting her skirt to ankle height, she skipped down the stairs, issuing orders to the Mistedge soldiers.

''Fetch me hot water from the kitchen. Have a servant retrieve the cache of healing herbs from the pantry. There's needle and thread in Darianne's old room.''

Darianne! She raced back to her husband, supported by two very confused knights. ''I forgot all about Darianne. Titus hit her so hard—''

''Cyrus is with her at Mistedge. She's f-fine,'' Ozbern stammered. ''Lady Wren?''

Relief lasted only a moment before being replaced with urgency. ''I am glad to hear my foster parents are well, and I'll wish to hear of them later. But there is work to be done. Ozbern, place my husband on the table so I may see to his wounds. Sir Clement, bring all the injured, be they Mistedge or Cravenmoor, here to the great hall to be tended. I'll need five or six women to clean cuts with a mixture of thyme and lady's mantle. Another group of the same number to tear bandages.'' She paused, then stretched her hand toward their heads. ''What are you waiting for? Must I box some ears?''

Bewildered, Ozbern and Sir Clement dropped Falke on the table. ''Nay, Lady Wren.''

''I'll explain later.'' 'Twas all the clarification he could offer his friends before his wife pointed them in the direction of their tasks.

Seated on the trestle table, he waited patiently as Gwendolyn had a bowl of clean, warm water and a cloth brought to her. As she separated his wool tunic from the wound, she issued commands to the confused soldiers and peasants. By the time she was ready to sew his cut closed, Cravenmoor had regained a sense of order. The injured were being tended. Serfs busied themselves raking out the foul, blood-soaked rushes. And amazingly, Falke could detect the aroma of broth simmering in the kitchen.

''This will hurt.'' Gwendolyn showed him the threaded needle in her hand. Concern darkened her eyes as she leaned over him. ''A kiss for luck?''

Holding her hand in his, he pulled her close. ''Nay, Wife. A kiss for luck is a fickle thing—I never know whether 'tis good or bad fortune I will gain. 'Tis a kiss of love I seek. For love is ever true.''

And so she kissed him. A kiss full of love and devotion. A kiss that promised a fortune of passion-filled nights and a life of joy.

The kiss of an angel.

Epilogue

Falke paced along the mossy ground near the pond. Restless, he tossed a flat stone into the calm water and watched the ripples rack the red and orange leaves on its surface. Where was she? She had promised to be here.

"Falke?"

The rose bushes, now naked of blooms, shook as she walked down the narrow path to the clearing. She had her hair unbound, free to sway at her hips as she moved. Just as he liked, though when other men were about, he preferred it covered by a wimple.

Midday sunlight spattered her plain wool dress with light and he longed to caress each spot. To savor the taste of her. The smell of her. It had been too long since he had held her in his arms. "What took you so long?" he growled as he reached for her.

"I have work to do, my lord," she informed him regally, then dropped the blanket and basket she carried to return his embrace. "You are most fortunate that your wife allows you these rendezvous."

He gave her his most charming, devastatingly handsome smile. "My wife understands my needs." He ran his fingers along her spine, traced her shoulder blades and then gently cupped her heavy breasts. Passion flared, and he allowed her feel how hard his need already was.

"Your wife is extremely understanding." Pulling away from him, she spread out the blanket. As she leaned over, the loose drawstring at her shoulders allowed him a generous display of milky flesh. "I brought a basket to break our midday fast."

Joining her on the blanket, Falke guided her down on the soft wool. He kissed the pulsating hollow of her neck. "Food will not satisfy the fast I seek to break." He kissed the grotto between her breasts, his hunger growing at her sounds of pleasure. "I have not made love to you since this morning."

Laughing, Gwendolyn reminded him, "We cannot do this every day. Already there is talk of the lord and lady's disappearance each day."

"Let them talk." Falke smiled, his hands already beneath her gown, his fingers massaging her inner thighs, making her burn for him. "I have plans for you."

"Plans?" She sighed, not really interested in the answer. Falke had her in a euphoria of sensual delights. His hands slipped her gown off, exposing her sensitive skin to his every touch. The warmth of his chest against the stiff peaks of her breasts. The feel of his lips trailing kisses down her hip. The hot tip of his manhood at the apex of her womb.

Slowly he entered, groaning with pleasure as she wrapped herself around him. Delicious heat coursed through her, and she begged for more. He rocked his hips, sending shivers of desire darting through her body. Rotating his hips, he pushed deeper, harder, faster.

Ecstasy controlled her. Desire swept away her inhibitions. She arched her back, wanting more of him. Needing more of him. Falke did not leave her hungry. Hot pulses of his seed filled her, consumed her and drove her to the precipice of fulfillment. Then drove her over the edge.

She exploded, her body shuddering from fulfillment. Her heart filled with the enormity of her love for him. Falke had been her salvation from Titus, and she his salvation from self-doubt. Together, they had repaired Cravenmoor, both physically and mentally. With the stores from Cravenmoor to support them this lean season, Mistedge would also survive.

Languid with satisfaction and contentment Gwendolyn cuddled close to Falke. She wiggled her toes and said, "Mistedge and Cravenmoor are set to rights. You are well healed from your injuries. What more could you want?"

"I want a chorus," Falke whispered, sprinkling a line of kisses down her neck.

"A chorus?" she gasped, her body already reacting to Falke's caresses. "A chorus of what?"

Turning to her, his eyes dark with want, his body hard with desire, he laughed. "Of angels, of course-just like their mother."

* * * * *

TAKE A TRIP ACROSS AMERICA FROM SEA TO SHINING SEA WITH THESE HEARTFELT WESTERNS FROM

Harlequin® Historical

In March 2000, look for

THE BONNY BRIDE by **Deborah Hale**
(Nova Scotia, 1814)

and

ONCE A HERO by **Theresa Michaels**
(Arizona & New Mexico, 1893)

In April 2000, look for

THE MARRYING MAN by **Millie Criswell**
(West Virginia, 1800s)

and

HUNTER'S LAW by **Pat Tracy**
(Colorado, 1880s)

Harlequin Historicals
The way the past *should* have been.

Available at your favorite retail outlet.

HARLEQUIN®
Makes any time special ™

COMING NEXT MONTH FROM

HARLEQUIN HISTORICALS

- **THE BONNY BRIDE**
  by **Deborah Hale,** author of A GENTLEMAN OF SUBSTANCE
  Love or money? That is the decision a farmer's daughter must
  make when she sets sail for Nova Scotia as a mail-order bride
  to a wealthy man, and finds the love of her life on the voyage.
  HH #503 ISBN# 29103-5 $4.99 U.S./$5.99 CAN.

- **A WARRIOR'S KISS**
  by **Margaret Moore,** author of THE WELSHMAN'S BRIDE
  In this captivating medieval tale in the *Warrior Series,* a knight
  aspires to make a name for himself at the king's court, but finds
  his plans jeopardized when he falls in love with a woman who is
  a commoner.
  HH #504 ISBN# 29104-3 $4.99 U.S./$5.99 CAN.

- **ONCE A HERO**
  by **Theresa Michaels,** author of THE MERRY WIDOWS—
  SARAH
  A reluctant hero finds himself on a wild adventure when
  he rescues a beautiful woman and loses his heart in
  Theresa Michaels's dramatic return to her *Kincaid* series.
  HH #505 ISBN# 29105-1 $4.99 U.S./$5.99 CAN.

- **THE VIRGIN SPRING**
  by **Debra Lee Brown**
  This talented new author makes her debut with this stirring
  Scottish tale of a young clan laird who finds an amnesiac beauty
  beside a mythical spring.
  HH #506 ISBN# 29106-X $4.99 U.S./$5.99 CAN.

DON'T MISS ANY OF
THESE TERRIFIC NEW TITLES!

CNM0300